Ogre's Lament

Ogre's Lament

The Story of Don Luis

Stuart G. Yates

Also by Stuart G. Yates

Unflinching
In The Blood
To Die in Glory
Varangian
Varangian 2 (King of the Norse)
Burnt Offerings
Whipped Up
Splintered Ice
The Sandman Cometh
Roadkill
Tears in the Fabric of Time
Sallowed Blood
Lament for Darley Dene
The Tide of Terror

To the real Don Luis, who suffered so many taunts and so much spite, but rose above it all to become someone very special.

And to everyone else who has been bullied, this story is for you.

Contents

Chapter 1

A Village

The morning dawned much as any other, but many remembered this day as the last one of normality before death came to visit the silent streets. From afar, the old clock chimed out the hour as it always did, the peel of its bell cutting through the still air, shattering the quiet, but only briefly. Locals said the mechanism had come from Germany, or Italy. Nobody knew for certain and nobody really cared so long as it worked.

Luis Sanchez stepped out into the bright sunshine and took in a breath. Another beautiful day. For a moment, the sun shone within him and he hoped today might be a good day. His mood, however, soon changed as the mundane routine of each and every day bore down on him like a heavy weight. Thoughts turned to his mother lying in bed dying, his tiny sister Constanza sitting on the damp earthen floor, playing with the little wooden doll Luis had fashioned for her out of an old piece of wood. The images brought a sad, resigned smile to his lips. If only he could do more for them. If only he were older, bigger, stronger, somehow able to find a decent occupation and bring in more money. So many ifs and buts. He sighed, shoulders dropping, and resigned himself to the fact that right now, the only thing he could *ever* do was go to Señor Garcia's bakery to pick up the bread for the early-morning deliveries, and get through. What followed soon afterwards would be worse, and he knew that. The trek to school to face the baying of the children from the village. Home by two, sweeping out the house, making the meals, reading Constanza a story before bed. Always the constant round of monotony and despair.

The sunshine inside faded, despite the heat still burning his face. The day would be neither good nor indifferent, merely the same as every other.

Señor Garcia welcomed Luis with his usual growl. Already the bread lay on the table, bundled up for the various customers whose orders never changed. Luis knew them all by now, so no need for the list. Señor Garcia marvelled at this revelation when Luis first appeared at his doorstep not so many mornings ago, his eager face peering around the door entrance.

"I can help you with your deliveries, Señor Garcia," Luis had said, flashing his best smile.

Garcia paused from kneading the bread and frowned. "Why would I want you to do that?"

Luis stepped inside, waved his hand over the flour, water, waiting masses of soft, sticky dough. "Because you're a busy man and I've been watching you working hard, making your bread. After it's baked, you have to rush out and get the deliveries done before your next batch of bread burns. I could help."

"With the deliveries?" Garcia shook his head. "I'd have to pay you."

Luis had shrugged. "Yes, but maybe the money you give me would not be as much as the money lost from all that wasted bread, burnt whilst you rush around."

Garcia thought about the reasonableness of this. His mouth turned down at the corners and he appeared unconvinced. "You'd have to remember all the customers, where they lived. It would take months. I've been doing this for half a lifetime and I still manage to get some of them mixed up. I'd lose too much money. I'm sorry." He picked up a large handful of dough and slapped it down on the worktop, kneading it with those thick, strong fingers of his.

"I'll write them down," said Luis, stepping closer, wafting his hand through the great cloud of flour pluming up around the baker's hands. The baker had stopped, mouth open, stunned. Luis smiled when he saw the look of total incredulity on Garcia's face. "Yes, I can read *and* write, *Señor* Garcia."

Garcia put his hands on his hips and shook his head slowly. For the first and only time that Luis remembered, the man smiled. "Well, if the good Lord has seen fit to bless you with such a gift, then I don't see how I can deny you! You can start tomorrow, at six."

And so, every morning for the past three months, Luis had done just that. This morning was no different.

Without a word, he gathered up the bundles of bread as Garcia worked away at more dough. Luis stepped out into the street to begin his rounds.

Despite the early hour, the Sun beat down with relentless intensity. Summertime in the village was often unbearable. Riodelgado sat in a little valley, surrounded by the steep sides of the mountains, the heat funnelling downwards, hugging the streets, never managing to escape. The residents cooked in this natural oven and they grumbled and groaned constantly. No one liked the heat. They retreated into their dark, cramped homes, like so many tiny, nervous animals escaping from the danger of predators. They waited for the cool of the night to arrive before venturing outside again, to sit and talk. And talk. Constant talking.

Luis sauntered through the streets, placing a bundle of bread inside each customer's open door. Not everyone ordered bread; some did not have the money, others made their own. Times, however, were hard, the lack of rain turning the ground iron-hard, crops unable to flourish. Coupled with this, news of the War filtered through every now and then, causing fear and concern amongst the villagers, numbing appetites. Recently things were not going well for the Spanish. Once, many years before Luis had been born, stories circulated of Spain defeating the heretics in the far north. But then the Swedes

4

came, followed by the French who joined with these Protestant upstarts to oppose the Imperialist cause. The forces of Spain soon became hard-pressed. Luis, when he heard the news from a one-eyed itinerant tradesman called Pablo, didn't believe the man's words at first. "But France is of the true religion," he'd blurted out.

Pablo had frowned, a gesture which made his single eye look quite terrifying. "How do you know anything about France?"

"I read it."

"You *read it...*?" Pablo had shaken his head. "What is the world coming to when a mere child can read..."

"It's true though, Señor Pablo. How can the Catholic French fight alongside the Swedes, who are *Protestants*?"

Pablo shook his head again, much more sadly this time. They sat by the dried riverbed, under the shade of the orange trees, not far from the tiny bridge. When he spoke again, Pablo's voice sounded resigned, almost sad. "Like everything else in this mad world, it's a mystery. Protestants fighting alongside Catholics, against *other* Catholics! Death is everywhere. I see so many horrors in my travels, and I hear tales of so many dreadful, inhuman things done to others. Things done in the name of religion, in the name of God." He shook his head. "We are in the end-of-days young Master Luis, the end-of-days."

Nevertheless, despite the War spreading, the tiny village of Riodelgado remained untouched by the scourges in the north. No soldiers ever came and the village carried on the way it always had, boiling in the summer, freezing in the brief winter.

A village like a hundred others in the mountains of Andalucía.

Until, one day, a soldier *did* come.

Chapter 2

A Soldier

Luis first spotted the man as he rode into the village square. A tall man astride a thin, over-laden horse, grey coat streaked with the sweat of a long ride. A soldier, that much was clear; sword at his hip, pistols in their holsters, breastplate protecting chest. He wore no helmet, instead a large, floppy hat, which cast his face in deep shadow. A bright red feather took all of Luis' attention, as the man's features, masked by the wide brim and a thick tangle of black beard, were difficult to work out. Except for the eyes, burning with an intensity Luis had seldom seen before. Dust covered the soldier like an extra coat, his poor steed stumbling forward to the drinking trough. They had obviously ridden for many miles in the searing, unrelenting heat. The horse dipped its head and drank. Luis, with only two more bundles left to deliver, sat down on the fountain steps next to the animal and studied the man keenly.

The soldier dismounted, stretched and sighed, his joints cracking. He pulled a bandana from around his neck, dipped it into the water beside his still drinking horse and washed himself, running the soaked piece of cloth over his face before pressing the material into his mouth. He dabbed his lips, stopped and noticed Luis as if for the first time, his eyes narrowing. Luis stiffened, a tiny thrill of fear running through him. The man's look seemed dark and terrible, as did the rest of him. A soldier, quick to judge, violence never far from the blade of his sword. Luis quickly averted his face and went to move away.

"Boy, wait there."

Luis froze, the gruff voice sharp, used to giving orders and no doubt expecting compliance. The man stepped closer, his air of supreme confidence unsettling.

"Where is everyone?"

Luis blinked. "Er... it is only early, sir. Most people will still be in their beds."

"Bah... *peasants*." He looked around, as if he were trying to find something that would prove the lie of Luis's words. Nothing else moved in the square. They were quite alone. The soldier exhaled and slumped down on the stone bench next to the fountain, coat and trousers creaking as he bent limbs. He motioned Luis to join him. For a moment he hesitated. "I don't bite, boy."

Luis forced a smile and sat down. The tangy mix of stale sweat and aged, cracked leather invaded his nostrils, and something else. Something he knew, had smelled many times before; the acrid stench of decay.

"What's your name, boy?"

"Luis, sir. Luis Sanchez."

The man cocked an eyebrow as he scanned Luis, from head to foot. Luis felt his stare and grew uncomfortable, edging away from him slightly. "You wear your hair long, like a girl," said the man, turning away to rifle inside a little pouch at his hip. "You must be a page, or a scholar perhaps."

Luis studied the man filling a white bone pipe with tobacco taken from the pouch. Once before had he seen this. The mayor often smoked a pipe, the only man in the village to do so. Tobacco was rare and expensive, brought in from the Americas. Luis knew where that was. He had pored over maps at his school and would often spend hours daydreaming of adventures in far off lands, of voyages across vast, open seas, of mountains and valleys and—

"Are you listening to me?"

Luis snapped his head around, blinking rapidly. The man's eyes burned with anger and the atmosphere became charged with danger. Luis held up his hand, alarmed. "I'm sorry, sir. I was thinking, and I meant no disrespect." He tried a smile, but the man's expression did not change.

"Thinking about what?"

Swallowing hard, Luis pointed towards the pipe. "Tobacco. Our mayor, he has a pipe. Rare things. Expensive."

"Expensive..." The man's voice drifted away and he sat back, closed his eyes and sucked on his pipe. His mouth made tiny popping sounds and smoke trailed white into the air.

The relief was palpable, the moment of danger past. Nevertheless, Luis remained upright, anxious not to allow his imaginings to return and so receive another sharp rebuke. So he sat and he waited, whilst the soldier quietly puffed away.

They remained like that for some time, neither speaking nor moving. Luis concentrated on his heartbeat, struggling to keep it steady. He had an urge to run, but he overcame it, grinding his teeth, keeping his eyes firmly fixed on the soldier as the man's lips popped around the stem of the pipe.

The horse shook its head and abruptly, the soldier stood up. He knocked out the old tobacco against the fountain step, then stuffed the pipe back inside the pouch. "A tavern."

"Excuse me?"

"Is a tavern close by, where I can find refreshment? Stable my horse?"

Looking up at him, Luis marvelled at the man's size. The buff leather coat strained across wide shoulders, arms thick and strong, legs, like coiled springs of steel, stuffed inside long riding boots. Sheer strength oozed from every pore. Even Fernando, the village blacksmith, couldn't compare with this man. What stories he must have, what tales to tell of battles fought, cities besieged, all the things he'd seen, the places visited.

"Have you never seen a soldier before boy?"

Luis shook his head, and for a moment allowed his imagination to wander, pictures of distant castles, endless forests, rivers of silver, adventures invading his mind, sending him far away.

A crack of laughter shattered his imaginings. He gasped and held his breath, waiting for the reprimand. But this time the man did not seem vexed, merely curious. Luis let out a slow sigh of relief. "No, sir, I've never seen a soldier. Never."

"So none have ever passed this way?"

"None."

"Are you certain?"

Luis nodded. The man seemed satisfied, pulled in a breath and adjusted his belt. "So... tavern?"

"Filipe runs an inn, sir. Up the main road," Luis stood and pointed towards the hill that ran from the square. "Just after the bridge. You can't miss it. Or the mayor, he sometimes lets out rooms I believe."

A moment of tension returned, the man's shoulders tightening. "Filipe's will suffice." He took up the reins and lifted himself into the saddle. The horse stamped at the ground, annoyed to be moving so soon.

Luis patted the horse's neck. It nuzzled into him and he stroked its soft nose. "You have come a long way."

The soldier studied Luis intensely. "You're not just a country bumpkin, boy. I can see that. You are a scholar, then?"

"Yes, sir. I like to think of myself as such."

"Peasants are ignorant, stupid. Dangerous. But you... you are different. And that, my friend," he struck the horse's flanks and began to move away, "makes you even more dangerous. We shall meet again, Luis Sanchez. Farewell... and thank you."

Luis stood still, contemplating the man's words. *Different...* Yes, he was different; he knew that much, the other children of the village reminded him of it every day. But the soldier meant something more, a difference which '... *makes you even more dangerous.*' Those words, curious, made no kind of sense to Luis at all. How could he, little Luis, be dangerous? If anyone was dangerous, it was he—the soldier. He had an air about him of barely contained fury, as if he struggled constantly to keep it at bay. Violence was his companion, his friend, his constant. And now he was here, in Riodelgado. But why? That was the biggest question of them all.

Chapter 3

The Bullies

After he placed the last bundle of bread inside the door of the Ramirez family, Luis relaxed his breathing, dropping his shoulders as the stress left him. Another day of deliveries done. He relished these moments, when he could simply be.

He stood against a wall, under the shade of an orange tree, and searched the sky. No sign of any cloud. Already the temperature had risen to uncomfortable levels. From down the way came the sounds of morning, a village slowly waking up. A baby crying, parents running around to find food scraps, an old man opening bedroom shutters and wheezing in a great gulp of air. From afar someone else coughing violently, sounding as if they were bringing up their entire lungs. A woman calling to her neighbour, barking out the usual '*Buenos dias*' that they had exchanged everyday for the past fifty odd years. Luis listened and he breathed it all in. His village. His world.

He called back at his house to check that his mother and sister were all right. His mother was sat up in bed, dragging a comb through her hair. She looked a little better, some colour returned to her cheeks, but Luis knew not to build his hopes up. She often rallied like this, however the illness which had ravaged her for so long eventually returned, often with a vengeance.

For now, at least, face flushed and eyes bright, she seemed in livelier spirits than she had been when he left.

"Luis," she cried as he came through her door, her face breaking into a smile. He rushed over and fell into her arms. She hugged him tightly and he snuggled into her shoulder, breathing in her perfume.

"You are feeling a little better?" He rocked back, so he could take in the details of her face.

She nodded. "A little." She placed the comb on her bedside table. "It is very hot today."

She often changed the subject like this whenever conversations turned to her illness. It was almost as if by not talking about it, in some bizarre way, the illness might become less. Luis, despite knowing this not to be so, much preferred to keep his mother in good spirits, so he decided to tell her of his earlier encounter in the square. "I met someone today. A stranger."

"Really?" She appeared indifferent and adjusted her nightdress. "And where did he come from, this stranger, or was it a 'she'?"

"No, a man. A soldier."

Her right eye narrowed. A slight holding of the breath. Luis noticed, but made no comment. "A soldier? Interesting. What's a soldier doing all the way down here?"

"He didn't say. I told him where to find a room, over at Filipe's."

"A room?" She smoothed down the side of her hair. Her gaze did not meet his. "That means he might be staying. Did he tell you his name?"

"No, mama. Why, do you think you might know him?" He wasn't sure why he asked, but something about her changed attitude unsettled him. Might the mention of a soldier be the precursor to something more sinister in her view?

She gave a quick giggle, "Know him? Goodness me, no. I don't think I have ever met a soldier... at least, not for many years."

Luis swung his legs over the bed and stood up. "Well, I'm sure he won't be staying for long. Nothing of very much interest for a soldier, here in the village."

She pressed her lips together, her eyes peering beyond him, her voice distant as she said, "No. That much is true."

"I have to be going. I'll see to Constanza, give her some breakfast, then I'll walk up to school."

He leaned forward and kissed his mother on the cheek. She reached over, a thin hand stroking his face. "Luis..."

"Yes, mama?"

"Be careful."

"Careful? Of what, mama?"

She shrugged. "Just... Be careful."

He laughed and turned to go. When he reached the door, she shouted out to him, "And Luis—if you get the chance—find out his name."

Frowning, Luis left her and went to the kitchen to prepare something for his sister to eat.

What did his mother mean by that, he wondered as he made his way down the slope towards the square. Why would his mother be interested in a strange soldier's name? She had said she didn't know any, had never met any, so why the interest? And the way she had become nervous, almost afraid at the mention of him. All of this was very curious. He couldn't remember his mother ever telling him to 'be careful', but to mention it this morning, after the meeting with the soldier, just seemed strange, a little too much of a coincidence. He was sure she was holding something back, keeping a secret or knowledge of something from him. Whatever it was, he would have to wait and see.

By now the early morning bustle had given way to the resigned and much calmer atmosphere of a small village gripped by strength sapping heat. Groups of men gathered on street corners, discussing what work they might be able to find. The olives were as yet unready to be gathered and, until they were, employment of any kind was scarce. Only some two hundred people resided in the village, but most of them lived on the borderline of starvation, desperate to find ways and means to feed their families.

Luis was perhaps luckier than most. The pittance he earned from the baker meant that at least he could provide one meal a day for his mother and sister. Many in the village couldn't even do that.

At the fountain, where he had spoken to the soldier not two hours earlier, a small bunch of boys gathered. Often they would find work to do out in the fields, picking out the stones from the hard, unforgiving ground. They had to move fast, as by midday the heat was so intense that no one, not even flies, ventured outside. Lounging around, as they always seemed to do, one of their favourite, early morning sports was to goad and abuse Luis. When they noticed him, their spirits became much more buoyant. Luis saw it and groaned.

"Here he is," began Alvaro, their leader, almost as soon as Luis came into view. A large, brutish looking lad of around fifteen, what Alvaro lacked in intelligence he made up for in sheer physical strength. Highly regarded by the local farmers, he always took particular pleasure in inflicting pain and misery on Luis. "Look at him, prancing around like a dancer in a bordello. Hey, Luigi, show us a dance!"

The other boys roared at this, the purposeful distortion of Luis's name. Luis kept his eyes averted, head down. He had long become accustomed to the tirade that greeted him most mornings. He wished there was another route he could take to his tutor's house, but there was none. Consequently, virtually every morning would find him forced to run the gauntlet of abuse. He gritted his teeth and marched on.

Two of the boys stepped out and barred his way. Luis sighed, resigned to what would come next. *Señor* Martinez, his tutor, would be angry when Luis explained what had happened, always saying the same thing, 'Luis, for the Lord's sake, why don't you fight back? Stand up to them Luis, don't allow yourself to be disrespected in this way.' It was all right for *Señor* Martinez to give such advice, he was a grown man, people revered him. No one would dare hurl insults at him. Luis, for his part, had long since learned that it was better to simply soak all the abuse up rather than try to retaliate. He had done so once and Alvaro had slapped him across the ear. The sting of the blow, the ringing that went on in his head for at least two days afterwards, was a memory more painful than the slap itself. So he let his shoulders drop and he sighed, preparing himself for the usual onslaught.

"You heard Alvaro," said another, a short and swarthy looking tough by the name of Carlos. Luis feared him more than almost all of the others put together. Excepting Alvaro, of course. "Let's see you dance."

"Please Carlos," Luis said in a small voice and made to go past.

Carlos, sensing Luis's despair, grinned at the prospect of some fun. He stepped up to the others in blocking Luis's path. "Dear me, Luis, refusing our request? We can't have that—we want entertaining, Luis."

"That's right," said a thin boy named Francisco. Jet-black hair and jet-black eyes which smouldered with unrelenting fury. Luis wondered if he were angry only towards Luis, or possibly the entire world. He didn't think he had ever seen the boy happy. Some said his father had fought with the Imperialist *tercios* at the battle of *Lutzen* and had died there. No one could be certain as news rarely filtered through about the War in the north. Luis believed the possibility Francisco might never see his father again, must affect him in some way. Almost a kindred spirit, Luis had often played with the idea that they could be friends. After all, he had lost his father too. Today, he was like the rest. Mean, mocking. He prodded Luis in the chest, sneering. "Dance for us, Luis."

Luis looked wildly from face to face, finally settling on Alvaro, who beamed, slapping one of the other toughs on the shoulder. "We are about to see the great dancing Luis. Come on, let's get moving." He slowly began to clap his hands and stamp his foot. Soon the others took up the cue, a steady beat designed to goad Luis into moving.

"I can't dance," Luis said through clenched teeth. "Why do we have to go through this every morning?"

"Because you're a girl," said Francisco, reaching over and flicking Luis's long hair. "Look at that! *Caballero*! You wear your hair like a girl's, so dance like a girl."

Carlos stepped closer and Luis gasped when he saw the thin blade in the boy's hand. "Shall I cut it off for you, Luis? Eh? Would you like that, make you like the rest of us?"

"You keep that away from me, Carlos." Luis instinctively stepped back, only to find himself right up against Alvaro, who leaned over him and breathed down into his ear.

"*Dance!*"

Letting his shoulders drop even lower, Luis looked down at his feet. No one ever came to help him, no doubt enjoying the show themselves. A few old, tired men looked on, sitting against the wall, their faces blank. Luis wished he had the strength, the courage to fight back. But he had neither. So, tentatively at first, he began to shuffle his feet from side to side as the baying applause gathered momentum. Gradually he lifted up his knees and danced in earnest. With his eyes closed, battling to keep back the tears, he tried to lose himself in his thoughts. Memories of when he was younger, with his father taking him up on his shoulders, walking him out across the fields and into the forest. The miles they walked, the things they talked about. Distant lands, people who spoke strange tongues, oceans and ships and cities that swarmed with thousands of citizens; tales of monsters, giants and dwarfs. They all thrilled him, especially the tale of the ogre who lived in the mountains nearby. An ogre that could sometimes be heard roaring in the distant valleys as hunger gnawed at his very soul. He would come down into the village and prey on some unfortunate who happened to be out after dark. No one else ever spoke about the ogre, but

Luis believed that was because they all feared that the mere mention of his name would bring him back down in to the village, to feast once again on children and grown-ups alike.

A great cheer sprang up and Luis snapped himself out of his dreaming. The boys had gathered around in a tight circle to enjoy the show and applauded loudly. Luis, dancing like a maniac, had earned their appreciation. He stopped and stood, hands on hips, breathing hard, sweat running down the bridge of his nose.

Alvaro stepped up and clapped Luis on the back. "That was a fine display, Luis. Tomorrow, we want you to dress up in a hat."

"With a feather," chirped in Carlos.

"Yes, with a feather. Then you'll be a proper *Caballero*."

Luis groaned again, already thinking of a plan to outwit them, anything that would mean he wouldn't have to go through this ignominy again. He hefted his bag and went to move away.

"Enjoy your lessons, Luis."

Luis looked up into Alvaro's cruel eyes. He could see the loathing simmering away in those deep, black rimmed orbs. Luis knew how much these ignorant, uneducated boys hated him. They hated him for the fact he could read and write, that he stopped at the bridge to look at the mountains, and in the cool of the evening he would stretch himself out in the grass and pick out the stars. They hated him for the fact that Luis had dreams, aspirations. That if anyone could, he would be the one to leave the village one day and make something of himself in that hardest and cruellest of worlds. Not them. Oh no, they would live out their lives here, dead by the time they were fifty, broken arms and broken backs, bodies worn out by the daily, unremitting toil of working in the fields. Not a life for Luis. So, the hatred. The envy. Luis didn't know which was worse.

Leaving the cackling voices behind, Luis trudged up the narrow footpath that climbed towards his tutor's home. As he took the first step, he caught something out of the corner of his eye.

Some way off, the soldier stood leaning nonchalantly under the shade of an orange tree, arms folded, smoking his long, thin pipe. A ghost of a smile flickered across his lips, a forefinger tipping the brim of his hat in greeting. Luis gave a tiny smile, then hurried up the path.

He must have seen it all, he thought, the taunting, the jostling, the humiliation.

And he hadn't helped.

Chapter 4

The Teacher

Señor Martinez greeted Luis with his usual dour expression, piercing eyes searching him under bristling brows. Wiry and bent over by the years, Señor Martinez still bore the stature of a well-respected man, a certain arrogance rooted in his strong jaw, the slightly turned down corners of his mouth. He did not suffer fools lightly, this old music teacher who had, so the stories went, once tutored the king's son in Madrid. For Luis to have discovered such a man as this, in this forgotten backwater of a dried-up village, was good fortune indeed. That he did not charge Luis a single peseta, even better. "There's something about you that I like," the old man had said when he first came across Luis a few years before. "Come and talk to me and I will open your eyes to a whole new world." So Luis did, and every morning since, excepting Saturdays and Sundays, he went to Martinez's simple house and worked through his studies. Soon, it became routine. Not a painful one, however; one borne from necessity. Luis might find himself trapped here forever without his tutoring. Riodelgado, the world's end.

"You're late again," said Martinez without anger. "They belittled you did they, as usual?"

Luis placed his bag on the table and slowly pulled out his books and the quill he'd borrowed from Martinez some days before. "Only a little."

"Bah!" Martinez slammed the flat of his hand down on the table. "When are you going to stand up to them, meet them full on and end all of this? Heh?"

Luis had no answer. He had been through this conversation any number of times and he was bored with it. He sat down and began to sharpen the nib of his quill. "There is a soldier come to the village," he said, quickly changing the subject. "I met him this morning."

"German?"

"No. Spanish, I think."

"You think? Don't you know? What was he, a mercenary?"

Luis frowned. "*Mercenary*?"

"Soldier of fortune—one who fights for the highest bidder. Now the war is almost over many such men will be roaming the countryside, looking for employment." Martinez sucked his teeth. "Or trouble."

"Well, he was certainly a soldier. He had a sword and pistols. A rougher looking man I have yet to see. He looked as if he had been travelling for days, perhaps even weeks." Luis carefully put the quill down and smoothed open the page of his copybook. "The war is over, you say? When did that happen?"

"I can't begin to know." Martinez disappeared for a moment into the tiny kitchen adjacent to the room and returned with a basket of bread. He placed it down before Luis, together with a slab of cheese. "Eat your breakfast, Luis. You can't learn on an empty stomach."

Luis smiled. The old man could always sense Luis's need for food, probably by simply listening to the rumblings coming from deep inside his young scholar.

Chewing through the bread, Luis asked again, "So, the war. When did it end?"

"I said I *don't know*. Pablo told me some weeks ago." Martinez pushed over a jug of fresh water. Luis poured himself a mug full. "Apparently a peace agreement has been signed by all the countries involved. Somehow, I suspect the struggle between Spain and France will only grow worse." He lowered his eyes, as well as his voice. "*Much* worse."

"Can that be possible?" Luis took a large drink. It tasted fresh and sweet. "I have heard it said that this war has been the worst in all recorded history. Hundreds of thousands of people killed, either by fighting or plague. Whole cities burned to the ground, miles upon miles of farmland throughout Germany salted, blighted forever."

"You know much, Luis. All of this from Pablo?"

Luis nodded, nibbling at a piece of cheese. "Mostly. Mother also told me some things."

"Yes, well... she would know."

Martinez slid over a wrinkled piece of parchment. "Enough talk of war, Luis. Your Latin requires urgent attention." Luis sighed, drained his mug and settled down to some study.

At the door, a few hours later, Martinez placed a tightly wrapped bundle of bread and cheese into Luis's hand, together with a small stone bottle of wine. "Tomorrow we will talk of some history, Luis. Geography too. That way you can make sense of all these things you keep hearing and all these strangers you keep meeting."

Luis gave an awkward smile, a little embarrassed. He stuffed the food and drink into his bag. "Thank you, Señor Martinez."

"And learn your verbs, Luis. You won't get anywhere without knowing them."

Luis waved goodbye to the old tutor and made his way back down into the square. Almost at once he broke out in sweat. The heat had become unbearable and not a soul was out. At least this meant he would not have to suffer another bout of bullying. The intense sunlight, however, was almost as bad, making his head hurt with all the frowning. By the time he reached his house, he was soaked through with perspiration, but all of this discomfort vanished when he saw old Señora Gomez standing at the doorway, wringing her hands.

"Oh Luis," she said, coming forward at a rush. She clamped her hands on his shoulders.

"What is it?" He could see by her flushed face something serious had happened. She shuffled into the house, wringing her hands again, and slumped down on a rickety old chair, mumbling incoherently. "Señora Gomez, tell me what's happened – is it Mamá?"

Luis dumped his bag down and rushed towards his mother's room. Señora Gomez caught him by the arm. "No, your mother is sleeping. Please don't disturb her. It's Constanza. She is not well. I have taken her to my house, kept her in bed, given her some broth."

"Constanza?" Luis felt his stomach pitch over. "But, what is it? A fever?" He was wild with worry. How could this have happened? When he had left them this morning they both seemed bright enough. Señora Gomez always came in to stay with them for a few hours whilst he worked and studied. To discover his sister was ill shocked him, turning his legs to jelly and he sat down on his bed, pressing his hands against his face.

Señora Gomez knelt down next to him. "She is very weak, with some kind of fever." She shook her head. "You should have told me."

Luis gaped at her. "I didn't know. When I left this morning, everything was fine. Even Mamá seemed better, more cheerful." He put his face in his hands, leaning forward, the news becoming too much all of a sudden. "I can't believe this."

She placed a hand gently on his arm. "You need some rest as well. You do too much, what with your bread deliveries and that... *school*. Can't you give it up?"

He brought his head up from his hands. "And what would I do with my life then, Señora Gomez? Become a farmer, perhaps? A worker in the fields?"

She shook her head, looking sad. "What will you become if you continue with your studies?"

"I will go to university, Señora Gomez. Madrid, possibly even Paris. I will learn to be a doctor."

"*A doctor.*" She shook her head again, this time more vigorously. "My, what silly dreams you have." She bent forward, her face very close. "I know you want to do what is best for your mother and sister, Luis, but you have to understand that this is the real world in which you live, not some fairytale. Studies and education are not for the likes of us. We are peasants, Luis. We always will be." She smiled. "You have to think of your mother. I am afraid she is not long for this world. I would prepare yourself, Luis."

"Prepare myself for what, Señora Gomez?"

"I think you know." She patted his knee and stood up, groaning a little as she did so, showing the few teeth she still had remaining. "My aching bones." Slowly she shuffled towards the door. "When your mother awakes, tell her about Constanza. Then, I suggest you go and visit the priest."

Chapter 5

The Priest

With great reverence, Luis gently eased open the heavy oak door of the church and poked his head inside.

The welcome coolness of the interior almost made him swoon and he paused. He held onto the back of the nearest pew for a moment before padding down the aisle towards the far end and the ornate altar, set upon its dais. Careful not to make a sound, he stepped up onto the raised stage. He glanced around nervously, picking out the life-size effigies of the Virgin Mother and the Lord Jesus, both of whom peered down at him with their unblinking, challenging eyes. *Show respect, Luis,* they were saying. *We know what is in your heart.*

He heard a sharp cough from beyond in the vestry and he waited, heart pounding. He shouldn't be here, the area off-limits to anyone but the clergy, or the invited. Nevertheless, he had to speak to the priest.

There was much to sort out—last-rites, burials. He steeled his heart, took a deep breath and crossed the dais to the little door of the vestry. He gave two, short raps.

The door wrenched open and the priest, draped in his black shroud of a cassock, stood breathing hard, dishevelled and sweating. For a moment, Luis thought the man might scold him, out of surprise or anger. Perhaps even fear? His eyes were round, startled. Luis let out his breath as the priest spoke, in a voice full of relief. "Ah, Luis. It's you." He nodded his head a few times and stepped aside, ushering Luis inside. "I was expecting someone else, that's all."

Father Brialles had been the village priest for as long as Luis could remember. A quiet, reclusive man, often found down by the river, Bible in hand, lost in the Holy Scriptures, or in thought. People looked up to him, hoping his intimate contact with God would protect them in a world gone mad. So far, as everyone believed, it seemed to work. Brialles kept them safe, with God's good grace.

Luis stepped inside the vestry. On a thin trestle table a canvas bag lay open, partly filled with various bits of ornamental paraphernalia: silver candlesticks, gold crucifixes, the odd small painting. Luis took it all in, questions beginning to formulate in his head. Before he could speak, Father Brialles launched himself into an explanation. "I can't leave things to chance, Luis. I have to protect the church treasures. That's what I'm doing, you see." He went over to the bag and pulled it further apart, making room for more sacred items.

Stepping up closer, Luis cast his hand over the assembled pieces. "But Father, protected from what?"

"Protestants, of course! The war grows closer, Luis. Once they get here, they will plunder churches such as this and tear them down. They have no thought for sanctity, Protestants. None at all."

"Father, Don Martinez told me today the war is over, that a peace treaty has been signed. The Protestants won't be coming here; it's over, Father."

For a moment Brialles stopped, pondering this news. He soon dismissed it, stuffing a couple of gold serving bowls into the bag. "I don't believe it. How can Martinez know such things?"

"Pablo told him."

"Ah well, there you are. That idiot itinerate spreads nothing but rumour and gossips, touting them as truth! The man is not to be trusted, Luis. You'll do well to remember that."

Luis noted what a hurry the priest was in, scurrying this way and that, hardly pausing for breath as he spoke, stuffing more sacred pieces inside the bag until it bulged. "We can never be too careful, Luis. All sorts of strangers wander around, most of them dangerous. Thieves, vagabonds, cut-throats. Nobody is safe nowadays. This used to be a quiet, peaceful place, in which people could live a simple, untroubled life." He paused, closed his eyes and sighed. "Not anymore. And I'm sad for it, Luis. Sad, and a little afraid." He looked down and seemed satisfied that he had gathered as much as he could. He pulled the draw-strings together and secured the bag with a knot. A smile spread across his face. "There! Now I can get ready to leave."

"Leave? But Father, you can't go, not now."

"Why ever not?"

"It's my mother, Father. Señora Gomez said I should prepare myself, that I should speak to you about what needs to be done..." He swallowed, casting his eyes downwards. "To get ready for when my mother..." His voice cracked and he turned away.

"Luis, please."

"I'm sorry, Father." Luis straightened himself. "If you could just come, just for a moment."

Brialles rubbed his chin, his breathing becoming erratic, eyes darting around the small, cramped room. "I can't do anything now, Luis. It's just not feasible."

"Feasible? But Father, I think she's dying."

"Then there is little we can do anyway, is there? Luis," he held onto Luis's arm, gripping it hard. "You must be strong. Your mother has been so ill for so long and she is due to cross into the realm of our Lord very soon. Pray for her, Luis, with all your heart and I am sure she will be received into His kingdom."

"Please, Father, she needs you to be with her. To give her your blessing. I'm begging you!"

Luis had always found Brialles to be a kindly and caring man. Often, at the end of Sunday service, he would come up to Luis and share some time with him, asking him about his mother and Constanza. He never appeared rushed or impatient. Not like now.

Now, he was a changed man, consumed with panic and a desire to escape.

"I can't Luis, I have to go."

He grabbed hold of the bag and hefted it down from the table, but he lost his grip and it fell to the ground with a crash. He cursed and Luis, startled, stepped back. He wondered what else was inside, what other treasures Brialles had secreted away. For the first time in his life, he began to question the priest's motives. "Father, surely you don't have to go right now, this very second."

Brialles groaned loudly as he swung the bag over his shoulder. Bowed down with its weight, he shuffled towards the door. "I do, Luis. You see, the war really has come to Riodelgado, and I have not a moment to spare before the Protestants begin to tear down this holy place!"

Like a light going on in his head, Luis suddenly saw everything in perfect clarity. The reason for the priest's haste, his fear of Protestants, a projection of his fear of something else.

The soldier.

Chapter 6

Mention of Ogres

The village-crier sounded in good voice as Luis returned home. To be entirely accurate the crier was on loan from the neighbouring, and far more prosperous, village of Casasierra, which lay at the top of the mountain pass to the west. Casasierra was an old place, its colourful history dotted with meetings and incidents with the Moors, people who had shaped the cultural heritage of the surrounding area. It had thrived, its position on the main route to Anteguerra meant trade flourished. Within a few decades its prosperity was such it became the premier village of the Axarquia. Whenever the mayor of Riodelgado sent a request, Casasierra responded by loaning its dignitaries.

A considerable number of people gathered in the square as the crier stood upon a makeshift platform and read from a scroll. Squeezing his way to the front of the throng, Luis looked up at the large man as he boomed, "A meeting has been called for this evening, at the village hall, as the clock strikes six. All who can are asked to attend." He rolled up his scroll and stepped down into the crowd and began to push his way between them. One man took him by the arm, face twisted in fear. "A meeting? What sort of meeting?"

"Just be there, Señor Rey."

"Yes, but what is it about, man? Is it plague?"

Someone else must have caught the question; a murmur like a wave ran through the people. Other voices rang out, alarmed, scared.

"*Plague*?" A terrified woman's voice hit high notes. "We have plague here?"

With a blink, the murmur became a loud clarion and amongst the shrill cries someone fell to their knees, hands raised in supplication, "Mother of God!"

Soon others joined in the building panic, like a squabble of farmyard hens, all clucking and flapping with increasing terror.

The crier threw up his hands, shouting above the noise, "Listen, it is *not* plague! Please, just come to the meeting." Relief began to settle, but the eyes of the crowd still reflected their uncertainty, their fear.

"Are you certain it is not plague?"

"Absolutely. On my mother's life."

The village-crier was a large, imposing man, isolated somewhat because of his status. The only time he ever spoke was when he had messages to convey. But he could read, and Luis had spoken to him on a few occasions, sharing stories, sometimes reading snippets of letters or poems. His name was Jorge, but Luis knew little else about him, apart from the deep respect and trust people gave to him. Luis was certain of one thing—what the man said was true. There was no plague in Riodelgado.

He told his mother of the meeting. Propped up in bed, her face like crumpled parchment, eyes sunken, lifeless, she listened in silence. Luis sat beside her, her liver-spotted hand in his, twisted into a sort of claw. When did she get to be so old? Luis had no sense of the years slipping by, every day the same, a long, drawn out path, never altering its course. Until now.

"Did Jorge say what it was about?"

Luis shook his head. "Only that it wasn't about plague."

"Hah! Then it probably is."

"Mama, you are so cynical."

She measured him with one, piercing eye. "These words, Luis, where do they come from? Cynical? What is that?"

"Oh, you know, you question everything, doubt everything. Experience has taught you things are rarely as they seem."

"I'd call that honesty, Luis."

He smiled and stood up. "I will go to the meeting and later tell you what happened. I don't think Jorge was lying, Mama. It's not plague."

"It is probably something worse."

"Worse? Is there anything worse than plague, Mama?"

"Oh yes, Luis. People are far worse. If it's not plague, then this will have something to do with people, mark my words."

Calling in on Señora Gomez, he noticed Constanza had rallied somewhat. Her cheeks and forehead still burned, but at least she was quiet, sleeping in a little truckle bed that Señora Gomez had made up for her. Luis thanked her and went to make his way down to the village hall when old man Gomez caught him at the entrance to the house. A short, brutish man; some said he used to be a fisherman, working out of Malaga. His language, always blunt and coarse, matched his features well.

"It might be plague."

Luis took a long breath. If he heard that word once more, he knew he would scream. These people were obsessed. Trapped in their petty, insignificant little lives, their limited knowledge of the world gave them a caustic view of everything. On the whole, good, honest folk, but quick to judge, relying more on gossip rather than actual facts. The truth was not something they readily accepted, preferring to rely on their own prejudices to guide them through the quicksand of life.

"Yes, Señor Gomez, but it probably isn't plague. Jorge said as much."

"How do you know he spoke the truth, how can you tell? What are you, ten years of age?"

Luis battled hard to keep the anger from his voice. "I'm fourteen, Señor Gomez. Fifteen in October."

"Fifteen? And you think you understand the world, do you? Have you ever seen a plague victim?"

"No, thank God. Have you?"

He frowned and for a moment looked indecisive. "Not as such. But I know what it can do."

"We *all* know that, Señor Gomez." Luis exhaled slowly. "If it were plague, then there would be cases here, wouldn't there? Many people would already be struck down."

"Your mother might have it. Have you thought of that?"

"For pity's sake, my mother hasn't got plague, Señor Gomez!" He pulled in a breath, exasperated. "My mother is dying, but not from plague. We're God-fearing people; we go to church every Sunday. Plague is not going to visit us." He was about to add he rarely saw Gomez there, but thought better of it. Gomez annoyed him, so unlike his wife, a kind and giving woman, never a bad word crossing her lips. This man was an oaf and Luis wondered how men and women actually became couples. Something must have attracted them to one another a hundred years ago when Gomez first met his wife, although he couldn't for the life of him understand what. Why someone as pleasant as Señora Gomez ended up with such a brute was a mystery. Luis kept his thoughts to himself, not wishing to bring the man to anger. So he smiled instead, as sweetly as possible. "It'll all become clear later, after the meeting. Then we'll know whether it's plague or not."

He stopped at the corner and sighed. As Luis expected, gathered outside the village hall were the local toughs. Carlos spotted him and his eyes lit up, he shoved Francisco in the arm and pointed. "Here he is, our little Señorita!"

Altogether, perhaps four or five of them sprawled themselves in the doorway, one of them sitting on the steps, his long legs sticking out, forcing people to negotiate a path around him. He didn't care.

Alvaro leered. "Ah, our good and kind Luis. Don Luis, with all that hair. Are you a Don already, Luis, a gentleman?"

Luis looked away. Other people arrived and he fell in behind them, hoping for some sort of protection. The bell tolled, the meeting was about to begin. He walked past Carlos, brushing close, smelling the stench of his sweat. A toothless grin loomed as Carlos barred his way and prodded him in the chest with a thick index finger. "Gentlemen say 'excuse me', Luis."

The air crackled with tension, the on-lookers probably hopeful of confrontation, waiting expectantly for this flashpoint to explode into an exchange of blows. Luis, however, merely smiled and the moment passed. "Do excuse me, Carlos, but may I pass?"

Carlos bowed, waving his arm extravagantly, "Enter, kind sir!"

They all laughed and with their mockery ringing in his ears, Luis stepped into the small hall.

It seethed with people, packed inside so tightly they were like one, formless creature. The mayor sat on the stage behind a large table, flanked by two other men whom Luis, standing at the back, could not make out. A clump of villagers, buzzing like a thousand bees, masked his view, and a thick fug of sweat rose from their unwashed bodies, clogging his nostrils, bringing bile into his throat. He opened his mouth to breathe and wished he had arrived earlier and found a place at the front.

The mayor brought his gavel down several times and waited. The talking continued unabated. A further bout of hammering, louder this time, and the murmuring gradually ceased. Everyone stood in expectation of what was to come.

"This will not take long," began the mayor, rising up out of his seat.

"Is it plague?" A voice, from the far side cried out. Luis couldn't see who it was.

The mayor closed his eyes briefly, looking pained. "Let me reassure everyone here, this has nothing to do with plague."

No one appeared convinced as the voices rang out:

"What is it then?"

"It's your duty to tell us!"

"It must be plague. Why else would you bring us here?"

The mayor's patience snapped and, instead of the gavel, he brought his fist down with a slam on the tabletop. A stunned silence followed. "For the love of God, will you let me speak?" He measured them all with his harsh gaze, scanning over the anxious faces. "It is *not* plague. I want you to listen carefully to what

I have to say, then you can ask your questions when I am finished."

A slight murmur, a few clipped comments, and the people settled. Luis could hear his own heart pounding in his chest. He had never experienced such a collective sense of expectation and concern in all his life.

"This morning I received a visitor. From the north." Another ripple ran through the crowd. The mayor held up his hand. "It seems the war that has blighted the whole of Europe for the past thirty years has come to an end." A few gasps. A tiny cheer of, 'Thank God!' The mayor nodded. "Yes. A peace agreement has been signed, in Germany. We have been fortunate that, by the grace of God, the worst excesses of this most terrible of conflicts have not visited our village, or the rest of Andalucía. But, as you know, several of our men went off to war, to fight for the Emperor, and none of them have come back." There was some mutterings and shuffling of feet. More than one family had lost sons, fathers and husbands. Luis thought of his own father for a moment and a stab of sadness hit him. "However, we now face very real and unexpected dangers. Many soldiers are unemployed. Mercenaries. I don't have to tell you about the dreadful, wicked things done by these men. They are out of work and are on the move. Already stories are filtering through of incidents in the north and northeast. Men have spilled over from the borders with France, pillaging villages, ransacking property, burning down homes, murdering the innocent." The murmuring grew as people reacted to these revelations with raised voices and exchanges of anxious, frightened looks; old and young, everyone knew of the horrors. Pablo had brought news many times. When Magdeburg had burned, the images he conjured were so dreadful, so appalling that some of the villagers had fainted. Luis's own father had told him the story and, although it was old, it remained vivid. And terrible.

"Please listen!" The mayor pounded the gavel as the clamour grew more urgent. "I have here the visitor I spoke of." He gestured towards the man on his right. A hush descended and Luis clamped his hand over his mouth as he recognised who it was—the soldier!

He stood to his full, impressive height. His breastplate had gone, but his thick buff coat gave truth to his profession. Around his waist, a broad leather belt held a sword and dagger and, for good measure, a pistol. Armed and ready, but for what, Luis asked himself.

"I'm not used to this," he began, black eyes like pebbles, holding the gaze of the now hushed crowd, "but I have a voice, one my men respect. I'll ask you to do the same, until I am finished." None of the assembly commented, all of them stunned. "I have travelled far, and for many months to reach here, a journey of hundreds of miles. Along the way, I have seen things that would make your head spin, fought in battles, watched people die. Killing is my profession." A slight tremor ran through the hall, which he ignored and continued without pause, "Like so many, I was employed in the service of his divine Emperor, fighting against the scourge of the Protestants. However, the last few years have proved bloodier than any I can remember." He clenched his teeth, which flashed white in a burnished face, framed by the thick black hair and tight beard. "The most resolute of our enemies are the French. They have sold their souls to the devil, throwing in their lot with the Swedes. A treaty has been signed and a sort of peace allowed to settle." He shook his head. "It will not last. Even as I speak, armies are gathering in the far north and I do not believe much time will pass until fighting breaks out again. This time, the war will be between Spain and France and it will decide the fate of Europe!" The crowd could no longer contain itself. A multitude of voices spoke at once, urgent and afraid; the roars of men and the gasps of women, all edged with uncertainty. The sound increased as people jostled and span around, faces aghast, eyes wide, all of them asking the same question, '*Will war come here?*' Luis could barely move, trapped between two bulky bodies, and he had to fight to free himself from the pressure. In so doing he managed to gain a better viewpoint in the aisle, directly opposite the soldier, who lowered his head, shook his curly mane of hair and turned his eyes upward.

"There is more," he said.

The gibbering continued, no one taking notice, except for Luis who watched, mesmerised as the soldier reached for his pistol, brought it out and fired into the ceiling.

The place fell into stunned silence. Everyone waited, all peering at the drifting smoke that trailed from the barrel of the gun. The soldier's voice cut through their ragged thoughts. "In a year, maybe two, the struggle will begin anew. The dangers, however, may come sooner. At this very moment, as your mayor told you, soldiers sweep across the border and with them other things which are making their way here. Unspeakable things, which have lurked hidden, waiting until such a time as this."

"What *things*?"

The soldier looked down at his hands and the pistol. Lost in thought, perhaps wondering what words to choose. He sighed, voice now low and ominous. "I have seen it. Coming here, riding through the mountains. My horse took fright at something and bolted. I fought hard to maintain control, but I knew what had caused the animal to react in such a way, as I had seen it, smelled its stink."

Everyone waited, silent, intense. Luis hardly dared breathe.

Impatience grew too great for one man, who blurted, "For pity's sake, tell us what you saw!"

The soldier took a few breaths. "It is like a man, but not like a man. That is the closest I can give to an explanation. I first heard about it in camp, just outside *Donauwörth*. I dismissed the rumours, thinking them the flight of fancy, childish stories meant for bedtime, to frighten children into behaving. But now..."
He shook his head. "Now, I am not so certain. I saw it, you see, standing on top of an escarpment, and I

noted its size, its barrel chest, the long, heavy arms, the short, squat legs, as thick as tree trunks. The wide, drooling mouth." He slowly raised his head, casting his eyes over his captured audience. "An ogre."

What began as a trickle soon developed into a loud cacophony of uproarious laughter, led by a small group over in the far corner. One man bayed like a mule, a friend slapping him on the back as he joined in. Another heaved, bent double, throat retching, eyes streaming. Luis saw them, suspected it was more an outpouring of relief than real humour. Others, however, were less disparaging. The villagers had been down this road before. Ogres, trolls, witches. Often seen, experienced, talked about, only those never blighted by such things would dismiss the notion out of hand. God-fearing these people might be, but none of them ventured out after dark. Not because of wolves, but because of the evil that roamed in the mountains at night.

"Fernando Perello," snapped the mayor, standing up next to the soldier, his head bright red with seething fury. He wagged his finger to the men in the corner. "Hold your inane cackling. You are a fool and an ignorant buffoon! You know nothing of any of this and you hide your fear beneath this mindless laughter. Be still!"

Perello looked around as every eye turned to him and he spread out his hands, "But this is nonsense. I've been to sea, travelled right across the Mediterranean, visited North Africa. These stories are created to keep people quiet, to stop them asking questions." He jutted his chin towards the soldier. "Like you said, they are for children."

"Not my child," said the other man on the stage as he stood. He was not like the others. He seemed shrunken, old before his time, his face white, eyes red-rimmed as if he were ill, sick with fever. He ran a trembling hand through his hair.

The mayor, lips squeezed together, laid a hand gently on the man's shoulder. "This is Tomas, as most of you know. Last night, he arrived home after spending another day in the fields, gathering what he could for his family. The sun had already gone down." The mayor nodded towards the man to continue.

Tomas took a breath. "My house, as some of you know, is next to the bridge, not far from the mayor's own home. A path runs down to there from the mountains. I'd come back from the fields, my old mule weighed down with what I had gathered, and as I drew closer to my home a terrible feeling overcame me. A feeling of dread. I knew, as I turned the corner, something was not right. The door to my home was open, you see. I ran up, certain something was wrong. When I got there, I looked inside and my wife..." His voice broke and he fell back down into his chair, burying his face in his hands, overcome with grief, his cries heartbreaking as he began to weep loudly.

The mayor slowly reached out his hand and again patted the man's shoulder. "Spare yourself, Tomas." He looked at the audience, silent once more. Even Perello had ceased his laughter. "Tomas's wife had been murdered. Her throat ripped out." The crowd swayed backwards as if struck by some gigantic, invisible fist. Someone cried out, a single piercing shriek of despair. "He came running to me, to tell me. As soon as I went to see for myself what had happened, I understood." He pulled in a long breath, as if mustering his strength, possibly even his courage. "The little child, a girl called Lourdes, had gone. Taken."

Luis gasped. "Taken?"

Eyes snapped round towards him and Luis felt the heat burning through his cheeks. He had called out without thinking, and now wished he hadn't been so bold as the villagers stared at him, open-mouthed.

"Yes, Luis," said the mayor, picking him out, knowing exactly where he stood. His eyes remained hard. "The house had been ransacked, turned upside down, everything smashed and broken. Amongst the ruin of his home, Tomas's wife lay dead. Lourdes, her bedclothes torn away, had disappeared. A trail of blood ran from the house and up the pathway. My good friend here," he indicated the soldier, who still stood, head down, "whom I met by chance, helped me track the trail, but it soon petered out. Nevertheless, it was clear for us to see, that the footprints in the ground had been made, not by a man or a horse, but by something else."

Slowly the soldier looked up, his eyes blank, his voice flat, "I know it for what it is. And now you know too what is coming into your village, leaving death and terror in its wake. An ogre."

Chapter 7

Footsteps in the Night

That evening, Constanza was well enough to come home. Señora Gomez, waiting inside the house, met Luis as he returned from the meeting and rushed towards him, her face etched with concern. Before she even spoke, he raised his hand, smiling, "It's not plague, Señora Gomez, I promise you. You can rest easy."

"Thank the Lord," she said beaming, the colour returning to her cheeks. "If poor Constanza... Well, I'm sure you understand what I mean."

He reached down and picked his sister up. She snuggled into his neck making tiny cooing noises and he kissed the top of her head. "You've been very kind, Señora Gomez. Thank you."

"Don't mention it." She stroked the little girl's hair. "If you need me, you know where to find me."

"Thank you. Good night."

She closed the door quietly behind her.

Putting Constanza down on the tiny truckle bed, Luis padded through to his mother's room. She was asleep, her chest rising and falling erratically, a rasping wheeze coming from her clogged lungs, making a sound like a small, wounded animal. He bent over and kissed her cheek. A thin film of perspiration covered her brow and he gently pushed away the damp hair from her skin. She moaned and turned over onto her side. He waited, checking she still slept. Satisfied, he left her alone and went back into the kitchen to prepare some scraps for Constanza and himself to eat. It had been lentils and beans last time. It would be the same again tonight.

Something woke him in the middle of the night and he sat bolt upright, senses alerted. At first he thought someone had forced their way inside the house and he waited, rigid with fear, heart pounding, not knowing what to do. The silence yawned around him and gradually he allowed himself to relax. No burglar had broken in. He threw back the covers and reached over for the single oil lamp his family possessed. He groped for the flint in the darkness and managed to strike it and ignite the wick. He turned it low, as the oil had almost all gone, and crept across the room to the door and shone the weak light around.

The door remained bolted from the inside. Most local people kept their doors open, but ever since his father had left, Luis had always preferred to lock the house whenever they went to sleep. Thieves were unheard of, but sometimes a passing traveller wandered into the village, someone that nobody knew. Like the soldier. It was always best to keep safe and sound, especially at night.

Luis went and checked on his mother, whose chest still rumbled, but she remained undisturbed. He returned to Constanza, who had flung off her covers and lay on her back, arms and legs spread-eagled. He chuckled to himself, put the lamp on the floor beside the truckle bed, and tidied up her clothes. As he straightened up, the noise came again.

A muffled cry, like a low whine. It stopped, abruptly cut off, as if a hand had clamped itself over the mouth. Luis stood in the half-darkness, unable to move, every sense alive with terror.

The seconds stretched out and he waited, not daring to breathe. Then, from out of the close, oppressive night, another sound, quite distinct, was coming closer.

The crunch of booted feet on gravel.

From somewhere, he forced his muscles to life and turned down the lamp. He crouched, peering towards the door. He didn't know why, but he felt sure whoever was out there had stopped and listened as intensely as he.

The tiniest noise, a flexing of limbs, followed by a slow exhalation of breath, terrible, unearthly. Luis put his trembling hand over his mouth to hold down the whimper of dread that boiled up in his throat.

It snuffled. Right outside the door, listening, waiting. Then the crunching of boots again, receding into the distance.

Unable to move, fear turning his legs to jelly and his stomach to water, Luis counted to sixty, not daring to believe the moment had passed. Drained, he sat on his haunches until the first light of dawn peeked through the crack at the bottom of the door.

Chapter 8

Señora Gomez

Mama still slept as Luis busied himself, preparing for the day. His little sister shuffled around in the kitchen area and Luis smiled down at her, stroked her hair, gazed into her round, saucer-like eyes, big enough to swallow him up whole. "Oh Constanza," he breathed, the horrors of the previous night receding as daylight once more overcame the darkness. It was a much colder morning than of late, the threat of rain heavy in the atmosphere. He pushed open the shutters and leaned out, taking in some air. Constanza tugged at his trousers. She wanted her breakfast. Luis sighed, over-burdened by all the responsibility, the endless repetition of the days, the monotony of a routine he loathed.

He smiled at her, knowing none of it was her fault and, with a sense of guilt beginning to develop, he stooped down next to her and hugged her tight. "Oh

Constanza," he repeated, pressing her head into his neck, "when are we ever going to be free?"

Luis held her close for a long time. Letting her go, he turned to the table, took out a roll of bread, broke it in two and chopped up a tomato. Placing the 'feast' onto a wooden platter, he motioned Constanza to the table, where she sat and began to demolish her meal.

He watched her quietly. She never complained, simply accepted her life, knowing nothing was ever going to come along to change things because this was how it was. How could she think otherwise? Too young to understand that life was full of constant struggle, woe and danger. Blissfully ignorant of the hardships to come, when Mama would no longer be here, she met each new dawn with a ready smile, unaware that Luis would have to move away some time soon, make his fortune elsewhere. The confines of the village would not keep him prisoner forever. One day he would leave, but not yet. Right now, there were still things to do, like deliver bread.

Where was Señora Gomez?

Luis opened the door and stepped outside, checking the narrow street. No one. The day had barely begun and Luis began to suspect he had risen too early. The next-door neighbour's cockerel had already started its early morning call. Plenty of others roosted in the village, and the daily competition of which one could shout the loudest was well under way. The one over the back always set up its competing cry at the same time every morning. So he wasn't early. Señora Gomez was late.

Sighing, Luis looked back at Constanza as she nibbled the last of her bread roll. "I'm just going to check on Señora Gomez," he explained, "I won't be long." She giggled, waving to him, and he stepped outside into the morning sunshine.

Señora Gomez did not live far. As Luis came round the first corner, his eyes fell on the old lady's home and a chill ran through him. Something wasn't right, the terror of what had happened in the night returning to his thoughts as he spotted the door to the Gomez household was slightly ajar. Luis slowed down, checked both ends of the street, and moved to the door with great caution.

Cold fingers of dread played with the nape of his neck as he pushed the door open with his fingertips. All loomed black inside, a deathly silence enveloping the place, so quiet he could hear the thumping of his heart. He took a breath and crossed the threshold, taking a moment to allow his eyes to become accustomed to the gloom. He chanced a look inside.

The room was in darkness, the shutters still closed. It was difficult to make anything out, but the smell rendered sight redundant at that moment. A thick, nauseous stench hit the back of his throat and made him gag. He turned and stuck his head outside again, breathing in the air. He gave up a little prayer of thanks for the cold, which helped to clear his nostrils of the awful, acrid smell.

Taking another, much deeper breath, he went back inside. He knew the layout of the house sufficiently well to find the main window. He wheeled to his left, skirting the odd bit of furniture, and pulled back the shutters. The light flooded in and he winced, took another lungful of air, and turned around.

For a moment, he thought he had the wrong house. The contents of the room lay strewn across the earthen floor, either deliberately knocked over or broken, as if a whirlwind had ripped through, smashing everything in its path. The large oaken table lay upturned on its edge, plates, lamps, cutlery, old bits of food, hurled in all directions. Hard backed chairs, smashed, jagged timber strewn in bits, thrown into far corners. An old chest, lid pulled back, contents flung around with little care or respect. Blankets, more plates, family heirlooms. The scene of a mad struggle, not a whirlwind at all.

In the far corner, still half covered by the gloom, a body.

Luis didn't need to move closer to realise it was Señora Gomez. His stomach yawned, the terrible dread of knowing overwhelming him.

She lay on her back, legs spread out, feet uncovered, her body twisted in an impossible angle; she didn't move. He gazed at her for a long time before finding the courage to whisper, "Señora Gomez?" He waited, open mouthed, hoping for a reply, or a movement. Anything.

Some of the debris covered her head, and he needed to know if she were still alive. He had to force himself to step closer, his feet refusing to respond at first, as if clamped to the ground. Something drove him on, curiosity, disbelief, a hope that perhaps the old woman still breathed, he couldn't say. Despite his dread, he knew he had to see, so he forced himself to move. He got down on his haunches, studied her. The chest did not rise. He closed his eyes and held his breath, not because of the stench, but in an effort to prepare himself for the sight which waited for him. When he pulled back the odd bits of material and wood which masked her face and looked, he felt his stomach turn. He rocked backwards, pushing his palms into the ground to stop himself from collapsing. He took a grip on a broken chair and struggled to his feet. He stumbled like someone drunk towards the door, hand clamped over his mouth, the vomit spurting through his fingers. Out in the street, he fell onto his knees and retched loudly.

He now knew what the smell was. The stench of death.

When he found the courage to stand again, he gave himself a few moments to steady his breathing. The thought of going back inside, to see it again, did he have the strength? He knew he had to, if only to confirm his worst fears, so he turned and groped forward.

The old woman lay on her back, as before. Not a dream, not a wild imagining of his fertile brain. Her torso was twisted at an impossible angle, her head pointing in the other direction, body wrung like an old rag, soaked in red. The blood, already congealed, had bloomed from the vicious, gaping tear in her throat. Flies obscured her face, but he knew it was she. Those wide, open eyes told him so. Señora Gomez. Kind, Dear Señora Gomez. Murdered.

He hung onto the doorframe and his self-control evaporated. He began to cry. The world collapsed all around him as the enormity of what had happened struck home. He did not care if his sobs brought others to the house. He slid down into the dirt and sat, knees against his chest and gave himself up to his grief, body convulsing from loud, prolonged wails of despair and anguish. What now of his life, without this kindly old woman to see to Constanza? How to continue his job delivering bread, go to his classes, better himself, do all the things he had ever dreamed. Señora Gomez had been his lifeline, his helping hand, always there to comfort the family, see to Constanza, sit with Mama. Luis put his head back, awash with tears, and cursed his existence, his bad luck, his…

He stopped, becoming angry with himself, an over-whelming feeling of guilt and shame overcoming him. How could he think of his own situation at a time like this? That poor woman, lying in that cold, dark room, ripped apart by some mad beast, had lost her life. And here he was, feeling sorry for himself! He cursed, clenched his fists and pounded the ground. There would be time enough for such, selfish thoughts. Right now, he needed to alert others, get an investigation started, apprehend the fiend responsible for such a heinous crime.

He got to his feet, breathing hard, ignoring the smell, his mind ripped open by blackened shards of memory from the charnel house that had been the home of his friend. Questions, cold and clinical, came to the fore. Who had done this and why? The old woman was not wealthy, possessed few belongings. No more, or less, than anyone else in the village. But whoever had attacked her was looking for something. Something of value. She had tried to prevent them from destroying her possessions and had paid for her efforts with her life, over-powered in a ghastly, insane act of unimaginable violence.

A new, even more terrible thought took root in his mind. The sounds he had heard in the night must have been the noise of the struggle, and then, afterwards, the murderer had stood outside his own door, listening. Luis pressed his fingers into his eyes, waves of nausea mixed with terror washing over him. He battled to keep himself under control, but the horror of it became too much and he vomited again, his whole body heaving, dispelling the last vestiges of its contents into the dirt. It was pure bile now and still he retched, spluttering, face glistening with sweat, drool dripping down his chin, throat burning with stomach acid. He pressed the back of his hand against his mouth, squeezed his eyes shut. The murderer, whoever it was, would have done for him, of that he was certain. The danger remained, the killer abroad in those narrow, twisting streets. He shook his head and, blinking in the growing heat, forced himself to break in to a wavering run, to find the mayor and raise the alarm.

The village seemed so much larger that morning, and he struggled over the last few steps to the mayor's residence. His mind returned over and over to the image of poor Señora Gomez, lying there in that dark room, alone, the horror of what had befallen her oozing out of every piece of broken furniture, just as her lifeblood had run thick across the floor. With the scene indelibly seared into his consciousness, he wondered how would he ever be able to sleep untroubled again.

As he reached the great wrought-iron gates of the mayor's house, Luis paused and ran through the horror of what he had seen. However hard he tried, he could make no sense of it. Nothing in his life so far had equipped him for anything like this. He had listened to tales about the war, the terrible excesses, the mindless brutality, but they dwelled on the other side of reality, a million miles away. Mere stories, conjured up to send children to bed with nightmares. The soldier had said as much, about ogres. Fairytales. This, however, this was something more. Real, vivid and immediate. Death had come tramping down the streets of his village, and in a few brief, terrible moments, had taken Señora Gomez away. There was no reason to it all, none that he could see. And if an old, defenceless woman could lose her life in such a way, what for the rest of the villagers, the ones who did possess items of value? Luis knew that his life, and the lives of everyone in Riodelgado, would never be the same again. He looked up at the sky, pure blue, not a single cloud to mar the view. Some would call it a paradise and perhaps it once was. But no longer. A sigh rattled in his throat, and he pushed open the gates and trudged up the broad, winding path to the great house.

He climbed the steps and peered upwards. All was quiet, the house standing silent and resentful. Like an unwelcome visitor, Luis stood, in two minds as to what to do. He had never been here before, despite it being so close to his own home. The one substantial building in Riodelgado, a village of a few huddled adobe buildings, dominated by this veritable mansion. How had the mayor acquired the wealth to build such a place and yet not lavish any of it upon the villagers? Such questions he had pondered on many times, but knew he should not voice. No one should ever question the power, authority or business of the mayor. No questions about anything.

Luis prepared himself and knocked on the thick, solid door. After a pause, he tried again, louder this time. Soon he was hammering with both fists. With no effect, Luis stepped back and scanned the upper storey. Perhaps there was no need to question the Mayor, but the dreadful deed needed explaining. So, taking a deep breath, Luis shouted, *"Señor mayor! Señor, come quickly!"*

He waited, and when there was no response, he bent down and shovelled up a handful of gravel and hurled them, with all his might, towards the first floor shuttered room. The tiny stones pinged against the wood, showering back down on him. Still nothing. Exasperated, he flung himself at the door, pounding it, yelling, "*Señor mayor, Señor mayor, please, come quickly!*"

The door was torn open so abruptly, that Luis almost stumbled forward onto his face. The Mayor stood, still in his nightgown, hair wild, eyes bulging, rage mixing with confusion, his mouth opening in a scream, "What in the name of God do you want at this hour?"

Luis took only a second to recover before he ploughed on, "Señor mayor, please, you must follow me, to the home of Señora Gomez, to see what has happened!"

The mayor glared, shook his head and ran a hand through his tangled hair, "How dare you come bursting into my home like this, you impudent pup. I'll have you flogged for this, dragging me out of bed at this ungodly hour!"

"*Please!*" Luis, unable to contain his patience or his respect any longer, grabbed the mayor by the front of his shirt and shook him, "For the love of God, you must come. It's Señora Gomez. She's been murdered!"

The mayor stepped back into the street, face ashen, tears dripping down his cheeks. For a good few minutes he stood unable to speak, gazing into nothingness. At last, he turned his wide eyes towards Luis and spoke, voice very low, trembling. "You... you found her like this?"

Luis nodded. "She usually comes to look after my sister, but after her usual time had passed, I became worried, so I came here to see what had happened." Luis looked back down the street. Talking about Constanza reminded him she remained alone in the house and had been for far too long. He made to return to his home.

"Wait a moment," spluttered the mayor, taking hold of Luis's shoulder. "Wait! I want you to go to the priest, you hear me? Run as fast as you can, tell him to come here. He'll know what to do."

"But Constanza –"

"Take a few minutes to check on her, Luis, but then run all the way to Brialles!"

Without hesitation, Luis set off.

It took but a few moments to verify Constanza was safe. She had gone into Mama's room, snuggled up close to her, and both of them lay in the little bed, fast asleep. He let out a long sigh of relief and whispered a small prayer of thanks. He left and broke into a run, dashing through the still quiet streets. He made one more detour before making to the church, this time to the baker's. Garcia looked up from behind his bench, great clouds of flour dust masking the look on his face.

"And what time do you call this, Luis?" He stopped, noticing Luis's anguished look, dropped the lump of dough in his hands and frowned. "Luis...? What has happened?"

"I'm sorry, Señor Garcia. It's old Señora Gomez, she's..." He couldn't bear to finish his sentence. Time was pressing, and the image of her destroyed body loomed up in his mind's eye again. He wiped his nose with the back of his hand. "I have to go to the priest, Señor Garcia. I have to fetch him."

He set off, not pausing to look back as Garcia's voice shouted out, "But the deliveries, Luis…"

They would have to wait. Everything would have to wait. Señora Gomez was dead, and at that moment, nothing else mattered.

Chapter 9

Chance Meeting

The church was deserted and, as before, the coldness struck him like a fist. Usually welcome due to the oppressive heat, the events of the morning changed his view of everything. Luis eased open the door as the first spattering of rain began to fall. In a land sucked dry of moisture, this too would have been welcomed, but not today. He peered into the interior and, for the second time that day, sensed something was wrong.

He took a deep breath, knowing he had to continue. His mind filled with apocalyptic images, of devils and demons prodding and stabbing with forks and firebrands. Señora Gomez dead, her body defiled, and now here, the terrible promise of something similar. He cursed his trepidation, fuelled by dread. Could Brialles also be dead? He stopped, waited, stared into the church interior, the whitewashed walls staring back at him, their brightness hurting eyes wet with tears. The village, visited by a monster, a fiend, exacting terrible acts upon the weak and helpless, the feckless, the selfish. A creature from hell, punishing sins past and present. Is that what all this was? Señora Gomez was none of those. A good woman, kind, helpful. Why should she be a victim of such callous disregard for life? Brialles may have answers. A man of God, he would understand.

Luis pressed his lips together and marched straight down the aisle towards the vestry where he had met up with the priest previously. His footsteps echoed throughout the cavernous, empty space, reverberating back at him in a kind of cruel mockery, the emptiness of that hallowed place like the hopelessness beating erratically in his heart...

When he put his head around the vestry door, the cold, empty room stared back at him, dashing any hope of a repeat meeting.

Swept clean, nothing remained in that place, not even the dust. Father Brialles had done as he had said: everything, all of the valuables, removed, all the accoutrements of the church service gone. As for the priest himself, there was no clue; even his robes of office were taken. Luis stepped across the threshold and stared unfocused at the far wall. He was at a loss what to do next, and then something moved behind him and he span around and almost cried out in surprise.

Filling the doorway, sucking on his pipe, stood the soldier.

He smiled. "So, Luis. We meet again."

Something in his easy manner caused Luis to stiffen, the man's unnatural smile forced, unfriendly, more of a sneer, perhaps even a snarl.

Luis trapped, his only escape route blocked by the soldier, shot his eyes around the room, searching out another exit. An old, forgotten door, a secret passage maybe. Often churches had them. There was nothing. His shoulders sagged, resigned to defeat, the terror building inside forcing him to break out in a sweat.

"What's the matter?" The man's tone sounded relaxed, but the situation was far from relaxed. Why was he here, and why now?

Luis spread out his hands. "I need to talk to Father Brialles, it's very urgent."

The man cocked a single eyebrow. "Really? Why, what's happened?"

"I can only tell the Father. I'm sorry."

"No matter." He smiled his oily smile again. His fingers crept to his belt and began to play absently with the hilt of his dagger. "But you need to understand one thing, Luis. The Father has gone."

"Gone?" Luis didn't understand. "Gone where? When? How long ago?"

The soldier shrugged. "I don't know. I came to see him, to talk to him about the ogre, and this is all I found. An empty church. The man has fled, Luis. Run away."

"Run away...?" He shook his head, looking down at the floor. "No, he couldn't, not now."

"What has happened? Tell me—I might be able to help."

Yes, you might. Luis looked into those cruel eyes, recognised the simmering threat of violence. The ability to kill someone without conscience. Someone like Señora Gomez. He swallowed hard. "The mayor sent me."

"Did he indeed. And why would he need a priest? Is he dying?"

"Dying?" Luis almost laughed. "No, of course not! He sent me to tell the good Father about Señora Gomez." Luis stopped, cursing himself for being so stupid, to have been lured into the trap of revealing all. What a fool he was!

"Señora Gomez? She's your neighbour, isn't she?" He gently played with the hilt of the dagger. "Has something happened to her?"

Luis knew he should simply clam up, speak no more about what had occurred. But the soldier's eyes were boring into his very soul, seeking out the truth. There would be no denying him. And, as if to underline the fact, the man, with deliberate slowness, drew the dagger from its scabbard and began to scratch at his cheek with the blade.

"She's..." Luis couldn't take his eyes off the cruel looking weapon. If the man pushed any harder, he would open up his own skin. The dagger seemed impossibly sharp. "She's been murdered," he blurted out at last.

A long silence followed, during which the soldier pulled back the dagger and scrutinised the point. He appeared calm, Luis' words causing no surprise. Luis waited, every sense buzzing with trepidation. At any moment, that hand would blur, the knife thrust plunging into his heart, extinguishing life in an instant. But when the hand did move, it was to slide the dagger back into its scabbard and he stood up straight. "Well, in that case, I think it's time we visited the mayor to tell him about our absent priest."

Luis dared not wipe the sweat beading across his upper lip. He released his breath with controlled slowness, not wanting the soldier to guess what thoughts were coursing through his mind. "And Señora Gomez?"

"Oh, she's not absent, Luis. She's dead, you said so yourself."

Luis bristled at the bad joke and did his best to harden his jaw, not to allow his emotions to show. "She was a good lady, and someone has murdered her."

The soldier held up his hand. "And we'll find the culprit, have no fear."

Luis gaped. "You think you know who it is?"

"I think I know who it *might* be." He winked, stepping aside to let Luis through. "But first, I need to speak to the mayor."

Luis felt a slight lightening of the spirit, suspecting he had misjudged the soldier. No killer would so readily allow a witness to a murder to live, let alone visit the mayor. "Very well," he said, keeping his voice even, "and me? What shall I do?"

"You?" The soldier's forehead creased in thought. "I think the best thing for you to do, Luis, is to go about your normal business. You have classes, do you not?" Luis nodded. "Then I suggest you go there."

Luis didn't need telling twice. He pushed past him, anxious to be free of that oppressive room. The stench of leather from the soldier's buff-jacket almost overwhelmed him. And something else too, a sudden thought. Luis stopped, frowning, and looked at the soldier. "But my sister, I can't just—"

Without warning, the soldier laid a heavy hand on Luis's shoulder. "Don't worry, Luis. I'll call in on my way. Everything will be fine."

Luis ran the back of his hand across his mouth. To trust this man, to allow him to step inside his own home and care for Constanza. A terrible anxiety nagged away at Luis, but he knew he had little real choice. The village had changed, its usual serenity replaced by fear. Time could never be reversed; the days of slow, quiet, untroubled normality gone. Nothing, to parody the man's words, would ever be fine again.

Chapter 10

A Map

Luis wandered down to the bridge, taking the long way around to his old tutor's home. Leaning over the stonewall, he absently dropped pebbles into the thin trickle of water below. Soon, this too would dry up and no further substantial rain would fall until next March. Some in Riodelgado spoke about late November being always wet, but Luis was not so sure. All of his Christmases had been bright and dry. As far as he remembered anyway. Memories, of course, played tricks. Just like the water. And soldiers.

Soldiers?

Luis raised his head, eyes scanning the horizon. He hadn't been wrong. He'd heard them before he saw them. Four cavalrymen, black as night, riding over the furthest hillside, making their way steadily towards the outskirts of the village. Luis, becoming afraid, dipped down behind the wall, holding his breath, hoping they hadn't seen him.

They came closer, the pounding of the hooves on the dry, unforgiving earth amplified the sound, the relentless drumming setting his teeth on edge. He leaned against the side of the wall, keeping himself as small as possible, dread coursing through him, turning his stomach to mush. Throughout the War, no soldiers had ever come this way, but now that the conflict was over, they came. And for what? Luis could not answer this question, but the many possibilities created such a terrible sense of unease he had to struggle to regulate his breathing. If they realized he was there, he knew for certain they would kill him.

So close were they now he could smell them, hear the horses dipping their heads into what was left of the stream, tongues lapping greedily at the water. They must have been riding for hours, days. But why here, why in Riodelgado?

A harsh bark, a snap in a foreign tongue, and they spurred their mounts and pushed them up the furthest bank in the direction of the village. Not Spanish voices, not voices that sounded like anything Luis had ever heard before. Rough, brutal men, used to getting their own way. Dangerous voices, dangerous men.

As the pounding of the hooves receded, he craned his head over the edge and studied them riding up the hillside. Three wore helmets, great silver things with plumes, the sun glinted off the metal, scaled tails protected their necks. He recognised them as so-called lobster pots. The fourth sported a floppy hat, not unlike the one who had come to the village only yesterday. A black feather dominated the crown. Perhaps their similarity to the original soldier was because they came from the same, what? Army? They might know one another, which would make their number five. Five soldiers, in a tiny place like Riodelgado.

Luis stood up, dusting off his knees, and turned, deciding to continue towards the house of Señor Martinez; the old tutor would know what to make of this, perhaps offer up some explanation.

"You are afraid of them, Luis?"

An involuntary cry spurted from his mouth at the sound of the voice, and Luis swung round, heart jumping wildly and he saw Carlos standing close, in full view. The tormentor, alone this time, smirked.

Luis exhaled and ran the flat of his hand over his face, wiping away the sweat. "Carlos, you almost scared me to death."

Carlos stepped forward, his eyes narrowing, "I've been watching you for some time, the way you reacted to those men. What are you frightened of? Who were they?"

"Soldiers, by the look of them. Where were you?"

Carlos nodded towards a tiny, squat building set back from the dirt track road. A hovel, its roof almost collapsed, rickety door hanging from its rusted hinges, the whole lot not much bigger than a pigpen. "My home." Luis didn't say anything. He had no idea Carlos lived there, nor that he was as poor as the dilapidated dwelling seemed to suggest. "I was in the garden, digging out the weeds, trying to make sure our beans and carrots grow well, when I heard them.

I looked out through the gate and then saw you." That smirk again, heavy with disdain and loathing. "Scared you, didn't they Luis? I wonder why."

Despite being on his own, Carlos still maintained an air of sneering indifference, of malice and heartlessness. Perhaps not as forcibly, but there nevertheless. Luis ran his wet palm down the side of his trousers and shook his head. "Anyone would be."

Carlos didn't reply and turned to look at the hillside. Luis followed his gaze. The soldiers had disappeared. "They seemed to know which way to go," said Carlos. "Perhaps they've been here before, or even come from here."

"No, they weren't Spaniards. I heard them speaking."

"Are you sure? Not Catalans, or Portuguese?"

Luis pressed his lips together, "I think I'd recognise those, Carlos." He shrugged his shoulders, "Germans, Dutch perhaps. Definitely not Spanish." He went to step past the other boy, but Carlos blocked his path. "I have to go Carlos, I'm late. Something terrible has happened, and I need to tell Señor Martinez."

"What do you mean? Terrible, like what?"

"You'll find out."

Luis took another step. Carlos put the palm of his hand against Luis's chest, the fingers curling around the top of his blouson. The pressure applied, Luis felt his stomach loosen as he looked deep into his adversary's cruel, unblinking eyes. "I said, *something terrible, like what*?"

Carlos, alone or not, was a formidable opponent. His hard, flat face, betrayed no emotion, but an expectation lingered there. He had asked the question, he demanded the answer. Luis made swift calculations. There was no reason why Luis shouldn't tell him about Señora Gomez; fairly soon everyone would know anyway as news of the horrific event ripped through the entire village like wildfire. But it was Carlos' manner than irked Luis so much, his arrogance, and above all else that terrible threat of sudden violence making him hesitate.

Carlos's eyes slowly narrowed, becoming mere slits. Luis knew that an outburst was close, so he steadied his breathing, keeping his voice low and even as he spoke. "Señora Gomez has been killed, murdered. Late last night. I found her this morning, and now I have to tell Señor Martinez."

Almost at once, something changed in Carlos's demeanour. His face crumpled, leaking colour. He stepped away, his mouth hanging open, and he shook his head, stupefied. No arrogance now in his voice, replaced by the frightened, confused uttering of a child, "You found her? Dead?" Luis nodded and a shudder ran through Carlos' body. His eyes gazed into a point way beyond in the distance, as if in that one moment he saw every image of his past being played out before him, and the tears welled up under the bottom lid of his eyes. "She's my aunty," he said, in a croaked whisper.

Luis stood, stunned. He had no idea of their relationship. If he had, he would have been a little gentler, letting the news out slowly, with more compassion. Señora Gomez was Carlos's aunty? How could hard, unbending Carlos have such a kind, thoughtful old lady as a relative?

Carlos, dumbstruck, stumbled back a few steps and fell down in the track, staring into nothingness, all of the fight and arrogance gone from him in an instant. Luis wondered what to do, feeling he should say something, put a hand on his shoulder, reassure him, anything. He knew he couldn't; too much had passed between them, too much hurt, so he shuffled off, keeping his footfall soft. He didn't look back until he came to the foot of a narrow, winding path that ran up to Señor Martinez's house and saw Carlos, still sitting, motionless. Luis's heart went out to the bully and he wished he could console him, be his friend. But Carlos would refuse any offer of condolence with a bitter cry and an accompanying fist.

Sighing, Luis turned. He doubted he and Carlos could ever be anything more than enemies. Even loss was not enough to span the gulf of malevolence between them. With his head hung low, he continued on his way.

Señor Martinez listened without comment as Luis told him all about what had happened. Only when he came to the part about the soldier at the church, did the old tutor stir, muttering something.

Luis spread out his hands. "Why would Father Brialles go away, Señor Martinez? What does he have to fear?"

Martinez rubbed his chin. "Much," was all he said. He stood up and went over to a large bureau-type desk, rolling up the lid with a clatter. He rummaged around and gave a little cry of triumph and turned around, face beaming. "Let me show you this, Luis, something which might make things somewhat clearer. Then, I think we will curtail our studies for today. You need to be with your family."

He motioned for Luis to join him at the large table and Martinez spread out the document he had found in the desk. Luis came up to the old man's shoulder and looked down. It was a map.

"Europe," explained Martinez, tracing his finger around the outline of a country in the south. "This is Spain, a peninsula, with Portugal to the west and France to the north." He jabbed at a large area of blue. "The Mediterranean, the cradle of European civilisation."

"Cradle? You mean, for a baby? Civilisation started here? In Spain?"

"No, not Spain. Here." He tapped an area in the east. "Just beyond this map, is Egypt. The Middle East. The Holy Land and Jerusalem. Where Our Lord walked and preached. We owe everything we are to what happened there."

Luis scanned the entire map, all the different shapes, the rivers and mountains, the names of cities and towns. A bewildering array of unknown and unexplained lands. He grinned. "I never knew it was so big," he said in awe.

"This map is about a hundred years old," said Martinez. "It has been with my family all that time." He ran his finger up from Spain up to the north and stopped somewhere in the middle. "The War has been raging right across this area, Luis. This is the Holy Roman Empire, a collection of princedoms and dukedoms that have fought against each other for a whole lifetime. The French are attempting to make this land their own and I fear, Spain will try and stop them."

"You mean, the War will go on?"

The old man straightened, winced a little and pressed his hand into the small of his back. "In another guise, I suspect. Spain is on the brink, Luis. Once, we were a great power, with an empire stretching right across the globe. We ruled lands in the Americas, so vast and rich we became the wealthiest nation on earth. Our armies were the best and for a hundred and fifty years we dominated Europe. But now, the dawn of a new era has arrived. If France overcomes us, it will be they who will become the dominant power, the new rulers of Europe."

Luis scratched his head, then waved his hand over the map. "But all of this, it is so far away. What has any of this struggle got to do with soldiers arriving in Riodelgado?"

"I'm not sure. But there has to be a link in some way. The distances are not so far to have prevented your soldier friend from coming here." Martinez pulled up a chair and settled himself down with a grunt. "You said you met him again, at the church?"

"Yes. And on the way here, I saw more."

"More?" Martinez frowned, face becoming serious. He gripped Luis's arm with such strength the boy gasped. "You have seen more soldiers? When? Why didn't you tell me?"

Fear, more than pain, forced Luis to rip himself free of his tutor's grip. "Señor Martinez! What is the matter?" He rubbed his arm briskly whilst Martinez scowled. "I was going to tell you, but then you showed me the map... Is this news important?"

"*Important*?" Martinez brought his fist down onto the map with a smash and stood up, moving with surprising speed towards his drinks' cabinet. Luis watched as the old man tore open the cap from a wide, squat bottle and poured out a generous measure of deep, ruby wine. Without hesitating, Martinez swallowed the entire glassful in one and gasped. He leaned against the cabinet, his breathing ragged, and his voice sounded brittle and afraid as he spoke, without turning: "Yes, Luis, it is important—*very.*" He poured himself another glassful, his hand shaking. This time he sipped at the liquid, taking his time, savouring the taste. He turned. "I'm sorry, this has come as a shock. First Señora Gomez, and now these... men. You spoke to them?"

"No. I don't think they even saw me. But Carlos did, and when I told him about Señora Gomez, he broke down. He was her nephew."

Martinez nodded and took another large mouthful. He grew calmer, more like his old self. "If you see them again, steer well clear, Luis, do you understand? They are dangerous men. Dark times have come to

Riodelgado. I always feared one day they would, but it is a surprise nevertheless. And, an unwelcome one." As if reaching a sudden decision, he moved over to the table and folded up the map. He thrust it towards Luis. "Take this, study it. Don't come back, not for a few days. Then we will talk again." He smiled, the usual warmth returning, features soft and kind. "I'm sorry for startling you, Luis." Luis took the proffered map and looked down at it in his hands. Martinez placed a hand on the boy's shoulder. "The world has come knocking on our door, Luis. We have no choice but to let it in."

Luis frowned deeply but the old tutor said nothing more and Luis left, wondering what Señor Martinez's parting words meant.

Chapter 11

Into Pieces

Rushing down the steep path, Luis was mindful that he had been away too long and that no one would be looking after Constanza. The soldier had said he would call in, but the very idea of that was unnerving. To allow a complete stranger into his home, to be with his mother and sister, both of whom were so defenceless, conjured up a whole host of dreadful, nightmarish thoughts. Above all else, the idea of the soldier knowing where he lived troubled Luis. Had the soldier followed him, or visited the village last night? With his stomach churning, Luis speeded up his walk until it became more of a run.

In his desire to get home, with head down, the map gripped in his fist, he didn't see them until it was too late. He should have known, he should have realised, but his mind was too full of worries and concerns. The first indication of their presence was when he turned the corner, and Carlos' voice rang out, "Hey, look who it is, a pretty girl come to say hello. Where have you been all my life?"

The guffaws from the gang were so loud they must have resounded throughout the whole village. Luis stopped, breathing hard, desperate to get home, but knowing that if they sensed his anxiety it would be perfect fuel for their goading. So he stood and waited.

Pushing themselves away from the fountain, they circled him, their faces full of sneers and leers. One of them flicked Luis's hair, calling him 'a fop!' Another pushed him in the back, 'Where's your dress, little girl?' Luis stood and he took it, biting back the tears of frustration and anger that brewed inside.

Then Alvaro spotted the map. The big thug made a lunge for it but Luis, quicker, skipped out of range. The relief was only momentary. From behind, out of sight, strong arms grabbed him, seizing him in a crushing bear hug. It was Carlos, and he was laughing down Luis's ear.

"What have we here?" Alvaro snatched the map and unfolded it. He studied it, tongue tipping his top lip. "Interesting. Is this part of your studies, Luis?"

"What is it?" asked Francisco, straining to see.

"It's a map," said Luis, trying to struggle free. But it was useless; Carlos, too strong, tightened his hold. Luis sagged, the fight draining from him. "It's of no value, Alvaro, I swear."

"That means it probably is," cackled Carlos, squeezing a bit tighter.

"No!" Luis struggled to keep the desperation out of his voice, "I promise you, it's just an old, useless map.

Nothing more. Please, give it back." He knew, deep down, that the more he tried to convince them, the more unconvinced they would become, but he little choice. The fear of them destroying it, ripping it up; what would Señor Martinez say then?

"It's very old," said Francisco, peering over Alvaro's shoulder. "We could sell it."

"Buy some food, have a party!" Manuel, who had made this announcement, took up a little jig, hands above his head, clicking his fingers. The others roared with appreciation, clapping their hands in unison, laughing loudly.

"So," Alvaro's voice rose above the clamour and silenced them. He grinned, wafted the map in front of Luis' face. "It's valuable, yes?"

Luis closed his eyes. What was the point, they were going to take the map, sell it to someone for a few miserable coins, and Señor Martinez would scold him for being so cowardly. Dejected, he merely shook his head.

"Ah, Luis," said Alvaro, putting his fingers under Luis's chin and tilting his head back. "Don't get upset. We're all friends together, right?" He turned around to his acolytes, spreading out his hands theatrically, "Am I not right?"

They all cheered and Luis wished he could disappear, or even die. Grim, terrible acceptance of the fate that awaited him sapped the strength from his body.

Alvaro jutted his face close to Luis's, hissing through clenched teeth, "I know it's not worth a sot, Luis." Luis looked up from under his brows, studying

Alvaro keenly. He wondered where all this was leading. "But to you, I think it is worth much more than money, eh?" He stepped back, folding the map up again, this time in a twisted, creased mockery of its former pristine condition. Without a pause, he struck Luis hard across the face with it. Luis cried out, the others whooped with glee. He brought his face up, glared at Alvaro, a new intense anger over-taking him as he watched the swaggering bully slowly begin, as Luis had feared, to the tear the map up into a multitude of tiny pieces, tossing the remnants into the air, where soon they floated back down to the ground, like so many snowflakes. But instead of melting, they settled in the dirt and mocked Luis for his weakness. Alvaro laughed and dusted his hands together for a job well done.

Luis closed his eyes, defeat complete. *Why*. That was the only word that ran through his mind. *Why*. Carlos released him, the fun ended and Luis dropped to his knees, head down, hands coming up to cover his face. He sobbed, his body convulsing as the little gang began to drift away, leaving their prey, and the only emotion Luis had was shame, shame at not having the strength to stand up to them, to stop them.

When he couldn't cry anymore, his throat raw, his eyes unable to focus properly, Luis sat back, taking in shuddering breaths, trying to break through the ignominy and recover some sense of self-worth. He blinked a few times, rubbed his eyes with his fists and looked around at the scattered remnants of the map.

Another wave of hopelessness washed over him as he saw that the map was beyond saving. Some pieces spiralled away in the light breeze, others lay at the bottom of the fountain, soaking in the damp silt. He reached out and picked up a nearby piece. It showed part of Spain. Anger came, like a slow-burner, building up in intensity, until at last he couldn't contain himself any longer and he screwed up the scrap of parchment, making a tight fist. He threw back his head and cried out. Cursing the world, his life, everything and everybody that had ever lived, he looked up into the azure blue sky and silently prayed for strength. Then he closed his eyes, waiting for the embers to cool, and gradually, feeling a little stronger, he climbed to his feet and took the first tentative step towards his home.

Almost at once, he saw a figure come around the corner, tramping across the village square, the heavy tread of his boots sending up tiny pirouettes of dust, leading a miserable looking mule, over-laden with bags. His face, half in shadow from the wide-brimmed straw hat he wore, seemed streaked with black soot, and he trudged with the air of someone who had come a long way, his shoulders round, bearing the heaviness of exhaustion.

Luis, weak and defeated, experienced a tiny tickle of happiness at the man's arrival. He smiled as the man drew closer. "Pablo," he said, his voice a mere croak.

The traveller stopped, cocked his head to one side and pursed his lips. "Oh no, not again. What have they done to you this time, Luis?"

Luis shrugged. "No more than usual." He kicked at some scattered pieces of the map that lay at his feet. "This was Señor Martinez's map. He gave it to me to study. They destroyed it."

Pablo clamped his lips together, exhaling hard through his nose. "Are you hurt?"

"No. At least, not my body." He forced a smile. "I could deal with that, Pablo." Luis shook his head and slumped down onto the fountain's stone seat. The traveller moved closer and placed his arm gently around the boy's shoulders. "It won't last forever." His face brightened and he turned to rummage through his saddlebags. After a moment, he turned again and handed Luis a dull, warped coin. "It's German, from Bavaria. I thought you might like it."

Luis turned the coin over in his fingers and smiled. The profile of an old king, almost totally worn away, dominated one side, the obverse a smudged eagle. "Thank you." He slipped it into his pocket and together they made their way up the slope towards Luis' home.

The narrow street that led to his house stood just a few dozen paces before the bridge that crossed the river from which the village derived its name. On the far side was the tavern in which Felipe scratched a living from the few locals and itinerants that frequented its walls. Reined outside, with their heads hanging low, stood four horses, sorry looking beasts, manes matted, coats streaked with dried sweat. Their backs groaned under the combined weight of heavy leather saddles and bulging saddlebags.

Pablo stopped and laid his hand on Luis' shoulder. "You have seen the owners of those horses?"

Luis noted the tone in Pablo's voice, not so unlike Carlos' when he heard the news of his aunty. Shock, mingled with dread. "I saw them earlier, coming over the hill at the far end of the village. Why, do you know who they are?"

Pablo looked down, and although his eyes were steady, Luis knew the man struggled to keep himself calm. The way his lips quivered slightly, the tiny tic in his temple. "I know *about* them," he said and turned again to study the four mounts. "I passed them earlier this morning, on the road to Anteguerra."

"You were all the way there, and you turned back? Why would you do that?"

Pablo shook his head, his voice becoming distant, almost as if he were speaking to himself. "I wasn't sure if they would come here, so I followed them for a while. I lost them in one of the mountain passes, but something about them caused me to become fearful, so I changed my course and head here." He turned once more to Luis. "I wasn't' sure, but now that I know, I've got to warn the mayor of their arrival before it's too late."

"I don't understand, Pablo. Warn us? Who are they, what do they want?"

Pablo stood for a long time, his breathing heavy, laboured. "Those men, they are the Devil's own,

Luis." He stiffened, "I want you to go and tell the mayor that these men have arrived. If you see that other soldier, you must tell him also."

"How do you know all this, Pablo? The *other* soldier?"

"Call it my sixth-sense, if you like." He gave a wry smile. "No, I saw him. And it is clear he is not all that close to those others. An acquaintance, rather than a friend."

"If you say so, Pablo, but I don't know how you know all this. You call it a sixth sense? I'm not so sure. How do you come by this information?"

"I listen, I watch, I sift. I've been walking these trails for years, my little friend. And if there is one thing I know better than most, it's human nature. Now, deliver my message to the mayor whilst I continue to find out what I can."

A new heaviness of limbs and spirit came over Luis. He'd had this conversation before, with the mayor himself. Forever pulled this way and that, with no control over his own decisions, he'd had enough of being everyone's servant. He sighed, knowing he had little choice. "All right, but first I have to go home, Pablo, I have to check that Constanza is well."

Pablo stared into the distance, tongue running over his bottom lip, thinking. "The mayor has to know. Perhaps he could gather some men together..." After a moment's consideration he shook his head. "Perhaps not. Go home Luis, then to the mayor. Tell him what I have said. That the Devil's own have come to *Rio Delgado*."

Chapter 12

The Devil's Own

Stepping through the door was like entering a different world. It had been bright outside, but here all was gloom and darkness. The fug from the soldiers' pipes obscured the details of the room, but Pablo knew it well enough from many visits and he crossed through the thick, stinking pall to the bar.

Felipe appeared from out of the murkiness, wiping his large hands over his apron. "You're back," he muttered.

Pablo nodded, leaning across the counter, quickly peering towards the four soldiers who all sat around a table, tankards and a large plate of bread and meat in front of them. None of them acknowledged the traveller's presence, a fact that Pablo felt grateful for. He eyed them for a second. A lifetime of surviving on his wits and intuition had equipped him with many abilities. One of these was assessing situations quickly. He felt the tension in the room as if it were a living thing, closing in on him, and his throat became dry and tight and he turned again to Filipe. "Water."

Filipe poured water into a cup from a large flagon of water and handed it over. Pablo drank it down, and coughed. The water eased his throat a little, but did nothing to wash away the feelings of unease.

He frowned at Filipe, hoping that the innkeeper would take the meaning. He did, throwing a quick glance towards the soldiers, then back to Pablo. He shook his head once.

Pablo nodded and turned to go.

He hadn't noticed anything, not seen or heard any movement whatsoever, not even the scraping of a chair. But there, as if materialising from the air itself, one of the soldiers stood in front of him. A big man, square headed, brutish looking jaw and broken nose. A deep scar ran from the corner of his right eye down to the side of his mouth. It seemed to glow, even in the gloom. Pablo's knees began to buckle and he had to hold onto the counter to prevent himself from falling.

"I know you."

The man spoke in Spanish, but with an accent. German. Pablo's one good eye darted around the room, seeking an escape route. The other soldiers turned their faces towards him, sat and waited, spectators, cruel smiles splitting their hard faces.

A noise, like the scraping of metal against stone, and the point of a dagger jabbed under Pablo's chin. Gasping, Pablo tried to back off but the solid edge of the counter dug hard into his back, preventing any such movement. He winced. Forward or back, pain welcomed him.

"I said, I know you," the man hissed. He applied more pressure, tilting Pablo's head further back. "I've seen you somewhere. Tell me where."

Pablo, his throat so dry he could hardly swallow, nodded. "Yes," he managed. "On the road. I'm a traveller."

"Spy, more like."

Oh my God, he means to kill me! Pablo threw out his hands, a gesture which caused the soldier to instantly jerk forward, his knee ramming upwards between Pablo's legs. A pain like fire erupted through his groin, followed by an overwhelming desire to be sick. He lurched forward, clamping his hands over the epicentre of eruption, retched loudly and collapsed to his knees, bent double, forehead against the floor.

The other men laughed. Pablo could hear them, through the surging waves of agony. He had never known anything like this, in all his years. Fear, so intense it became a living thing, consuming him, the overwhelming sensation taking hold of his entire being. From somewhere something heavy gripped his shoulder and pushed him backwards with a sharp jolt. He hit the ground, curled up tight, whimpering.

"*Stop!*"

A voice from the distance. A long way off, from the far end of a winding black tunnel. Filipe's voice.

"*Please,* he is no spy, he is what he says, just a weary traveller. He often calls here, bringing us news."

"If I see him again, I'll rip out his lungs, you understand me?"

"Yes. But please, let him be. I beg you."

Through eyes blurred as if peering through a swirling mist, Pablo saw hands taking hold of him, helping him to sit up. Through a red veil, he made out the door and through it the light of the day, a beacon of safety. If he could reach it, all would be well and good. He could continue with his life, keeping himself to himself, living on his wits. Wits which had failed him this day. How had he not heard him, how had he not assessed the danger?

Filipe wiped Pablo's face with a cool, damp cloth and Pablo smiled, recovered a little, becoming aware of his surroundings, the pain easing at last. The nausea remained heavy and thick in his stomach, a reminder of the attack, but he had strength enough to walk unaided and he staggered, like a drunkard, to the door.

The light hit him like a blow, forcing him to recoil, and he brought up his hand to shield his eyes from the glare. A stab of pain again in his loins and he swayed over to the bridge, leaned over the parapet and vomited into the pathetic trickle of a river below. He sucked in quick, sharp breaths and, groaning, he slid down to the ground and sat with his back against the wall and shivered in shame and horror. Throat like sand, he took gulps of air through his mouth and thanked God he had survived. He closed his eyes and tried to settle himself. When he felt able, he got to his feet and slowly made his way to Luis's home.

Luis looked up as the figure of man filled the doorway. He stepped back, knocking over his chair, letting out a cry of alarm. But then the man's voice came and Luis relaxed as Pablo spoke: "Oh Luis, please..." He stumbled forward and Luis quickly came around the table and caught him as the man fell forward. He was too heavy for Luis to prevent him from hitting the ground, but his intervention softened the impact a little. Luis rolled Pablo over onto his back and gazed down at the man's stricken face.

"Pablo, what in Heaven's name has happened to you?"

The man croaked something indecipherable and Luis rushed over to the kitchen and poured some water from the jug into the one, wooden goblet the family possessed. He came back, stooped down and supported Pablo's head as he gently tipped the goblet to the man's lips.

Pablo coughed and spluttered as the water hit his mouth. Gradually he relaxed as the liquid got to work and restored some of his strength. Luis dabbed at the man's forehead and saw the one good eye regaining some of its former lustre.

Sitting up, Pablo ran a hand over his face, took the goblet from Luis and drained it. He shook his head. "My God, Luis. They nearly killed me."

"Who? The soldiers? What happened, what did they do?"

Pablo held up his hand, "Enough to say they didn't succeed! They think I am a spy and have threatened me that if they see me again..." His voice trailed away.

Luis helped Pablo to his feet and then guided him to a hard-backed chair, where he sat and stared out across the room. "They are Germans," he said after a short pause. "They must have come down from the fighting in the north. Mercenaries, soldiers of fortune, willing to cut your throat for a scrap of bread. I've met their like a hundred times, but the man who attacked me," Pablo shook his head. "He was like no other. Strong, like a bull. And quiet. I didn't notice him until it was too late, then," he slammed his fist into the palm of his other hand, "as quick as that, he hit me. I didn't stand a chance." Luis poured him another drink from the jug and Pablo took it and drank. "Thank you, Luis. Your family, did you find them well."

"Very well. Constanza is sleeping with Mama, but someone had been here, made them some food, tidied up, stayed with them."

"Who?"

Luis shook his head. "The soldier, the one in the square." Pablo stared, demanding further explanation. "He said he would, you see. He met me at the church, told me to go to the mayor's whilst he called in on Mama and Constanza. I was on my way when I saw you."

"The one who has spoken of an ogre, in the mountains?"

"Yes. He seems to know more than he's letting on."

Pablo sniggered and finished off the water, turning the empty goblet around in his hands. "I'm not so sure about all that, Luis. I think it's a smoke screen, designed to prevent anyone from going up into the mountains. He's a liar and you shouldn't trust him, despite what he might have done for you and your family. And these other soldiers, I think they are connected in some way. They seemed to be waiting, not in any rush to move away."

"But what about Señora Gomez? She's been murdered."

"I don't know, but it's strange that all of this should happen as soon as that soldier appears. This was a quiet place before he came."

"I have to go to the Mayor, let him know what has happened. Father Brialles has gone, taken everything from the church, all the gold, the silverware. Did you know that? Pablo, what is going on?"

"I haven't a clue, Luis. But I'll say this, I think you should stay out of it. You're only a boy, and your mother and sister need you. They are you first concern, Luis. Leave the other troubles to the authorities. Stay home, continue with your studies, and one day all of this will be nothing more than a bad dream."

"My studies? How am I supposed to continue with them? Señora Gomez was the only person who ever helped me, and now…" He shook his head. "No, I will have to give them up, I have no choice."

"But you can't, Luis." Pablo's hand shot forward, seizing Luis', squeezing hard. "What will become of you Luis, if you give it all up, eh? What will become of your dreams?"

"I will have to forget about them, Pablo." He pulled his hand away and sat back, looking down at the table. "They were stupid dreams, anyway. To be a writer!" He gave a single, sharp laugh. "I dreamed of being another Cervantes, that I would one day write a great novel and become famous. *Don Luis*, that is what they would call me. But now... Now, everything has disappeared because life has played its hand and all my cards are useless."

"Life is not a game, Luis. We are not dealt anything; we make our own choices, take our own luck."

"You believe that, Pablo? I don't. I believe some people are given all the luck in the world, always dealt the best hands, whilst some of us are destined to scrape around in the filth until the day we die."

"You're too cynical, Luis. You shouldn't think like that, not whilst you're so young, with so much yet to discover."

"I didn't used to think like this, Pablo. But with Señora Gomez dead, everything has changed and become very simple." He leaned forward, putting his chin on his hands. "My family. I have to look after them. That's my life now."

Pablo sighed and stood up. "I left my mule just the other side of the bridge. I'll go and fetch her, then I'm leaving, and I don't know when I will return."

Luis pulled out something from inside his shirt and smoothed it down on the tabletop. It was a piece of the map Señor Martinez had given him. "This is Spain," said Luis. "One day I wanted to travel, like you. Go to all the places I have only dreamed about."

"It might be best if you tempered your ambitions, Luis. The world is a fascinating place, but it is also one filled with uncertainty and danger. The war continues to rage in the north. Who knows when it will end."

"But it will end, Pablo."

The traveller smiled, "Yes. It will, and with God's good grace, we will live through it."

"I think that, perhaps, this tiny fragment of the map is a sign. A sign that one day, a very, very long way off, I might be able to salvage something of my ambitions. A grain of hope, Pablo. That is what will keep me going."

Pablo laid his hand on Luis's shoulder. "Your words show how determined you really are, Luis, so hold onto them, and your dreams, even if you have to put them aside for a little while. I am in awe of the strength you show, for one so young, I honestly am." He smiled, and the warmth glowed from his battered face. "God bless you, Luis. Take care of your family, but mostly, take care of yourself."

He turned and strode out into the burning day.

Luis sat and gazed at the open doorway. Strength? What strength did he have? Where was it when those boys did what they did? No, he had no strength. Just an acceptance of how cruel and merciless life could be.

From within, his mother's voice called to him. Weak, pathetic. Luis knew she was close to the end and then it would be just him and Constanza.

The two of them, to face the cruel world together.

Chapter 13

The Morning Blight

Luis awoke with a start.

For a moment, he wondered where he was and his eyes snapped left and right, trying to make out any familiar shapes or items of furniture. The room, draped in partial darkness was thick with steaming, suffocating air. He ran a hand over a face that dripped with sweat. The curse of summer nights. Heat.

He knew it was his house. The dream of figures standing over him, faceless and huge, had all gone now. By the weak, grey light struggling through gaps in the door, the room and the things inside took shape. His home. His life.

Groping over to the kitchen, he poured water over his hands from the jug and swilled his face. He stood there, head down, letting the water drip into the basin beneath. Next to it a knife, the only cooking implement he possessed of any worth. Sharp enough to slice through the toughest cut of meat, whenever they could afford any meat. Slowly Luis hefted the heavy blade in his hand.

It wasn't the dream that had woken him.

He knew that now.

He whirled around, the blade coming up defensively and the charge of fear crushed his chest, forcing him to groan. His hand trembled, the strength drained from limbs. The soldier reached out and gently took the knife from Luis's grip.

"Dangerous," the man breathed.

"What...?" Luis shook his head, allowing himself to slip to the floor, his legs no longer able to support him.

The soldier carefully placed the blade on the table, swept up the water jug and, within a blink, tipped its contents over Luis's head. The boy coughed, but was grateful for the sensation. It brought the senses back, refreshed his mind, snapped him back into the present. He got to his feet, wiping both hands over his face.

"You should always lock your door, Luis. You never know who might wander in."

"I must have fallen asleep." Luis turned and looked out through the open shutters. He took in a deep breath. The first streaks of the approaching dawn, like ragged tears in the fabric of the night sliced through the sky, offered up a glimmer of hope that today might be a better day. Always the hope, a tiny shaft of optimism, every morning. And every morning, the reality that life was always going to be hard and bleak and sometimes, like now, dangerous, consumed those same hopes. Luis turned, the feeble light enabling him to make out the man's features. "How long have you been here?"

"Most of the night. I came earlier, to see to your sister and your mother." He paused. "She is very ill, Luis. You know that."

"It's not plague," he said quickly.

"I didn't think it was. I've seen plague. Watched people die of it. Not pretty."

"You've seen...?" Luis had no understanding of how anyone, even a man such as this, could experience such things and still retain the will to carry on. He quickly changed the subject, the nightmare vision of plague too much for this time of the morning. "Thank you, for what you have done."

The man shrugged and turned around, leaning back against the table. His leather coat creaked as he folded his arms across his chest. "You saw some soldiers yesterday, so I understand."

"How do you know that?"

He looked askance at the boy and tapped the side of his nose. "I have my ways. Four of them, yes?"

"I think Pablo had a taste of the type of men they are. He was attacked by one of them."

"They fought with Pappenheim at Lutzen. Hard men. Fearless. Not many like them left."

"You know them?"

The soldier laughed at the incredulity in Luis's voice. "Oh yes, I know them very well." He reached over and ruffled the boy's hair. "I was their commander. Their leader." He pushed himself off the table and strode back across the main room to the doorway, where he stopped and leaned against the frame. Very methodically, he brought out his pipe and began to pack it with tobacco. Luis wandered over to join him. A belt of almost pure white was coming up over the hillside. It did little to cheer Luis's mood. The arrival of the soldiers, what had happened to Pablo and the death of Señora Gomez had all combined to turn his safe little village into a portal of danger. But why had they come now, these soldiers? He looked up at the man standing next to him. "If you know them," he said, "then you'll know what they're doing here."

The man laughed. "I said I was their leader, Luis. Not their nursemaid. And besides," he paused, his thumb pressing down in the pipe bowl, "I am not their leader any longer. They take orders from no man. Not now."

"Then, what *do* they want?"

He tapped Luis's chest with the stem of the pipe. "That, my friend, we will have to find out."

Garcia looked up through a cloud of white flour, pressing his fists down hard in the dough. "My God, Luis, I didn't think I'd be seeing you again!"

Luis cocked his head. "Why? I need this job, Mr Garcia. I can still do the deliveries whilst Constanza sleeps. By the time I've finished, she'll just be getting up in time for breakfast."

"Well, if you think it's feasible."

"I do."

Garcia smiled. "Good. I'm glad." He nodded to a pile of bundled bread placed at the far end of the table. "It's all there."

Luis went to go, but Garcia stopped him with a cry. "Luis! Just before you go—these men, these soldiers. You saw them?"

How did news travel so fast? Luis nodded. "Yes. Four of them. They're staying a Felipe's."

Garcia nodded, still kneading bread. "And that other one, the very tall man. You've spoken to him, haven't you?"

For a reason he couldn't understand, Luis thought it best to remain neutral, not give too much away. It was all idle gossip, of course, but Garcia's mood had altered, become tense. Did he have an inkling as to what these men wanted, what they planned to do? "Yes, but only briefly."

Garcia nodded. "I fear that their presence will bring nothing but pain and misery to our village, Luis." He stopped kneading and leaned forward, his eyes holding Luis. "We all need to be on our guard."

Luis stared wide-eyed at the baker. His voice, so flat, so ominous, made his heart skip a beat. Slowly, fear, like a lead weight, came crushing down across his chest again, making breathing difficult. Without hesitation, Luis quickly collected the bundles of bread together and rushed out to begin his delivery round.

Luis raced through the deliveries, finishing them much more quickly than he had ever done previously. The baker's tone, more than his words, affected him greatly. The arrival of the soldiers had brought a great black cloud with them, and it hung over the village like funeral drapes. Black, cold, horrible. It made him shiver just to think about it.

Walking back along the high road which circled the village and would eventually bring him back down into the square, he saw a large body of men gathering together outside the gates of the Mayor's *hacienda*. They appeared agitated, with their serious faces and quick, jabbering speech. As Luis approached, he picked up one or two snatched sentences. '*I blame them, all of them... Only a boy, it's not right... It has to be as the soldier said... But there's no reason for it... Does there have to be a reason... It's food, that's all it is... Mother of God, how can you even think such a thing...*'

"Enough!"

Luis gave a start and turned to see the Mayor, dressed in his clothes of office, opening his gates and stepping out to confront the men. Flanked by two guards, pole arms shimmering in the bright sunshine, he waited with hands on hips, a hard, serious look on his face.

The group of men grew quiet, bowing respectfully, they shuffled their feet, crushed by embarrassment. None looked towards their mayor.

"I can hear your gibberish from my house!" He stuck his thumbs in his belt and glared at the assembly. "I'm sick of this kind of talk, this title-tattle, do you hear me? l want you to listen carefully, to the *truth*." He took a breath. " So far all we know is that the boy has gone missing. His mother woke this morning to find the front door forced open, the place ransacked and the boy's bed empty. She went outside and discovered tracks leading up to the mountain. She then rushed here to tell me what had happened."

One man piped up loudly, "Why didn't she wake up if the place had been ransacked?"

"Drunk probably," said another.

"Was she even there? I know that woman, never at home, always out with someone or other."

"Been 'out' with you, hasn't she, Nico?"

A wave of muttering and laughter rippled through the assembly.

"*Quiet!*" The Mayor blew out his cheeks, "All of this is not going to help us find the boy! I want you all to go home, prepare some food and drink for each of you, and pick up any weapons you might have. Even a pitchfork will do. I have a few swords down in the *plaza*, but no muskets I am afraid. None that work, anyway."

"Pistols? We must have some pistols. My old dad has a couple from the time of the Armada."

"Dear Lord, they won't work!"

"They might. I could give them a good clean, fire off a couple of rounds."

"Aye, and blow your own hand off when it backfires!"

Another burst of laughter. Luis crept closer until, at last, one of the men noticed him and glared, face like fury, eyes bulging. "What the Devil are you doing here?" The man raised his hand to strike Luis, but the Mayor was there first, catching the man by the wrist.

"Don't you raise your hand to this boy."

They all stopped, gaping at the Mayor. The two bodyguards moved forward, pole arms pointing forward, braced for attack.

"But you know who this is?" The same man, who had tried to hit Luis, tore his hand from the Mayor's grip. "This boy knows who murdered the old Gomez woman! And what has he done since, eh? I ask you." He turned his withering gaze upon Luis. "I'll tell you what he's done. Stayed inside his house, like the rat that he is. And you, Señor Mayor, with all your fine talk of pistols and swords, what have you done up until now?"

"Well, I'm doing something *now*, damn you."

"If you had acted sooner, Francisco would still be alive."

Luis gasped, the sound of the boy's name almost knocking him backwards. Francisco, one of his many tormentors, he was the one who was missing, snatched away in the night? Luis couldn't believe it. He stared towards the ground, unable to overcome the tightening of his guts, the rising panic, feeling more afraid than ever before in his life.

"These damn rumours!" screamed the Mayor. "That's all your good for, the lot of you." His head appeared to swell, cheeks bulging, blossoming bright crimson. He glared at the man who had spoken up so vehemently. "We don't know Francisco is dead, you idiot, all we know is he is no longer at home. That is why we are going to go up into the mountains to find him."

"This rat knows what has happened." The same man pointed an accusing finger towards Luis, who stood and gaped, his body trembling. "He knows that soldier, the one who came out of nowhere, the one who told us about the ogre. I saw them talking together, and I'll squeeze the damned life out of him if he doesn't tell us what's going on." Without warning, his hand shot forward to seize Luis by the throat. He shook him like a rag. "Tell us what you know, damn you!"

Luis's eyes rolled up inside his head, all of his senses jingled about like a coin in a bucket. The man kept shaking him and soon he could see nothing but blackness, followed by a sharp stabbing pain in the back of his head. The sky filled his vision, so blue, perfect. He wondered if he might see a bird, winging south, escaping to a happier, more contented world where...

He blinked open his eyes, full consciousness returning. He was on the ground, the hard cobbles pressed against his body. He went to move, but the man's red, contorted face loomed over him like some enraged demon, spittle hanging like silver threads from the corners of his open mouth. "Where is he?"

Something large and heavy swung through the air. Luis saw it from the corner of his eye, felt the sudden rush of a wind, then a crack, like a hammer striking wood. The man fell down next to him, hitting the ground hard, flat on his face. They lay side by side, and Luis stared into the man's unblinking eyes, eyes so wide, unseeing. A trail of thick blood drooled from shattered teeth and mouth. He didn't move. He was dead.

Luis yelped and scrambled to his feet, helped by rough hands hauling him upwards by the shoulders. He looked around. The bodyguard smiled.

"Luis." The Mayor turned Luis to face him, eyes full of concern. "Are you hurt?"

Luis took a moment, grappling with his senses, feeling as though the dreams of last night had returned. He wasn't sure if he still slept, or if this was truly reality. "No, Señor. Thank you." Things came into focus. The guards, the others, the man sprawled out in the dirt, half of his face smashed in. No one appeared concerned, or even surprised. All of it happened so quickly, so nonchalantly. He looked at the mayor, who still held him by the shoulder.

"I'll have no accusations thrown at this boy, do you hear? He had nothing to do with the old woman's death, and neither does he know anything about Francisco's disappearance."

"How can you be so sure?" The man called Nico asked, his courage still evident despite what had happened to his companion.

The Mayor's eyes narrowed. "Because I have a witness. Now, go back to your homes and do as I have said. We will gather in the *plaza* within the hour." The men shuffled and mumbled but nobody made any movement. "*Now!*"

They jumped at the sharp tone of the Mayor's voice and one by one they began to move away, although they still muttered their misgivings. Luis watched them go, and cautiously touched the back of his head.

"Are you sure you are all right?"

Luis dropped his hand. "Yes, thank you, Señor."

The mayor gave a thin smile. "Everything will become clear very soon, Luis, I swear to you. Until then, you have to stay safe." He nodded towards the bodyguards and the three of them tramped off down the road towards the *plaza* and the mayor's offices.

Luis turned to look at the prostrate man in the dirt. The blood trickling from the corner of his mouth made a tiny pool around what was left of his jaw. Luis balked as he saw the back of the man's head caved in where the pole arm had struck. He turned, closing his eyes, swallowing down the bile. It was the sight of the trauma he found sickening, not the death of the man himself. Luis felt nothing for him, so different to when he had discovered Señora Gomez. Was that because he cared for her, because he knew her, or because he depended upon her? Life was so cheap, he thought to himself. Not one of the men had so much as said a single word about the sudden explosion of violence that had destroyed the other's life. Everyone simply accepted it as just another occurrence, nothing special. And what would become of the body? Would it lie here, to rot in the sun, become food for scavenging dogs? Luis shivered as scenes of ripped flesh and jaws chomping on festering innards careered through his mind in a mad, hellish dance. God, what a world this was where no one cared anymore.

Another thought took hold, dark and disturbing, pushing away the others. If all this was so, then why did the mayor care so much about finding Francisco?

Chapter 14

Alvaro

The spring had gone out of his step now. He dragged his feet through the dust, head down, feeling so low, so deflated. He wished he was a grown man, strong and resourceful, he'd know what to do then. He'd lead them all up into the mountains, flush out the vile creature that had brought this blight to his village. No one would stand in his way, no one would dare.

"Well, well, if it isn't *Don* Luis."

Luis groaned inwardly. Alvaro. Of all the people to meet on such a day as this, why oh why was it always him? Would he never tire of playing these horrible, vindictive games?

Luis brought up his head and locked eyes with Alvaro's.

"Ooh," said the big bully, his hands reaching out in mock horror, "you look scary! What you trying to be, Luis? A man?"

"He'll never be a man," said Carlos, stepping up closer, flicking Luis's hair. "He's a fop. He's a fop with a mop!"

Sprawled out across the bridge, trying to find shelter in the tiny sliver of shadow cast by the wall, the other members of the gang began to stir. The sun burned with penetrating intensity this day, hurting eyes as it bounced of the white walls of the nearby buildings. Luis, however, didn't care. Having witnessed death, close up, nothing else mattered at all. He knew these boys wouldn't care, but they might care about something else. He set his jaw. "Haven't you heard?"

Alvaro frowned and exchanged a quick glance with Carlos, his lieutenant in terror. "Eh? Heard what?"

"I've told them," said Carlos, puffing out his chest, making a good show of being tough. "Told them about my aunty, so you can shut your mouth about that. It happens, people die."

Luis didn't pause. "About Francisco?"

The boys exchanged another glance, this time the air of infallibility beginning to flitter away. "Francisco? What about him?"

Luis took a moment, deliberately creating an air of suspense. When it looked as if Alvaro was about to explode, he said quietly, "He's been kidnapped."

The words took a moment to register. Alvaro furrowed his brows, as lights began to go on all over his face. "Kidnapped? What the hell are you talking about?"

"What I say. He's disappeared. I've just been talking to the mayor. They're going to meet in the *plaza*, go up to the mountains and flush out the ogre."

"You've been talking to the mayor?" Carlos sniggered, "Don't make us laugh." He pushed Luis hard in the chest, forcing him back a couple of steps. "Don't play games with us, you little rat. Tell us the truth or I'll wipe that girly grin off your face."

Carlos cocked his arm, the hand bunched into a fist, preparing to strike. From somewhere, before Luis could even think about it, the anger came to the fore and, breathing hard, he dashed Carlos's hand away as the punch came, looping in a wide arc, and struck the thug in the chest, palm out, hitting him hard just under the breastbone.

Everyone gasped. Carlos, stumbling backwards, fell down into the dirt and sat there, incredulity written across his features. Alvaro gave a little laugh, stunned by what had happened. Luis too realised what he had done and grew afraid, stomach turning to mush, throat growing dry. He thrust out his hands, babbling quickly, "Oh God, Carlos, I'm sorry, I never meant to…" Wild, desperate, his words tumbled out in a great gush, "What I said is true, it's Francisco, he's gone missing and they're going to find him, in the mountains, and they've got guns and swords, and they mean to capture the ogre, bring it back, end all of this killing, and poor Señora Gomez, maybe the same monster murdered her and…" His voice trailed away as despair overcame him.

Carlos climbed to his feet, face dark, eyes narrowed. But even as he clenched his fist and readied himself to attack, Alvaro stepped in, threw out an arm to bar his friend from doing anything. "Hold on, Carlos!" Alvaro measured Luis with a thoughtful look. "This is true, Luis? Because if you're lying, I'll—"

"It's true, Alvaro, I swear! The mayor has gathered together some men and they are going to go up into the mountains to kill the ogre and find Francisco."

"Because the ogre has him?" Sergio, one of the youngest of the little band with the face of an angel, glanced around him, eyes wide, the reality of everything gripping him with dread. "Oh my God, the ogre has him! What will we do, where can we go? Oh my God!" He pressed his hands against his face, broke down and began to cry. Two of the others went to him, held him, tried to reassure him, perhaps more for themselves as it became clear that everyone was deeply afraid.

Carlos stepped forward, eyes still dark. "You honestly spoke with the mayor?"

Luis nodded. "I think we should all go home. Lock our doors, that's the only way. Let the men sort this out."

"*Stay at home, lock our doors*?" Alvaro turned up the corner of his mouth, "Nah, that's not for me Luis. Maybe for you, big girl that you are. But not Alvaro. I'm going down to the plaza, join the men. My dad has a fowling piece; I'll get that, shoot the bugger!"

"I'm coming too," said Carlos. "I want to find and kill this ogre, after what it did to my aunty. I'm going to see its head stuck on a pole!"

Alvaro clapped him on the back. "Right, well said my friend. The rest of you get off home. And you," he placed his finger into Luis's chest, "we'll see to you later."

He swung round and, together with Carlos, marched off down to the plaza. Luis shook his head, then looked at the others. No one said a word. "Go home," he said quietly. "Lock the doors, tell your parents what I have told you. And stay alert, especially at night."

Luis moved on, crossed the bridge and turned into the narrow street that led to his own house. On the corner he stopped, looking down the hill he saw Carlos and Alvaro, heads held high, arms swinging, off to join the adventure. A wave of nausea washed over him and wondered if he would ever see either of them alive again.

Chapter 15

Memories in a Letter

Constanza ran into his arms as he came through the door. She held onto him, pressing her face into his chest and began to sob. "Louie," she said, not needing to say anymore.

Luis kissed the top of her head and gently led her into the house, sitting her down on one of the smaller wicker chairs they possessed. He dabbed at her eyes with a piece of cloth. "Are you hungry?" he asked.

"No. The kind man cooked me some broth."

"The kind man?" Luis frowned, but realised she talked about the soldier, who said he would visit her. He smiled, reached down for the doll he had made her. "I'm going to make you another one of these. Then you can play with them both." She grinned, clutching the little wooden doll in her tiny hands. He stroked her hair. "I'll go and check on Mama."

He padded through to the backroom. His mother sat propped up in bed, pillows stacked up behind her, head tilted to one side, mouth open, eyes closed. He stopped and watched her from the doorway. She seemed so small and frail, a mere shell of the once vibrant woman she used to be. He peeled back the layers of his memory, flickers of past moments from his short life. Smiles, laughter. How his father would pick him up on his shoulders, parade with him through the village. So proud. And his mother, eyes as clear as the day, laughing. Always laughing.

"Luis, is that you?"

From a distance, his mother's voice brought him back to the present. He shivered, pushed himself off the doorframe and stepped closer.

He knelt down beside her and saw the thin, grey skin of her face, like old parchment, dry and wrinkled with cracks so deep, they must have hurt. If he wanted, he could put his fingernail inside them. He resisted the urge to do so and held onto her skeletal, claw-like hand instead, bones so prominent it seemed they threatened to burst through the flesh. "How are you feeling?"

"Where have you been?" Her voice sounded weak, as she took almost all of her strength to form the words. She peered at him through yellow eyes, eyes that betrayed the depth of her sickness.

"I had to go to work, Mama. Like I always do."

"Someone was here. A man. Kind. He took care of Constanza." A forced smile. "He told me about Claudia."

Señora Gomez. Luis bowed his head. "An awful thing to see, Mama. And now, Francisco has gone missing. Mama, something terrible has come to this village."

"Soldiers."

"No, Mama, not them. An ogre."

Her head came up, eyes widening, colour returning impossibly to her cheeks. She pulled her hand out from under his and gripped his arm with surprising strength. "Luis, be careful what you say."

"It's true, Mama." Her sudden change unnerved him. A new energy, conjured from somewhere, seemed to flow through her, bringing vibrancy to her limbs. The mention of the word *ogre* had brought about this transformation, but why? He pressed on, "The soldier, the one who looked after you, he told us everything. This *thing* has come to our village and is hiding up in the mountains. The mayor has organised a band of armed men to go and flush it out, and find Francisco."

She pressed her fingers around her mouth, her eyes gazing directly towards him, like tiny balls of fire. "Holy Mother," she breathed, "it can't be true."

This news meant something to her, something way beyond the fairytale horrors and legends of fantastical creatures. Luis shuffled closer, eager to discover the reasons for his mother's growing alarm. "What can't be true, Mama? I need you to tell me, Mama."

The silence stretched out. From the main room came the sound of Constanza playing, her voice changing as she took on the roll of her doll. Cocooned and safe in the world her imagination had created. Ignorant, as yet, of the terror that stalked the narrow streets. Happy. Luis squeezed his mother's arm. "Please, Mama. Tell me what you know."

She looked away, the hand dropping from her mouth. The red flush left her cheeks, the greyness returning. She took a long time to consider what to do, and Luis waited, not daring to speak, knowing he was close to a revelation. At last, she turned to him again and her eyes blazed, wide and terrified. "It was years ago, not long after your second birthday. A child was discovered, a young girl. We learned later her name was Teresa. They found her behind Filipe's boarding house, in the old broken shed he used to stable his mule. She had had her throat cut." She paused, breathing hard, the memory bringing the distress back to her and her bottom lip trembled. "By the time they brought the body down into the plaza, the news had spread and everyone gathered there, to see her. Such a tiny thing, so white, so..." For a moment, Luis believed she would begin to weep, but she held her breath, stared into a place far, far away and continued, words measured and slow. "We were all so shocked. Nothing like this had ever happened before, and none of us knew what to believe as the rumours began. Some people said it was bandits come down from the hills, or mercenaries out for blood. But everyone questioned why such men, brutal as they were, would kill a little girl? Something happened to the village that day. As if a cloud had descended, one of fear and suspicion. Shame."

"Shame?"

She nodded. "Yes. Because, of course, they obvious answer soon became clear. The killer had to be one of us. A villager, a neighbour. But then, a few days later, another child disappeared. His name was Jose, a bright cheerful boy, not a bad bone in his body. A little like you, Luis. Good and kind-natured. He used to run errands for the old people in the village. One morning, he simply vanished. Your father went to speak to the mayor and the next thing I know, your father took a musket and set off for the mountains." She shook her head slowly. "Three days he was gone. Three days of dread and uncertainty. I could barely eat I was so sick with worry. And then, one morning, he returned," she nodded towards the door, "standing there, face like a stone. He was a different man from that day. Changed."

"*Changed*? In what way?"

"I don't know. Sad. Frightened. A bit of both. He sat at the table, head in his hands, and he stayed like that for hours, not speaking. I dare not ask him what had happened. Not long afterwards, the mayor came."

"Came here, to this house? The mayor?"

She smiled, reached out a hand to stroke his hair. "Amazing as it may sound, yes he did. He came to ask your father what he'd discovered."

"And did father tell him?"

Her face grew serious again and she pulled back her hand, exhaling slowly. "He told the mayor he had seen it, in the hills. He had followed the tracks for days, leading him deeper into the mountains, until early of the morning of the third day he caught sight of it again, and it had the boy, Jose."

Luis felt he chest tighten. "*It*, Mama? Father had seen *it*?"

She nodded again and closed her eyes. "Yes, as close as I am to you now. The ogre."

Silence. A long time passed before Luis could bring his senses under control, it felt like there was an olive press on his chest squeezing tight.

"He wrote a letter," she said. "I couldn't read it, of course, so it must have been for someone else. I'm not sure if he wrote it for the mayor or for you."

He blinked. "For me?"

"Your father always talked about the need for you to be educated, Luis, and he had put money aside for the day when you would be old enough to go to school. He'd taught himself to read and write, or so he told me, but he only ever wanted the best for you." She patted his hand. "That is why he went up to the mountains, to find the ogre. He was afraid it would come for you."

"But you said he'd seen it. Is that all? After he'd told the mayor, didn't he warn the village?"

"Of course. After he spoke to the mayor, he went to the plaza, gathered the people together, told them the news. Some scoffed, of course, called him names. Some said he had been drinking." She gave a single laugh. "Ignorance is the blight of the world, Luis. Everyone believing they know the truth, never accepting what is actually going on in front of their eyes. Fools everyone, nobody believed him, or offered to help. When he came back to the house, he sat down and wrote the letter." She put her head against the wall, suddenly appearing very old, her voice strained, tired. "He took his musket and left for a second time." Her eyes opened and they were wet. "I never saw him again."

He read the letter in silence. She had kept it all this time and now he held it in his hands, it was as if the sound of his father's voice returned to him from across the years.

When he finished, the tears rolled down his face unchecked. The words cut through him like knives, so sharp and incisive, causing him to hold nothing back.

He dragged his hand across his nose and sniffed loudly. "Have you ever shown this to anyone, Mama?"

"No."

"So nobody one knows what he said?"

"No one. I have locked it away all these years, waiting for the right moment because I always knew it would happen again, the killings. I also knew your father had discovered the answers." She smiled. "Now, tell me what he wrote."

Uncertainty coursed through him, twisting his guts, and he shuffled and gazed at the floor. He'd listened to her as she recalled the story father told her, but the letter was somewhat different. It contained so much more, so many other, revealing aspects, the reality coming into focus, the message clear. He coughed and forced himself to speak. "All is as you said, Mama." Luis stroked her hand, avoiding her eyes, not wishing her to catch the lies he had to tell. "Father warns me not to go into the mountains, to stay here and do my best to look after you. The ogre, he says, is very dangerous." He let his hand slip away from hers, ashamed the lies came so easily. He looked at the letter one more time. His eyes never left the page, though the words grew blurred, his mind on other things, consumed by the discovery of what his father had told him.

The truth.

Chapter 16

The Mountains

The glare of the sun bounced off the scorched, white earth, hurting his eyes, making him blink repeatedly. He quickened his pace, jaw set, the sharp incline and loose scree forced him to concentrate on every footfall lest he slip, turn an ankle or worse. His mouth gaped open, the stale, fetid air thick with the pulsating heat sapped his strength, but not his determination.

Earlier, his mother pleaded with him not to go, but he was adamant. "I have no choice." He held up the letter. "This proves as much."

"But you told me your father warned you to stay away."

Luis averted his eyes, thinking of a way out. Lies came easily it seemed to him, but this time he had no need to resort to fiction. "Yes, yes he did. But he also told me to keep you safe."

"Tell me everything the letter says, Luis."

"When I return."

He turned to go and her voice, splintered with emotion, crackled after him, "Wait...I don't want to lose you as well." He paused at the doorway, turned and smiled. He had nothing else to say.

He gave Constanza a bread roll and watched her eat. His heart ached with a pain beyond anything that had visited him before. The horror of death, even that could not compare. A black, unknowing chasm opened up before him, and the dread of what lay within caused his stomach to churn and his throat to turn dry. Constanza turned to him and he rose to go, unable to hold those round, innocent eyes. He left the house and even as he pounded down the track from his house, his mother's voice cut through the morning and into his heart, "*Luis!*" He put his head down, steeled himself against the yearning to run back and hold her and tell her he would never go, and carried on.

He stood in the *plaza*, a few paces to the rear of the small knot of men who had gathered in front of the village hall; a small, ancient building, its walls a maze of cracks and broken plaster. It served as the office of the mayor; nobody gave the time to maintain it. Nobody cared.

Luis imagined how it was, all those years ago, when his father stood in the same spot, waiting for the command. Now it was his turn, and he promised himself he would not fail.

"We have been visited by something so evil, so terrible," began the mayor, standing outside the main door of his office on a little dais of hastily nailed together slats of wood, "that no one will be safe until it is destroyed!" The men cheered and raised a selection of vicious looking weapons, pole arms, rusted swords and farming implements. "We will divide into two groups. The first, those of you with pitchforks and scythes, will approach the mountains from the main track. The other group, armed with what few muskets we have, will skirt around the western edge, the only other possible route. The plan is that the first group will flush the creature out, forcing it to run straight into the trap that the others will set." Another great cheer. Beaming, the mayor clapped his hands together, then produced a large pistol which he brandished and yelled, "Let us go!"

The mob, still cheering, began to break up into its allotted groups. Luis watched them silently, wondering what his father would think. He wished he had someone to bounce his thoughts and feelings off, but there was no one. Mother was far too ill, Señor Martinez had told him not to do 'anything rash' until everything was a lot more certain, Señor Garcia was never one for prolonged conversation, and Father Brialles had disappeared. The one man who might be able to give him some direction, Pablo, who fluttered in and out of the village like a moth around a candle, had also gone. Luis, totally alone, with only his own judgement to guide him, deliberated the right course to take, even now in that open square, with the sun so hot and the mood of the assembly so determined.

The picture of his mother reared up in his head, of her sickness, of Constanza so tiny, so needy. He watched the men march off and knew his duty demanded he stay, regardless of the anger that stiffened his limbs and had, for a few moments, determined his path. Seeing those men, what good could he possibly do? He turned to go.

"Thinking of joining them, Luis?"

The soldier, arms folded, leaned against the fountain, puffing on his pipe, his narrow eyes peering out from beneath the wide rim of his hat, studying him. Sprawled around him were the other soldiers, faces set hard like granite. None spoke, not a flicker of movement.

The soldier pushed himself forward, dusting off trousers thick with dust. He glanced towards the mob of villagers as they began to move away and shook his head, a thin smile crossing his lips.

"You would be wise to stay here, Luis. Watch over your family."

Perhaps the fact that the soldier's words echoed his own thoughts, or perhaps the intrusion alone, caused Luis to glower with anger. "What's going on?"

The soldier frowned. "I don't understand you, Luis. Going on? Nothing is 'going on', except that your fellow villagers are almost certainly marching off to disaster."

"Then why don't you warn them? It seems to be me that you know a good deal about what's happening."

"Not everything." He studied the men marching off up the street, their voices cheery, full of expectation, even joy. "You're right, I should try and say something, but your mayor, he's a stubborn fellow." He turned his face towards Luis. "Like so many, he doesn't listen to reason."

Luis sucked in a breath. "The reason being *what*, exactly?"

The soldier's eyes became cold and Luis was gripped with a sudden urge to run. He forced himself to hold his ground, his heartbeat thumped in his throat, making swallowing difficult. He waited.

The soldier studied the bowl of his pipe, his voice becoming a little gentler. "Like I said, Luis, it would be for the best if you stayed here and looked after your family."

He gave a flicker of a smile and motioned to the others, who began to move away, heavy black boots crunching over the gravel. As if resigned to their duty, they were expressionless, weighed down by something which drained them but which spurred them on.

Luis watched them move away in a different direction to the one take by the villagers and he deliberated over his next action. The soldier galled him, it set his teeth on edge. The unspoken words, a knowing of the truth, the arrogance and contempt; he pondered and knew he had only one course to take and prove them all wrong. He ignored the soldier's advice and trotted after the group of men with the scythes and the pitchforks, pushing all thoughts of his ailing mother to the back of his mind.

Keeping out of sight, Luis trailed the group of men as they made their way along the mountain path. An ancient track, cut out centuries before by Carthaginians, the story went, it was rarely used nowadays, except for people like Pablo. Treacherous, full of potholes and loose rocks which laid in wait to twist ankles or break limbs, it meandered through the mountains, rising steeply at one moment, then tumbling dangerously in another. The men's curses and sudden guffaws of laughter echoed amongst the soaring, stark sides of the craggy cliffs. Luis winced at the noise and wondered about the wisdom of such an advance. If an ogre did lurk amongst these mountains, then it and everything else within a thousand paces would have adequate warning of their approach. Perhaps this was the plan, to make as loud a racket as possible, force the creature out into the open where it could more easily be brought down. This was its habitat after all, an area rarely ventured into, fear and superstition creating its own, perverse barrier to exploration.

Luis stopped, anxious, doubting the collective intelligence of the men. He smacked his lips and wished he had brought water. In his haste to leave the house, common-sense had deserted him and now he cursed his stupidity, he swallowed hard, trying to cut through the constricting dryness of his throat. All he gained was a spate of violent coughing.

He froze with the thought that the men might hear, struggling to keep the coughs muffled by clamping both hands over his mouth. He crouched down behind a rock, heart pounding, eyes squeezed shut, as their footsteps approached, together with raised, furious voices, growing louder as they drew closer. Luis, sweat springing from every pore, pressed both hands hard against his mouth to prevent another bout of coughing, and so give away his hiding place. He could not, despite his best efforts, and he retched loudly, convulsed and bent double.

A strong hand took him by the shoulder, hauling him to his feet. Luis stood, dejected, feeling foolish and guilty. A group of men gathered in a loose circle, anger brimming over in their red faces. The man who had grabbed him glared with barely contained fury whilst the others huddled closer, eyes accusing and angry.

"What in the name of God are you doing here?"

Luis spread out his hands, palms upwards, trying to find the words. But none were adequate enough to explain away the situation, and his shoulders slumped, defeat complete. "I wanted to help," he said, voice low and pathetic.

"You get on back home," said one of the men. "We haven't got time to babysit."

The first man pushed Luis in the chest with a thick, meaty finger, as fat as a sausage. "You know something about all of this, I can feel it. You're always skulking around, sticking your nose in everyone's business."

"It was him who found the Gomez woman."

"Aye, then took up with that tinker, the one-eyed rat-faced one."

"Skulking, like you said, thinking he's so superior with his books and his letters. Get the truth from him, Sergio."

Sergio narrowed his eyes. "You know something, don't you, you little turd, that's for sure."

"No, I swear—"

Without warning, he back-handed Luis hard across the face. Luis's head rang like a bell struck by a hammer, a massive burst of pain spreading over his jaw, senses swirling in a maze of confusion and fear as his legs went from under him, muscles liquefied as the world cart wheeled over his head. A face came up close, so close he could smell the rancid breath; his stomach lurched.

"I will talk to you again, you little rat, and then I'll get the truth out of you if it's the last thing I do."

Luis wanted to shout out, tell him it was all a dreadful mistake. He had found Señora Gomez, already dead. He didn't know anything about what had happened, or why—how could he? His stomach heaved and he twisted away and vomited into the parched dirt. From a distance he heard their guffaws and the shame overwhelmed him. His throat burned, his eyes streamed, but worst of all, pain pulsed across his left cheek, travelling into his temples, his entire head a throbbing mass. He became dimly aware of the men drifting away and he sat in the dirt, gazing down at the ground. The man had hit him so hard, with such violence, he had had no time to prepare or defend himself. Dumped unceremoniously on the earth, belittled, and not one of the others spoke up or tried to prevent it, not one.

He touched his jaw and winced, the skin hot and swollen beneath his fingers. He pulled his hand away and saw the tiny spots of blood, he coughed again and spat out more blood. Pain he could handle. Wounds would heal. Damaged pride was another thing. The man had made a fool of him, just as the bullies down in the *plaza* did every morning. He put his face in his hand and asked himself how much longer he was going to take all of this. Señor Menendez advocated fighting back, making a stand. Well, perhaps the time had come. He'd be beaten black and blue of course by his tormentors, but at least they might respect him.

Luis climbed his feet, slapping away the dirt and the dust from his clothes, stood a moment to check his bearings before trudging back down the track. He had gone barely twenty or so paces before he was forced to stop, the ache in his jaw consuming every sense, sapping all of his energy. He found a large boulder and sat down, putting the side of his face into the palm of his hand. He rocked forwards and backwards, a little constant murmur oozing from his lips, unwanted and unconscious. After a few moments, he put his forefinger into his mouth and explored his teeth, one of them wobbled and he struggled to keep down the tears. The bastard had hit him so hard. Out of his bag he pulled a bandana and fashioned a sort of bandage for his mouth, tying it off in a knot on top of his head, and he wished there was water to wash away the blood. A solitary tear rolled down his cheek and he almost gave way to it all, the enclosing despair. All he had wanted to do was help, to find out what had happened, and they had treated him in the time-honoured way. They hated him because he was not like them. He had ambition and desire. They would live their lives in Riodelgado and die there, nameless, forgotten. And because he longed for something more meaningful they loathed him, mistook his thirst to learn for a belief he was better than them, superior. Fools they were, every one. He tried to open his mouth, but the pain was too much and he yelped, held onto his face and prayed for the agony to fade.

Damn them, damn them all. He'd not allow them to force him from finding out what lurked up in the mountains, the evil entity that had taken away his father, killed Francisco and Señora Gomez, perhaps countless others. He had no other agenda, but those men were afraid and suspicious. Easy enough to splatter a mere boy, quite another story to take on the likes of an ogre.

If there was an ogre, of course.

He leaned his face into his hand, hoping a slight application of pressure might relieve the swelling. He needed water, desperately. What a fool he was to come up here without anything to drink. A fool and a thoughtless idiot. The soldier had been right—his place was back home, with his mother and sister. Not flitting around here on some mad quest to—

An ear-piercing scream cut through his thoughts, snapping him back into the present and he sat up, straining to gauge the direction of the sound. Another, more prolonged this time, echoed around the soaring peaks, more terrible than the first. A retched, pain-racked squeal, like that of a wild animal caught in a trap.

A clamour of voices, raised in terror, coming down through the pass in a mad, urgent rush, drawing ever closer.

Without a pause, Luis dropped down behind the boulder, the pain in his jaw forgotten, as a band of men erupted from the furthest bend in the path. Craning over the top he watched them scurrying past, like frightened, wide-eyed rabbits, whimpering, blubbering, running forward blindly, stumbling over rocks and potholes, some falling, none of them stopping. A frenzy of yapping mouths and flailing arms. Luis stayed low, not daring for them to catch a glimpse of him. Even in their rout, they might pause and attack him again. The ignominy of it returned unheralded, the force of the blow and he put his tongue into the loose tooth and cursed. He chanced another look but could not see his attacker, the one called Sergio. The man's name stuck in his throat like something sharp and he coughed again. The pain winced through his face and he sat and waited, holding his head, until the last of them had disappeared in a cloud of dust and whimpering dread. He slumped down on top of the boulder and knew he should return home. Whatever had happened, he had no wish to discover it on his own.

Something stirred out the corner of his eye, and he froze. A large shape, moving way over on the far side amongst the olive trees that hugged each side of the path. Luis turned, focused his eyes on the undergrowth, hardly daring to breathe as he stared, his muscles calcified as a new terror seized him in its grip.

A massive smudge of black mingled in the dark green leaves of the olive-grove and a deep, rumbling sound emanated from the very earth, hollow, mournful. Luis waited, stone like, expecting any moment for the thing to come bursting out of the trees to attack him.

A loud rustle of broken branches, snapping twigs, as the shape pushed onward like a large animal forcing its way through the foliage, mindless of anything, unafraid, confident that no harm would befall it. A predator, strong and fearless.

A predator.

Luis forced himself to his feet and took a step backwards. He waited, mouth hanging open, struggling to control the growing urge to turn and run. Every shred of common sense told him to do so, to flee, and yet he knew that such a course would almost certainly bring his doom. With eyes never leaving the twisted tangle of trees, he took another step, careful not to give the thing a sound. He battled to still his heart, remain calm. But remaining calm was for Sunday afternoons and pleasant walks along the river bank, not here and now, in this clinging, cruel moment of horror. To be killed alone, no one to hear his cry, could anything be more terrible. It groaned, that nameless spectre, and the trees themselves shrank back as the deep black smudge loomed larger. The air grew leaden with danger, the threat reaching out to seize him and extinguish his life.

Tree branches parted. Luis screamed, self control deserting him, and he turned and ran, head down, not daring to look back, vaulting boulders and fallen tree trunks, arms pumping, lungs screaming, sprinting with wild, mindless abandon, fear giving him new energy. He didn't stop running until he fell through the open door of his house and lay face down on the earthen floor, his body consumed by exhaustion, but elation at being safe at last.

Chapter 17

Insights

Luis sat behind the door of his house, knees pressed against his chest, breathing hard. He stared into nothing, his fear total. Whatever the thing was in the mountains, it was huge. The men ran like frightened children, those same men who seemed so brave, so resolute a few moments before, reduced to quivering wrecks. Their screams had pierced the air after they first caught sight of it, or had it perhaps attacked them. He had no way of finding out, not wishing to confront them again so soon after they had belittled him.

Luis got to his feet, still shaking, and went over to the water jug. There was about a mouthful left, which meant he would have to go down to the *plaza* and fill it from the communal pump. He groaned, not relishing the thought. He traced a finger across the line of his swollen jaw and knew he didn't really have a choice.

He stared through the tiny window above the simple sink and wished he could leave, take his family and go. Far away. A new life, a new start. A distant place, where... he stopped and listened.

The house stood silent. Where was Constanza?

Gripped by a fear more terrible than anything he had experienced in the mountains, Luis ran into his mother's room. She was sleeping, her laboured breathing like the drone of bees. There was no sign of Constanza. He went back to the other room. His own bed lay in a heap in the corner, Constanza's next to it. Truckle beds, made from larch and moss, the wildlife within the warm sanctuary causing the whole structure to shift and sag and he shivered at the thought of all those bugs running through his hair, and anywhere else their curiosity led them.

He snapped his head around, angry. Where was Constanza? Grabbing the water jug, he ran out into the daylight, looking both left and right. The other houses in the street, white, crumbling adobe walls, single windows cut next to dilapidated doors, looked back at him, mocking his panic. No signs of life, not at this time of day. Mid-afternoon, the heat so intense only fools would venture outside. Fools or naughty little children. He secured the door and ran down to the *plaza*, hoping to find her there.

He did.

Constanza sat at the fountain, tiny stick-thin legs peeking out from the hem of her tattered dressed. She gasped when she saw him, her face lighting up like a beacon and she raced forward, arms wide, shouting,

"Louie!"Luis caught her in his arms, hugged her, letting the relief consume him. He hooked his hands under her armpits and spun her round. She giggled with delight and held onto him when he stopped, pressing her face against his chest. "Louie, where you been?"

He did not want to frighten her, not now after so much else had happened. He set her down, smoothed out her hair and smiled. "I went to see what the men were doing."

A frown creased her elfin face. "What happened to your face?"

He forced a laugh, stroked his cheek and shrugged. "It's nothing. I fell, hit a rock. I'll be all right."

"Someone has hit you."

Sometimes her instinctive ability to discern the truth surprised him and he grimaced. "No. I fell, as I followed them men into the mountains."

"And what were they doing?"

"Looking for something. Some one."

"A monster?"

Luis stayed still, looked down at her and tried to regulate his breathing. She gave a bemused expression then frowned again, "I want to know what happened to your face. Louie."

Luis had to struggle not to put his hand against his jaw line again. "I told you, I fell. The path, it was treacherous and I slipped in a pothole..." he smiled through the lie and knew she did not believe him.

From her expression it was obvious she didn't believe him and her mouth opened to speak but then her expression changed, eyes becoming wide as she looked past her brother's shoulder. She beamed. "It's you!"

Luis straightened and turned to meet the gaze of the soldier, who stood some way off, arms akimbo, expression inscrutable as usual.

Luis looked away, guilt and shame rising once more. "They went up into the mountains," he said quietly. "The men. I followed them."

"I know. And I seemed to recall telling you *not* to go with them."

"I couldn't help it."

"And what happened?"

Luis took a moment, his hand straying towards the swelling. He didn't want Constanza to hear the details, desperate not to frighten her. Yet, fear resonated in every corner of their village and he questioned the need to shield her from the truth. The terrible thought that the ogre might come into the village and strike again played around in his mind and he wrung his hands, not knowing what to do.

The soldier reached out and took the water jug from Luis's hand and, smiling, passed it over to Constanza. "Try and fill that as much as you can," he said.

She took up the challenge with childish eagerness and the soldier took Luis by the shoulder and turned him away. "There has been another attack."

Luis jumped. "*What*? When?"

"Another child. Whilst the mayor's valiant little band were tramping through the mountains with all the subtlety of a herd of cows, the monster came down and murdered another innocent." He nodded meaningfully towards Constanza, "I think it is even more imperative that you stay with your family, Luis." He turned to Luis once more, brows heavy. "Constantly." He reached out and with surprising kindness, touched Luis's cheek with the back of his hand. "That looks sore. Bathe it with cold water, try and reduce the swelling."

Luis felt his eyes growing moist. Such a brutal man and yet so concerned.

"You know who did this, don't you?"

The soldier betrayed no emotion. "I can guess. One of those *brave* stalwarts who marched to catch their quarry and ended up knocking down a young man, whose only thought was to understand what is happening in this God-forsaken place."

Luis gaped at him. "Sergio," he said, without thinking, then instantly regretted it as he saw a darkness creep over the soldier's face.

Before he could say anything more, Constanza gave a little cry and Luis turned to see her struggling with the over-full jug, water slopping over the rim. He went over to her, took the jug and smiled. "Well done, Constanza. Soon you'll be able to come and do this all by yourself." She giggled. Luis ran a little of the water over his hands then rubbed the back of his neck to try to cool himself down. He pulled out the kerchief he had used as a bandage, dipped it in the water trough and dabbed at his jaw. He sighed with relief as the pain subsided slightly. "I never thanked you for looking after Constanza the other day," he said, and turned, smiling towards the soldier.

But the soldier was not there.

Together they made their way back up the hill. Luis held the jug with great care, not wanting to spill a single drop. Ahead of him, Constanza skipped and hopped across the winding dirt track. Luis marvelled at the way she could find fun in almost everything she did. He offered up a little prayer of thanks to God for blessing him with a sister so easy to look after, who never strayed—apart from today—and who always had such a boundless capacity to amuse herself. He couldn't help but smile. A thought struck him, a question. Why had she gone down to the fountain? To fetch water, or had she been led down there by the soldier, and towards what end?

As they reached the turn in the road that would take them to their own little house, Luis saw the bunch of men gathered outside Filipe's guesthouse. The mayor stood before them, gesticulating with his hands, no doubt giving out more orders, most of which would be as useless as the last lot. Luis exhaled, growing depressed at the futility of it all, and continued on his way.

She told the story later, in the cool of their house over some pieces of broken bread and pitted olives, of what had transpired. "The man knocked on our door, Luis. When I opened it, he wasn't there, but I knew it was him—I could see him walking down the street, towards the square. So I followed him. That's where you found me." Luis didn't understand. Why could the soldier call and not wait for an answer? Unless it was to leave the house empty, apart from Mama of course. Empty for what purpose? He ran a hand through his hair, exhaustion overcoming him. A pain pulsed behind his eyes, but at least it had begun to recede a little and he didn't press his sister with any more questions.

At the end of the street, armed men stood guard.

Luis, after a supper of cold meat and bread, wandered outside to take in the air. The atmosphere was so thick he could have scooped it into a bowl for soup. When he turned to go back inside, he noticed a man posted at the bottom of the street. Curious, he told Constanza to stay indoors, and wandered down to talk to the man.

He was old, doubled over, leaning on a vicious looking halberd. A great floppy hat put most of his face in shadow, but as Luis neared, the man turned to reveal a face deeply etched with age, skin the colour and texture of unleven bread, dry and flaky. A straggly, iron-grey beard dropped down to an emaciated chest and his breathing rasped like clothes dragged across a washboard. Hardly the sort of person to inspire confidence.

"Good evening," he said, his voice coming from a throat coated in dry gravel.

Luis nodded. "Are you guarding us?"

"That's the idea." He jerked his head past Luis, towards his house, "There's another one of us at the top. Name of Mario. Big man."

"The blacksmith?" Luis felt a little reassured. Mario, as strong as a bull, put the fear of God into most people. But Luis wondered if the ogre would be in the least bit intimidated. He doubted it. "You will stay here all through the night?"

The old man nodded once. "We'll be relieved soon enough, hopefully..." He let his voice drift away. Something in his tone made Luis guess the idea of someone relieving him was more a vain hope than a guarantee.

"And what happens if you see the ogre?"

The man coughed and spat into the dirt. "Bah! There is no ogre, lad."

"But the mayor, he said—"

"Believe you me, I've lived in this Godforsaken place all my life and I know there isn't any ogre or monster, troll or goblin living up in those mountains."

Intrigued, Luis sat down on the wall of a nearby crumbled old building and leaned forward, elbows on knees. "What makes you say that?"

The man shrugged. "Because I *know*!" He stretched his back and settled himself to again lean against the halberd. "I fought for Tilly at the battle of the White Mountain, back in twenty. That was a hellish day, I can tell you. But nothing compared to what happened at Magdeburg eleven years later." He closed his eyes for a moment. "I remember him standing there, Tilly, the tears streaming down his face, but even he couldn't do anything to stop it. God died that day, or turned his back on us. Something happened, I know that."

"I don't understand. What do you mean 'he couldn't stop it'? Who couldn't stop what?"

"*Tilly*! Don't you listen, boy? Field Marshall of the Catholic forces against the scourge of the Protestant north. We butchered those swine at the White Mountain, heathens the lot of them." He spat again into the dirt. He shook his head as memories from his past ate away at him, face drawn as if in pain, his voice low. "Later, at Magdeburg, I learned that evil lies not in monsters and demons," he turned his screwed up eyes on Luis, "or ogres—but in men. ordinary men made inhuman by the excesses of war."

"What happened, at Magdeburg?"

The old soldier puffed up his chest and stared out across the broken houses towards the distant hills. For a moment, it didn't seem he would answer, his eyes grew dim, his face thoughtful. As Luis opened his mouth to prompt him, the old man spoke, voice low, sad. "We'd laid siege to it for months, but when we broke in…" He shook his head. "It was carnage. Our troops ran like packs of wild dogs through the city streets, butchering anyone we came across. Men, women, children, we skewered them all, and looted every house we fell upon. In the end, the drink overcame us, not any sense of piety or shame. God forgive us, we dropped down in the dirt and slept until Tilly raised us with shouts and threats, and we marched off, saddle bags bulging, bellies filled." He turned and stared at Luis. "I spent everything I had on women and drink, trying as best I could to rid my mind of those images of what we did, to clear my ears of the screams, the begging for mercy. So no, don't talk to me of ogres. The only ogre is us."

"You think that the one doing this, all of these murders, is a *man*?" The old soldier nodded. "But why? Why would any human being do such terrible things? What good could it do?"

"I'll tell you what I think," said the old soldier and beckoned Luis to step closer. But as uis went to stand up, a shadow crossed over them and both of them stood still.

"I *think* it is time for you to go back to your mother, Luis."

The mayor smiled broadly, a smile devoid of any humour or good feeling. He appeared drained, his mouth hung open slightly, moustache and beard bedraggled. Flexing his shoulders, the leather of his heavy, sweat-stained coat creaked. His wide-brimmed hat cast a deep shadow across his face, masking his features, just as the old soldier's did. Was this deliberate, Luis wondered. Looking closely, Luis realised that there was something about the mayor's manner telling him the man was close to edge. In his belt were stuffed two ornate pistols, at his hip a silver inlaid sword. A man prepared for battle, or anything else come to that.

The old soldier hacked again, deep furrows in his forehead. "What happened up in the mountains?"

The mayor pushed back his hat and Luis gasped at the man's ashen, strained look. "I wasn't at Magdeburg, Enrique," the old soldier muttered something and turned away, "but I know what I saw this day."

He laid a heavy hand on Luis's shoulders. "It took Sergio. We all saw it. One moment he was there, the next," he snapped his fingers, "gone!"

"Probably fell over a ravine," said Enrique without turning around.

"No, he didn't. The ogre took him." The mayor sighed, readjusted his hat and began to move off, "Old soldiers never lie, so they say." He chuckled, waddling down the pathway that led back to the bridge and his own home. "Stay indoors tonight, Luis. Stay close to your mother."

As he watched the mayor swagger into the distance, Luis knew he'd offered good advice. But old Enrique's words had struck home. Something wasn't right with any of this. The mayor seemed to be trying too hard to convince everyone that the ogre was real. As yet, no one had seen it. Even that shadow in the trees, could Luis honestly say it was an *ogre*? Obviously something roamed the stark, silent mountain, but what? The truth, almost certainly, lay in the fissures and caves of the cliffs, and Luis was determined to find out exactly what it was.

Chapter 18

The Old Soldier

Luis sat up, his face dripping with sweat. He wiped his wet forehead with his palm and brushed away the bugs running through his hair—he still hadn't cleared out his truckle bed. He stood up. The night had cooled a little, but he was as soaked as if he'd plunged into a river. Scraps of nightmare images returned, of grotesque beings, of sharp teeth and cavernous mouths. He shuddered and groped around for a cloth, or a rag, found one and did his best to dry himself off.

The remnants of the dream lingered. Despite what the old soldier said, Luis knew what he'd seen. The ogre. The dream confirmed it, and he would never deny a dream.

He was running, like someone blind, arms outstretched to ward off the branches of the olive trees, thousands of them packed so tightly they were almost as impenetrable as a solid wall. The deeper he went into the grove the more difficult movement became, legs leaden, breathing laboured, the air thick with heat, every step requiring a massive force of will. And yet, he knew he must keep going, because the shape behind him loomed ever closer, relentless in its pursuit. He could hear its breathing as it crashed through the trees, immense strength breaking through branches as if they were nothing but kindling for the fire. Deep growls, like the rumbling fury of mountain landslides, sent his senses whirling in terror, and he turned and saw the true horror of the thing that bore down upon him. It came bursting through the trees, huge, a great square head set upon wide shoulders, slavering mouth full of long pointed teeth, flat nose, dark green skin pulsating with a thick covering of puss-filled boils. Luis screamed as it lunged forward, its massive hands ready to seize him as if he were an insect, to crush and tear apart his limbs, and at that point he woke.

He looked at his hands and they trembled. The dream, so vivid, confirmed all of his darkest fears. The shadow from the mountains had manifested itself in his dream, confirming his deepest, most base fears. It was real!

From the far corner he heard a tiny whimper. Constanza stirred, turned over, kicking off her threadbare blanket. Luis smiled. He loved her more than life itself, and if he had the means he would take her from this place, provide for her, care for her. If he had the means...

He went into the tiny kitchen area, found the jug and poured water over his head. He stood, looking down, allowing the cooling effect of the water to bring back some sense of equilibrium. The heat sapped his energy, making every action so difficult. Even the effort of thinking took up most of his strength.

Thoughts, however, were difficult to oppress.

His mother's illness played on his mind the most, eating away at him like maggots on a corpse, every day burrowing further through his body towards his soul. Especially now, as darkness pressed around him in the early hours, the demons came visiting, testing his faith, filling him with dread. The facts were impossible to ignore; his mother's sickness grew worse with each passing day and the end would not be far away. He tried to drag his mind away from such thoughts, but they would not let him. How would he cope with the hurt of her passing? Pictures of her lying in her bed, suffering as she did, but alive. Still here to smile at him, stroke his cheek, reassure him. He wanted so much for her pain to cease, but even more he wanted her to be alive. He dropped his head. Her suffering would end soon, he knew it, and that made him sad and filled him with despair, for with her passing the real battle would begin. The battle to protect Constanza.

Luis didn't know who Constanza's father was. Mama never mentioned him, but Luis believed a link, a bond, still remained between them, and something more too. She always seemed to have enough money to add to Luis's pitiful earnings in order for them to buy food. Luis never asked, but he suspected the money came from Constanza's father.

A pistol shot, the sharp crack like a whip, rang out through the still night, splintering the silence. Luis ducked instinctively, eyes drawn to the front door, and waited on bended knee.

From the far distance came a voice, urgent and frightened, shouting, "*Murder!*" Someone pounded past the door, quickly followed by another. Luis held his position, mouth open, listening for further sounds. He crept forward and checked Constanza. Through the gloom he could make out her huddled shape, still asleep, unaware. He leaned forward and kissed her then, then tiptoed to the door.

He eased the ancient timbers open and they creaked and groaned with impossible loudness. He held his breath, waited, and when no responding cries of alarm greeted him, he took his chance and peered outside.

An eerie silence clung to the cracked and crumbling walls of the adobe houses close by. Keeping low, he took a few steps down the uneven street and peered towards where the old soldier had stood guard. The dawn had not yet begun its journey across the sky and the darkness lay like a thick blanket, shapes impossible to discern in the gloom. The whitewashed walls of the ancient buildings gave off a sort of light, but not enough to see things clearly. He crept forward, ready to run back if any wild creature reared up out of the darkness to attack him.

He stopped when he saw the shape, gripped with indecision. Should he turn and flee, or wait. The shape moved, sensing his presence. It was a man, and the musket in his hands glinted in the feeble starlight. "Who's there?"

"It is I. Luis Sanchez."

"Come closer so I can see you."

Holding his breath, Luis did as instructed. The man breathed a loud sigh and lowered the musket. "My God, lad, you scared me! What in all that's holy are you doing out at this time?"

Some of Luis' nervousness receded. "I heard a gun-shot and thought—"

Something lay on the ground next to man, a mound of discarded clothes and Luis felt his knees buckle as he recognised what it was. Not a mound of anything. A man. He snapped his eyes towards the other man, who still had the musket trained on him, and gasped, "Who is it?"

"Enrique."

His muscles grew slack and Luis crumpled to his knees, craning forward to confirm that dread news. The old man lay on his back, mouth wide open, black and toothless in a silent scream, a pistol in his hand, the massive gaping wound across his throat crusted with dried, black, evil looking blood.

Luis didn't have the strength to stand. Nothing more to do, the old man dead, murdered, another vic-tim claimed by the invisible assailant who walked the streets to butcher and maim. He felt a hand pressing on his shoulder and he turned to face the other. This close it became clear who it was. Mario, the black-smith. Good, kindly Mario.

"He managed to fire a shot before it overpowered him. Perhaps he wounded it." He frowned, face becoming a scowl. "I asked you a question, didn't I? What are you doing out here in the dead of night, eh?" Good, kindly Mario transformed into an accuser, suspicion lending his voice an ominous, angry tone.

Luis opened his mouth to speak as he made a feeble effort to stand, but his legs and feet were as water, with no strength. He reached out a hand to break his fall and pitched backwards as everything went black.

Voices woke him and he blinked open his eyes to stare into a vast open sky of perfect blue. He looked about him to focus on his surroundings and sat up. He winced as a stab of pain jabbed into his neck. His head throbbed and he reached to touch a large swelling on the back of his skull, as big as an egg. He winced again, teeth on edge, and studied his fingertips and the small spot of blood. The memory returned; Enrique, the dreadful contortion of death, the feeling of slipping into a black hole. He had fainted, cracked his head on the ground. And then what? He glanced over and saw a group of three or four men jabbering all at once to one another. With the dawn, everything became clear, including the fact that they had left him lying on the ground without a care. The thought didn't come as any real surprise. These people didn't give a fig about anyone except themselves. He set his jaw and stood up, dusting off his pants.

He caught the eye of one of the men, Mario the blacksmith, who threw his head skywards, prodded one of his companions and muttered something. The other man, a swarthy brute named Arturo, stepped towards Luis, his face dark. "What did you see?"

Luis blew out his cheeks. He was sore and hungry and had no idea what time it was. He could have been lying there for hours for all he knew. Constanza would need him, Mama too.

Arturo stabbed him in the chest with a hard finger. "I *said*, what did you see?"

"See?" Luis frowned. "I didn't see anything."

"Are you sure?"

"Of course I'm sure."

"Mario said you were out here, in the street. What were you doing?"

"I heard the shot, then came outside and saw…" He pointed to where the body of old Enrique still lay, eyes staring, seeing nothing. The open wound had by now closed up, the blood congealed and this, in a very horrible way, made the corpse appear even more ghastly than before. Luis turned away, clamping his hand over his mouth, suddenly feeling the urge to be sick.

"You're coming with me," said Arturo, taking Luis by the shoulder and turning to the others. "I'm going to take this one to the mayor. You'd better move the body."

Luis spluttered and coughed, tried to wrench himself free. The man's grip grew tighter. "I've done nothing," he blurted out, desperate now.

153

"Then you've got nothing to fear, have you."

As the knot of men grumbled loudly, Arturo pulled the struggling Luis along the narrow street towards the mayor's residence.

The mayor, hair tussled, face deep-lined with stress and strain, slumped down in a chair in his dining room and stared at the floor. Skin, already of a sickly pallor, went as white as chalk dust as Arturo told him about Enrique's death.

"Throat cut?" The mayor shook his head and, in a quiet voice, as if to himself, he added: "The same as old Gomez..."

Luis took this as his cue. He tore himself free from Arturo's grip and stepped forward, "Please, Señor. The old soldier, poor old Enrique, he told me a story before he... before he was killed."

The words struck the mayor with little effect. His eyes were blank, not registering anything, he put his chin in his hand and mumbled, "It's here, amongst us all, waiting... always waiting..."

"Señor, he spoke to me, told me something I think you should know."

"We found this boy in the street," said Arturo. "He's known for it, scurrying about in everybody else's business, trying to make himself out to be so bloody superior, better than us all with his—"

"That's not *true!*" Luis slammed his fists against his thighs. "I'm sick to the back teeth of you all, with your petty gossiping and your rumour mongering. Every day of my damned life you snigger and smirk,

154

condemning me without proof, using your ignorance as your only guide."

Arturo jutted his face into Luis'. "You were out in the street, you can't deny that."

"I heard the gunshot, you idiot!"

Arturo cocked his fist, ready to strike, and the mayor stood up, "Stop that, you fool. This boy has nothing to do with any murders, so get that notion out of your head right now."

The air grew still, the silence total. Arturo blinked a few times, allowed his arm to fall loose and formless.

The mayor patted Luis on the shoulder and smiled before returning to his seat, his voice low but nevertheless Luis found it menacing. "Tell me what the old man said."

Luis gave a sigh. It was time to get to the point. "He told me he had fought all over Europe, seen terrible things, that he had been here when the first killings had occurred, years and years ago—"

Arturo shifted, looked from Luis to the mayor, "*Other* killings?"

"Yes," continued Luis. "He told me all of this has happened before, some years ago. Not so bad, I don't think, but people died in suspicious circumstances. My mother said much the same thing."

"Your *mother*?" The mayor almost screamed the word and sprang to his feet, face red with rage. "Your mother doesn't know what time of day it is, never mind what happened years ago, you ignorant fool!" He took a few breaths, the redness gradually receding from his cheeks, and sat down. "Now, what else did the old soldier say?"

Luis took a moment, silently counting to ten, holding back his anger. How dare this man, whatever his position of authority, speak about his mother the way he had. Breathing hard, Luis said, "He told me that it wasn't an ogre doing these killings, but a man." His eyes narrowed. "And he paid with that information with his life."

"I was there when he said that," the mayor leaned forward menacingly, bunching his fist. "What did he say after I left damn you?"

Luis took a step back, afraid, but as he did, Arturo gripped around his throat from behind and hoisted him off his feet. Luis struggled in the hold, clawing at the man's forearms, kicking out in desperation. Arturo held on with ease as the mayor, seething with rage, stepped forward.

From somewhere amongst the dread and confusion, Luis realised this was not good. Something unknown and dreadful contorted the mayor's features, overcoming any sense of nobility or tolerance. A man out of control, but why, Luis did not understand. He wriggled, only causing Arturo to tighten the grip. Luis gagged.

The mayor stood so close, Luis could smell his decadent perfume. He clamped his hand around Luis's cheeks and squeezed, snarling through clenched teeth, "What did he say?"

Blood pounded in Luis' head, his eyes bulged. He could no longer focus, nor breathe as his tongue swelled to fill his mouth. The room span, the ceiling tipping back over his head and then, with the darkness enveloping him, Arturo released him and he fell to his knees, coughing, gulping in the air through a throat parched raw.

A foot on his chest pushed him over onto his back, the pain lancing through his body like a multitude of burning hot embers. He rolled onto his side, battling with the overwhelming horror threatening to send him spiralling into panic. The ground went in and out of focus and he groped with hands flat to try to find some leverage, to get himself to his feet, to run, escape.

A face loomed close. The face of the Mayor. No, not the Mayor. Arturo. No, not him... Luis didn't know to whom the face belonged, nor did he care.

"Damn your eyes," spat the mayor from a long way off, the fury in his voice bringing Luis back to the present with a start.

Luis sat up and touched the back of his head again. It felt sticky and wet and he did not dare to look and see how much blood there was this time.

"You pathetic excuse for a human being," the mayor yelled and put the heel of his boot against Luis' chest again and shoved him backwards.

Luis didn't wait for another blow. He scrambled to his feet and stood, swaying, breathing like a ragged, stricken beast close to death. The mayor, like a thing possessed, rushed forward, fingers spread like claws. Luis screamed and threw up his arms in a pathetic attempt to ward off the attack. It never came and he chanced a look and saw Arturo, holding the mayor around the body, grimacing with his efforts. "Lord Mayor, *please,* you will kill him; he is only a boy."

After a moment, the mayor relaxed, the wild look slipping away from his eyes, and Arturo released him from his hold. The Mayor giggled. "Yes, you're right, but a boy? Is that what you call him? A fop is what he is, a girl with that long, dangling hair. You don't belong here, boy! Neither you nor that accursed family of yours. Go back to your mother and tend to her, that's all you're good for." He whirled around and stomped off out of the room.

Arturo watched him go, then turned to look at Luis. "I've never seen him like that before. He's beside himself with rage. Why?"

Luis shook his head, looking at the blood on his palm, blood that leaked from the gash on his head. "I don't know."

"He's so *angry.* This business with the ogre," Arturo shook his head. "Are you sure you didn't see anything?"

"Positive. But...." Luis turned his gaze to the man's. "I know it is not an ogre that is murdering all these poor people."

"How do you know that?"

Luis closed his eyes. The throbbing in his head was growing worse. He needed to lie down, drink some water, try and sleep. "I must go home."

Arturo nodded. "Yes. And when you get there, don't venture out again. Not until this is over"

"That," said Luis, "might not be for some time, I think."

Chapter 19

A Brace of Pistols

He rushed through the village, the sharp slap of
his simple leather sandals over the cobbles the only
sound. A couple of men at the end of his street gave
him a hard look as he hurried by and he tried his
best not to meet their eyes. When they growled, however, he couldn't help but glance over to meet their
harsh stares. Did they blame him for Enrique's death,
or was there something more? Everyone seemed so
angry, so dead-set on throwing around their accusations like sand in the breeze. Accusations not based
on poof or anything other than the desire to hurt.

About a hundred paces or so from his house, he
stopped, listening. A dreadful, heaviness came over
him, pressing down on his shoulders, as if something
very large and very bad studied him, measuring his
every move. He whirled around, half expecting to see
the men brandishing weapons, bitter words erupting
from their cruel mouths. But there was nothing, only

the steady beat of his heart in his ears. A bead of sweat rolled down his face and gripped by a sudden, inexplicable dread, he broke into a run.

The house door yawned wide open.

For a moment everything went black.

He hadn't left the house open like this and images of Señora Gomez came to mind, the scene that met him when he discovered her broken corpse. He held onto the door well, a horrible plunging sensation pulling him down into a swirling, inky pit. He fought against it, hung on, took in deep, full breaths, and gradually recovered his senses. He wiped sweat from his brow and took a step inside.

The room appeared as if someone had turned everything upside down, hurling the contents everywhere. The truckle beds lay in a mess, ripped apart, the natural bedding tossed over the dirt floor. He walked through the room, feet crunching over broken bits of crockery and shattered furniture. Nothing remained intact and when he went into the kitchen area he found it too had received the same treatment. A scene of mad rampage, things pulled apart, possessions lying broken and wrecked, as if an army of scavengers had ran amuck through the tiny building, stripping everything bare. For what reason, a search for valuables? Thieves, robbers, come to steal anything they could find? Except that there wasn't anything to steal. A poor family, owning nothing of any real value, so why? Luis bent down and upturned an old, wicker chair. Someone had put a fist or a boot right through it.

And no sign of Constanza.

His heart pounding, stomach like water, dreading what he might next discover, Luis staggered in a daze to his mother's room.

The bed lay empty, sheets pulled back, the indention of her head still pressed into the thin, straw pillow.

He slid down the wall, all of his strength leaving him in that single instant.

Both of them, sister and mother, gone.

After what seemed like an age, he shook himself and knew he must move, but wasn't sure if he could. Uncertain what to do, where to go, who to tell, Luis sat with knees pulled up to his chest and stared into nothingness. He forced himself to concentrate his mind on what he could do. In his wildest dreams he never believed such a thing could happen. His mother, so ill, was incapable of dragging herself out of bed, even with Constanza's help. So how had she done so? He squeezed a finger and thumb into the corners of his eyes and tried to make some sense of it.

The answer came like a slap in the face. Someone else had taken both his mother and sister. They had broken in and kidnapped them both. But who, and why? And why tear apart the house? To search for something, something of value. He touched the inside pocket of his jacket and felt the outline of the letter his father had written to him. Could they have been looking for that, these nameless, mysterious intruders? Were the few scribbling of his dead father worth the lives of his mother and sister?

He couldn't stand it any longer. All of the fight and resistance went out of him in a rush and he plunged his face into his hands and cried.

Later, he found some water and splashed his face. He took an old rag, dabbed himself dry and scanned the destruction about the place. It would take hours, possibly days to put everything right. He didn't think he had the strength, or even the desire to do it. The people who had done this had not merely ransacked his home, they had besmirched his life. He didn't think he would ever be able to rest easy in this building again.

He went into his mother's room and began to search for a clue, anything that would lead him to the answers he so desperately needed. The old blanket box against the wall had been broken open, its contents tossed around. Nothing appeared to be missing, but then he wouldn't know because he had no idea what it was they were looking for. But one thing he did notice. The goblet, the metal goblet that he had found, that had gone. He frowned. Why would anyone take such a plain, unimposing item? None of it made any sense, and he wandered back into the kitchen.

Unable to find a scrap of food, he packed up his shoulder bag, slipped the large carving knife into his waistband and returned to the broken box hoping he would find what he wanted there. As luck would have it, he found it under a crumpled blanket; his father's old pistol, wrapped in an oil rag, untouched for years. He pulled away the cloth and smiled. Its reassuring weight gave him a new surge of confidence and he pulled back the hammer and released the trigger. Everything worked and he grinned. He wrapped the weapon up again and slipped it into the shoulder bag. With one last glance around the room he dipped through the door and went out into the street. The sun hit his face like a fist and he quickly returned inside and rooted around until he found an old hat. Cramming it down over his head, he pulled in a breath, and marched off into the heat towards the baker's.

Garcia glanced up as Luis came through the door. The baker shook his head. "I have heard the news about last night and what happened to you. Carted off the way you were, like a common criminal. What is happening to this place?" He leaned on the table with his fists. "Luis, you can't make any deliveries, it's too dangerous. I won't let you."

"Señor Garcia—"

The baker held up his hand, "I know you need the money, Luis. God knows we all do, but life is more important. Here," he bent down and brought up a tightly wrapped package and plonked it down on the table. "Take this. It's not much, just some rolls and a bit of cheese, but it'll be enough for today. Maybe even tomorrow if you're careful." He pushed it across the tabletop towards Luis.

Luis didn't know what to say. "Thank you, Señor."

"I wish I could do more. Don't worry about the deliveries, Luis. I'm going to shut up shop for a while anyway, perhaps go and join the town militia, try and get to the bottom of all these dreadful killings." The man's eyes bore into him.

Luis picked up the package and studied it. Something stopped him from telling Garcia about the disappearance of his mother. But he had to say something. "Awful about Enrique, isn't it?"

Garcia's head dropped. "I've known him all my life. A kind, gentle man, aged before his time. He fought in the War, you know."

"Yes, he told me. The White Mountain, I think he said. And Magdeburg."

"Yes. Magdeburg." Garcia came from around the table, wiping his hands on his apron. He placed his hands on Luis's shoulders. "Human beings are capable of the most dreadful things, Luis. If your father was here, he'd tell you."

Luis felt his heart suddenly clamp up and he stared into the baker's eyes. "My father? What do mean?"

Garcia stiffened, stepping back. "Nothing. I've said enough. You run off home now, see to your mother. She'll need you more than ever now."

With this cue, Luis made his decision to divulge what had happened. "Señor Garcia, my mother has gone."

The baker frowned, clearly not understanding Luis's words. "Gone?"

"Constanza too. I came back this morning to find them both missing and the house ransacked, as if someone had been in there, trying to find something."

"But..." Garcia shook his head, holding his chin with forefinger and thumb. "Luis, you need to go home, bar the door and wait. That's all you can do now."

"No, Señor, that is not all." Luis delved inside the shoulder bag and brought out the pistol. "I need powder and shot for this. Have you got any?"

The baker stared in disbelief at the weapon. "That's your father's," he said. "Where did you get it?"

Luis stopped. Something in the man's voice betrayed his fear. "What do you mean where did I get it? I found it in my house of course."

"But you couldn't have done, he—" Garcia stopped and his eyes became fixed on something beyond Luis. His expression changed, becoming hard, the light in his eyes dying down until they became like dull, black pearls.

Luis, sensing the change, turned and wished he already had the pistol prepared. The shape in the doorway cast a large shadow and Luis narrowed his eyes, trembling slightly, his mouth becoming dry.

The figure stepped through the door and now his features became clear. The soldier stood, legs planted apart, hands on hips. He leaned forward, jutting out his jaw. "Luis. It seems that every corner I turn, you are there."

"I could say the same about you, Señor."

The soldier pointed towards the pistol. "Yours?"

"My father's. I need shot and powder."

"You do? And why would that be?"

"Someone broke into my house and now my mother and sister have gone missing."

"I see."

Luis swallowed hard, stiffened his resolve, the sight of the soldier a catalyst for a renewed sense of determination. Nothing was going to divert him from his chosen path, not now. "I intend to find my mother and my sister, Señor. And I'll need this pistol for protection."

A slight smile crossed the soldier's lips. He reached over and tapped the handle of the carving knife in Luis's waistband. "You'll need more than that, my little friend." Slowly the soldier unbuckled his own belt from which hung a sword in its scabbard. He stepped close up to Luis and secured the belt around the boy's middle. He had to pull the belt as tight as it would go so that it wouldn't slip down. Even so, the scabbard end trailed against the ground. The soldier stepped back, looking pleased. "Your pistol is a good one, but a brace is far more effective." He pulled out one of his own pistols and rammed it into Luis' belt.

Luis, lost for words, ran a fingertip over the butt.

"Careful, it is already primed," said the soldier and took out two small pouches from the bag hanging over his shoulder. "Powder and shot. You know how to load these weapons?"

"Yes, Señor."

The soldier nodded and handed Luis the pouches. "And now you are ready, Luis. Ready to meet any enemy."

The baker, recovering himself, stepped up next to Luis and pulled him around by the shoulder. "Luis, for the love of God, this is madness. Think about what you're doing."

"Let him be, old man." The soldier cocked his head to one side. "Don't you want Luis to be a hero?"

"*I don't want him dead!*"

Again, the soldier smiled, but without humour. A dull, lifeless curling of the lips, that was all. "People sometimes have to die to be true heroes. Wouldn't you say?"

An awful silence fell down upon them then. From somewhere a mouse scurried along a wall, a bird sang its shrill song and the world continued to turn. Luis sniffed and pulled himself free of Garcia's grip. He swept up his father's pistol and dropped it into the bag, together with the pouches of ball and powder. He exhaled loudly. "I don't intend to die, Señor. I intend to find my mother and sister."

The soldier bowed, taking off his hat to wave it with an elaborate flourish, "Then I wish you God speed." He straightened and stepped aside. "*Don* Luis."

Chapter 20

The Cave

Almost as soon as he had stepped out into the morning light, the raised voices of the two men came to him through the open door. Luis stopped, put himself flat against the wall and listened.

Garcia's voice sounded strained. "Are you mad sending him out like that? If the boy is killed—"

"I have faith in him which is more, I wager, than you have."

"He's nothing but a boy, for God's sake."

"God has little to do with any of this, master baker. You know that better than anyone."

"If any harm comes to him—"

"You'll do as you've always done—knead your bread. You chose this life to hide behind, so get used to it."

The sound of a footfall broke his concentration and he span around to see one of the other soldiers coming up the track. He had a pot-helmet crammed on his head which made him appear much taller than he actually was. The nasal bar masked most of his features, except for his eyes, which glowed with a piercing light, a menace that Luis found strangely hypnotic. He stepped straight up to the house, paying Luis no mind, dipped his head and went inside the baker's.

Luis stayed still for a moment, then pushed himself from the wall and broke into a run. The conversation he had listened to brought a ball of nerves to knot inside his stomach. None of it made sense, with Garcia appearing to know the soldier with more than a degree of familiarity. Answers needed to be found, and as he pounded through the narrow streets, his mind whirled with where to begin; uncovering the many secrets, but more than anything else, the priority now had to be to find his family.

He settled into a steady jog and followed the familiar trail into the mountains. As he left the village and crossed over broken ground, the sweat streamed into his eyes, the oppressive heat making heavy weather of his progress. Within a few paces of the boulder behind which he had hidden yesterday, his clothes were soaked through and he stopped and peeled off his jacket. He took a drink from his canteen, wiped his forehead with his sleeve and gathered his strength. He pressed on.

Soon the abundance of olive trees gave way to wilder species, mingling with ornamental trees untended for many years. Here the air was thick with the scent of jasmine and he circled around an ancient, long-abandoned farm building, ghosts of its once impressive spread lingering in a single vivid blue jacaranda tree which burst through the broken walls, managing to maintain sense of forgotten grandeur.

The trail bent round to the right, then to the left, becoming narrower and more rock strewn as he moved ever upwards. This part of the trail was seldom visited nowadays, there being no reason for any of the villagers to come up this far. Any signs of order gave way to coarse bracken and the occasional fir tree, the vegetation sparse, arid and brittle. Luis couldn't remember the last time it had rained and now the very ground ached with thirst. This was a blighted landscape, suffering, withering, close to death.

He paused again, a few moments later, taking another drink. Something rustled over to his right and he whirled around, panic stricken, only to see a bird emerging from the undergrowth in a flurry of beating wings and coarse cries, undergrowth flying off skywards. He followed it with his eyes and wished he had its freedom. The silence settled again and Luis went to take another drink but thought better of it. He had to conserve what he had; there was little hope of finding any fresh water to replenish his canteen up here in this harsh, lonely place. Sitting down on an outcrop of rock, he took off his hat and fanned himself. Amongst the soaring mountains, the air was thick with humidity. Within an hour or so, it would become cooler, the altitude helping to ease the discomfort, bringing welcome relief from the constant, pressing heat.

He tramped on for another hour or so, but keeping time was difficult up here, with the landscape all so similar, the climb prolonged, winding, never ceasing. Its uniformity caused his mind to wander, to latch onto things not always pleasant. He thought about his village, the day-to-day passage of time with nothing much to do except read and tend to Constanza and his mother. He squeezed his eyes shut to prevent the tears. Constanza and his mother. He had to find them, and he felt certain they would be here, amongst these soaring, anonymous peaks. The thing that came into the village, to kill and cause havoc, that had to responsible. But who to believe? The mayor and his cronies, or Enrique, now dead, throat slit, to keep him quiet, prevent him from telling the truth? As a warning to anyone else who might ask too many questions? And, in the questioning, what might be unearthed? The truth of why the killings had taken place, why someone had taken his family away?

A noise, the crack of a broken branch, echoed like a gunshot across the shattered landscape. Luis jumped, and stopped. He scanned the grey rocks, punctuated with clumps of bracken and gorse, and allowed his eyes to roam to the distance, to a small copse and, further still, a wood. The sound emanated from there, and he waited. Luis had heard tales of wolves living in those woods. He fingered the pistol in his waistband. Wolves, hunting in packs. His shot with the pistol would have to be a good one. He had never fired a pistol in anger before, but knew what to do, how to load and aim. He'd put many a shot into a tree trunk before now, but the thought of killing even a wolf, filled him with dread. Could he do it? Extinguish a life? He remembered Enrique, laying there, his throat sliced through, the other man knocked down on the cobbles, brains dashed with no more thought than if he were an insect. Luis, a witness to death close up and intimate, hadn't so much as blinked. Somehow, the thought of killing a wolf held more significance than the death of that man. He wiped away the sweat and studied his hand, rock steady, and he frowned. Had he changed so much, in such a short time, that even the death of a human being no longer held any horror for him? He wanted to care, but he didn't. Not now, not when there were more important concerns. He settled his hat on his head and turned away to continue along the twisting trail, his stride strong and resolute.

After what seemed an eternity of mindless trudging, head down, knees bent, moving upwards, upwards, forever upwards, the trail finally came to an abrupt halt. A rock fall of great boulders lay like a man-made wall before him, blocking the path. The sweat ran down his face in rivulets and he looked in despair towards the top of the pile. He could climb it, if he had the time, but the day was giving way to early evening, the sun becoming lower in the sky. The temperature had dropped, as he knew it would, but the rocks radiated heat and gave no relief. He slumped down on the ground and hung his head, dejected. All this way, all this effort, to be defeated now. He cursed God, nature, his life. But most of all he cursed the ogre, for coming into his village and reaping havoc.

Climbing to his feet, he looked around. By the time he made his way back to the village, it would be night. The whole expedition would have been for nothing, a waste of time and effort. Disastrous. He hadn't gained anything by coming up here except for sore feet and an aching back. A great surge of anguish consumed him. His legs ached, his shoulders were sore where the straps of his pack had rubbed against his skin, and biting thirst made his throat feel constricted and dry as dust. It had all been for nothing.

Weighed down by these feelings of failure, he slowly began tramp back down the way he had come. He would have to try again tomorrow, taking the other route which skirted around the mountains to approach them from another direction. It would probably be a tougher climb and he would have to pace himself, plan on taking two days to reach the mountains proper. Such a trek would require more water, more food, compel him to seek out places to rest for the night. Finding shelter in this hostile place would not be easy, but if—

He froze. There, not a hundred steps to his right, he saw it. The faint flickering of a campfire. He stooped down on his haunches, screwing up his eyes, focusing on the light. Definitely a fire, no mistake about it. There were caves over there, he recalled. If he had prepared his route better, he could have made for them and used them as a resting place to stay in through the night. The question for the moment, however, was who sheltered there now?

Luis eased out the pistol from his waistband, checked the priming pan and, keeping the weapon drawn, he moved towards the light of the fire, mindful of each step he took. He kept low, slipping from one clump of bracken to the next, careful not to make any sound. He remembered the noise from the woods, so he stopped every so often, checked the ground, measured his breathing. He had no wish to alert whoever it was camping by the fire. He had no plan, only the desire to find out who it was and whether or not his mother and sister lay trussed up, captured. Luis doubted an ogre would need a fire to keep warm, but perhaps to roast the meat of its victims? The idea brought bile into his mouth and he gagged. He swallowed down the last of his water from the canteen, re-checked his pistol and pressed on.

It grew darker and with it came thoughts of spectres and demons lurking in the deep shadows, waiting to spring out on him, drag him off to their lairs to feast on his bones. His head snapped from left to right, eyes wide, the pistol shaking in his hands. It felt so much heavier now and he took no comfort from the fact that he had it. One shot, if he were lucky. He doubted he would have the chance to use his father's in the bag. It would have to be the sword and the knife. He fell down behind an uprooted tree and sat, breath coming in sharp gasps. What an idiot he'd been. What had been thinking, to come up here to face the dangers of the night. The terror. The unknown.

He wanted to cry, but he battled to keep control. Thoughts of his mother and little Constanza renewed his strength and determination. They were the reasons he had come here, and they were reasons enough. Life without them would be no kind of life at all. He had to continue, no matter what. Pulling in a huge gulp of air, he stood up and moved forward.

Caution abandoned, he quickened his pace, desperate to reach his goal, find his loved ones. A few paces and he scrambled up a slight rise and came to the fire, spluttering in the entrance to a wide slit of a cave. A few meagre blackened twigs spat and crackled, sending up little flurries of red and orange sparks, close to going out. Luis got down on his knees. Bones lay scattered on the ground, picked clean and terror gripped tight around his throat. So this was it. The ogre's lair. He glanced around, checking that the beast was not in close proximity, then edged towards the cave. Nothing but a cut in the side of the mountain he couldn't clearly make out the interior. He ducked down, did his best, but saw no evidence of habitation. Perhaps the creature used this spot to feast before moving on. He stared at the embers again, surmising that the meal must have just ended. The fire, still smouldering, the bones recently stripped, everything pointed to this place having been abandoned very recently, possibly within the last hour. Luis pushed through the dying embers with the toe of his shoe. Why, he mused, why leave all of this here, so that anyone could find it. Like a beacon.

Or a trap.

Too late he realised what a fool he'd been. He readied himself to, but before he even took a step a great arm caught him from behind, clamping around his throat, lifting him bodily off the ground. Luis kicked out, squirming in the grip, but the creature was too strong, stronger than anyone he could imagine. The hand squeezed like a vice, crushing him. He couldn't breathe, the pressure too great. He thrashed, tried to scream, but it was useless, the force of the arm across his throat restricting any sound he could make. More pressure and he felt like his head would explode like an over-ripe melon. His fingers grew numb, the pistol slipping from his grasp, and the night began to close in as the great throb continued in his head. A pounding pulse, over and over, growing in intensity, pressing outwards against his skull. No other thoughts came into his mind, every fibre of his being consumed by the pressure in his skull. Nothing to think about. Only the heavy, pounding pulse. And the blackness.

Alvaro skirted along the far side of the escarpment. He'd broken away from the knot of men as they tramped along the trail, none of them knowing how far to go or which direction to take. Impatient, Alvaro took his chance and slipped away unseen.

As he rounded the mountain, he looked across at the rolling countryside, the undulations of the hills, dotted with an abundance of olive and almond trees. The land groaned. Sweltering heat, sun scorched ground, baked iron hard, everything struggling to find moisture. The curse of summer.

A small mill stood some way off, lying in a slight dip. Alvaro narrowed his eyes and made out a thin plume of smoke trickling out of the roof. He knew the mill, but also knew it had stood empty for years and he didn't know anybody lived there still. He felt a thrill rush through him. The ogre's lair? He gripped the handle of the long, heavy knife in his waistband, gritted his teeth, and slowly made his way towards the building, his heart thumping with excitement, knowing this was his chance to prove himself, to be a man, a hero. As he scrambled closer, however, another feeling began to take firmer root. A feeling of dread.

Liquid, cold as ice, sharp and sudden, hit the back of Luis's throat and he sprang upwards, wide awake, coughing coarsely. The memory of the grip, the fiend at his throat, flashed into his mind and he grabbed for his sword. But the weapon was not there. Nor the pouch, his knife, nor anything that he had brought with him. Even his boots. He frowned. Where were his boots?

A shadow fell over him. He rolled over, scrambling to his feet, eyes wide, a croaked cry emitting from the depths of his being as he focused on the thing before him. A man, but not a man, a grotesque, twisted body with leering, drooling mouth.

He stood, impossibly huge, a water jug in his hand, his great head jutting forward.

And he was smiling.

Chapter 21

The Ogre

The light from the morning sun framed the huge figure in front of him, encircling his head in a kind of halo. Unable to discern the creature's features, Luis sensed its mouth was open, slavering, eager to feed. Luis pushed himself further into the tiny cave, arms held up to deflect any attack. The thing remained still, rooted to the ground, studying him. Luis wondered why the creature had not already attacked and devoured him, the fate no doubt of all the other unfortunates who had happened upon this place, or been taken by night time swoops into the village. The creature, full of anticipation for the feast to come, would extinguish his life in a wild orgy of sharp claws and vicious fangs. Hopes, dreams, plans, all gone to nothing. Mother, Constanza. Nothing.

"You hungry?"

Luis stopped, his mouth dropping open, unable to comprehend, the voice so much like a man's for a moment he thought it was a man. Perhaps this was the reason for its success. People lulled by its human sounding tone, believing a normal person spoke, allowed themselves to relax and then, without warning, the strike. The breaking of bones, the biting down of those huge, sharp teeth. He tried to retreat further, but he hit the dank, hard, unforgiving wall of the cave, cool and sharp against his body, the sensation snapping his thoughts back to what the creature asked. Hungry? Had it said such a thing to fatten him up? Into what kind of mad nightmare had he stumbled? He managed a feeble, 'No,' and shook his head, a dullard, accepting of his fate, resigned to death.

It stepped to the side and the sun hit Luis directly in the face and he winced, he turned his head away. The figure moved up beside him and squatted down, stinking of sweat and corruption, unwashed, untended, a base creature from the out of the pit. A thick, musty tang like rotted vegetation, shreds of victims' flesh lodged between jagged teeth, the stench of... Luis shuddered and forced himself to stare straight at his new companion.

The large hulking brute fell down beside him with a loud exhalation. Shoulders as wide as a doorway sprouted thick arms like gnarled tree trunks, forearms bristling with coarse, black hair. It wore a torn and ragged leather jerkin, loosely tied across the bulging chest with frayed bits of twine, and thin, ripped leggings. The head took most of Luis' attention. Bolted onto those shoulders, perfectly square and massive, topped with tussled brown hair. Heavy brows almost obscured small, piercing eyes, but eyes which were kind, intelligent. Not like an ogre at all, or at least not what Luis *imagined* an ogre to be like. A man. A big man, true enough, but nothing horrible or frightening, wrenched from the imagination of writers conjuring up spectres and ghouls.

"I think you are hungry," the man continued, face breaking into a wide smile. "You're just too frightened to say so." He stretched around to his side and produced a plate, filled with slivers of dried meat, a hunk of bread and an apple, sliced in half, the core gouged out. He thrust the food forward and grunted, "Take it."

Luis hesitated. Gazing at the offerings, he realised how hungry he was. His stomach joined in, rumbling loudly and the big man laughed.

"Don't be afraid," said the man, and he repeated, "Take it."

Luis examined the meat with his finger, poking and probing, half expecting it to spring to life or ooze with a fearful slime, even poison. The stranger watched him, smiling all the while and at last Luis took hold of the food and crammed it into his mouth without ceremony, desperate to fill his belly. It tasted delicious, not over salty and very lean. The bread too was warm, as if newly made. Within a few moments he had demolished everything and sat back, crunching down on the last of the apple.

The big man did not speak, never once taking his eyes off Luis, smiling, happy his companion had enjoyed the meal so much. He picked up the finished plate and pushed it in away. He threw Luis a cloth. "I have water, or milk if you prefer."

Luis coughed, some food catching in his throat, the man's words taking him by surprise. "*Milk?*"

The man nodded and went back into the corner of the cave and brought out an earthen pitcher. He poured Luis a generous measure of frothy milk into a wooden goblet and passed it across. Without hesitation Luis greedily drank it down. A little warm, but fresh and, like the food, delicious. He couldn't remember the last time he had drunk milk. Perhaps the previous Christmas, when old man Jose came into the village with his goats? Jose had disappeared soon afterwards and the goats with him and there had been no milk since.

Luis smacked his lips and wiped his mouth on the cloth. He stared at the empty goblet for a long time, his heartbeat settling, fear beginning to slip away, replaced by an increasing certainty that everyone, from the mayor downwards, had been mistaken in their presumptions. This man was no ogre, that much was clear, but who he was and why he lived amongst the unforgiving mountains remained a mystery. Luis looked up and found the man's eyes boring into him. He didn't look away. "Who are you?"

The man shrugged, the smile never leaving his face. He spread out his hands, palms upwards. "Who do you think I am? The ogre?"

Without thinking, Luis brought his knees up to his chest and wrapped his arms around them, as if protecting himself. He shook his head. "Ogre? What do *you* know of any ogre?"

The smile broadened. "Ah, I've hit a nerve all right, haven't I?" He laughed, a sound of falling boulders rumbling from his ample stomach. "Seems like everyone in that damned village believes there's an ogre lurking around up here." He thrust forward without warning, pulled back his cheeks with his fingers, stuck out his tongue and made a roaring sound. Luis yelped, hurled himself away, cowered and whimpered, the little child returning, fearful of night time shadows and goblins lurking in the darkened corners. The big man laughed again, and poured out more milk. Luis took the goblet without a word. "You people, you're all so ignorant."

This stranger was no simpleton that was for sure. Luis studied him closely, those huge, square shoulders, the solid knots of muscle like cannon balls in his arms. How could a human being become so large? He took a sip of milk, licked his lips, and asked again, "Who are you?"

With a deep sigh, the man stood. Luis gasped, but for a different reason this time. The man was bow-legged, as if he had spent most of his life on the back of a horse. Short and squat, they seemed too small to support the weight of his body. He walked over to the far side of the camp, in a rolling gait, arms hanging so low they almost brushed the ground. Señor Martinez had showed drawings Portuguese sailors had made of creatures discovered in a far-off lands. Dark places, unknown. Creatures like this, heavy-bodied with short, stumpy legs. Had this poor man, captured and brought back from a distant land, managed to break free and escape into these mountains?

The stranger turned and tilted his enormous head, smiling. He motioned him forward with a great slab of a hand. "Come over here."

Luis wondered what would happen next, but his fear had all but gone now. If the stranger wanted him dead, it would have already happened. He got to his feet, feet which were still bare, and stepped across the broken ground, wincing as his bare flesh trod on brittle stones and sharp twigs.

"Put on your boots."

Luis saw them propped up against the far side of the cave opening. He rushed over and pulled them on, not bothering with the laces. "I wasn't sure who you were, or what you wanted," said the man, "but I think I'm beginning to understand."

Luis stamped like a bird bringing up worms from the ground a couple of times. The familiar, comforting feel of the soft leather caused him to grin.

"Why are you here, in these mountains? Have you come to hunt me out?"

Luis stared, debating whether to be truthful or not.

"I know many of you come here to hunt. I've watched you all and sometimes I show myself, or shake a tree, and they run like children, screaming for their mama."

"There have been killings, in the village."

"And you thought it was me."

"An ogre. That is what the rumour is."

"You believe those stories?"

"I wasn't sure at first, but yes, I came up here to find an answer."

"To kill me."

He turned away, the resonance of his voice, so sad, coming down heavily upon Luis, filling him with guilt.

Luis followed him along a small, narrow path that twisted downwards and eventually plunged into a natural tunnel of over-hanging acacia and heavy scented yellow and white umbellifer. No wonder nobody had ever found this man, hidden within such a wilderness. They emerged into a large patch of scrubland, ringed by trees, amongst which lingered a herd of goats, chomping on bits of bracken and gorse. When the man approached, they set up a chorus of loud bleating and some wandered over to nuzzle up to him, pressing their faces into his hands, searching for titbits. Luis watched, fascinated.

"This is who I am," said the man with a smile, turning towards Luis. "My name is Salvador, and I am a goatherd."

They sat in the shade of the trees, surrounded by the chomping goats. Luis rested his head against a tree trunk, closed his eyes and asked, "Why have I never heard of you, or seen you?"

"You want the whole story?" Luis nodded, without opening his eyes. "Very well. It might help you understand something, but it may also sit uneasily on your shoulders. A burden, unwanted."

"You talk..." Luis studied him for the umpteenth time, all of his power and strength centred in his upper body, with legs feeble in comparison. "You talk like a man educated, Salvador, but also you talk in riddles."

He smiled, pulled out a piece of coarse grass and stuck it between his teeth. "Then I'll tell you the story and hopefully, all will become clearer."

He sat back, sucked on the stalk, and picked up a twig to begin tracing random designs within the dirt. "I learned most of it from my mother, of course. After my birth, she said everything was as it should be, but when I was about two summers old, something began to happen. My face changed, my body became bulkier whilst my legs remained small and weak. The other villagers, they would stop, point and stare, telling my mother I was not normal, that she had been cursed." He uttered the last word with venom, his voice sounding harsh and angry. "Like they always do, ignorant peasants that they are, they couldn't understand. They believed me to be the spawn of the Devil and they harassed and spat their venom at her relentlessly, hounding her as if *she* were the wicked one. So they forced her to bring me up here to the mountains, to die."

A terrible silence fell over them, causing even the goats to stop their munching. Luis stared at Salvador, open-mouthed, not daring to believe the inference of the man's words. His voice was little more than a croak when he asked, "They meant you to die?"

Salvador nodded. "That was their plan, for me to die from exposure. But my mother, God bless her, would come and tend to me every day, slipping out of the village whilst they all slept, to care for me, feed me. The years went by and I grew strong," he smiled. "As you can see."

"But," Luis shook his head, ashamed for being part of a community so superstitious, so callous, capable of imposing such suffering. Uncaring was one thing, but this, this was barbaric. "Salvador, that is so awful."

"I was different. Their small minds couldn't understand, so they rejected me. Out of sight is out of mind."

"Nevertheless, to deliberately kill a tiny child..." He ran a hand through his hair, thinking of Alvaro and Carlos, the way they taunted him, made his life a misery simply because *he* was different. It wasn't such a jump to accept they were capable of far greater cruelty, if they could get away with it. "Truth be told, I suppose I know something about how cruel people can be."

"You speak with meaning in your voice. Perhaps that is why you do not shun me."

"Shun you? Why should I *shun* you? You gave me food, looked after me." He spread out his hands. "All right, I admit I was frightened, but that was at first, when I thought you were..." His voice trailed off and, feeling a little ashamed, he looked away.

"Don't fret so, I quite understand. They think I am the ogre, all of them. Why wouldn't they—no one knew I survived up here, but they believed *something* roamed these mountains. So, the idea of an ogre came about, a hideous beast lurking amongst the caves and woods. This ogre became their scapegoat for every bad thing that befell the village. A child died, it was the ogre. The water dried up, it was the ogre damning up the river." He shook his head. "Simpletons. My mother visited me here and she would read to me." He saw Luis wide-eyed expression. "Oh yes, my mother could read. You know of the music teacher, Martinez?" Luis nodded once, holding his breath. "She was his daughter."

Luis clamped his hand over his mouth, the shock of the revelation hitting him like a punch. "Oh my God! Señor Martinez, he knew about this?"

"No. My mother couldn't bring herself to tell even him; it wouldn't be safe. The village elders would throw her in jail and send a search party to root me out, kill me. My legs," he slapped his thighs, "they aren't that much good for running. They would have hunted me down like a dog, strung me up. God knows what else." His face went dark and he hung his head. "I sometimes feel that I would have been better off dead. My life has never been easy. When my mother died..."

Luis watched him without speaking. He saw the single teardrop run down Salvador's face, hang from the tip of his nose for a moment before it dropped down into the earth.

Salvador wiped his eyes with the back of his hand. "I must have been your age when it happened. I don't know the details, but when she didn't come to see me I grew suspicious. I made my way down into the village and discovered the truth." He put his head against the tree and looked skywards. "I overheard conversations, learned how she'd died. From that moment, I had to fend for myself. And I have, living up here, amongst the trees, scrambling around, surviving. Most nights I would creep down into the village, find scraps of food. One or two of the villagers knew about me, helped me."

"Helped you? You mean some of them know who you are?" Luis could hardly believe it.

"Oh yes, one or two." He smiled. "Señora Gomez. I think you know her?"

This was too much. Luis bit his lip, trying to hold back his feelings, but he lost the struggle and the tears sprang out as the dam burst, all of his emotional turmoil coming to the surface in a rush. He put his face in his hands and surrendered to the despair that washed over him.

The only sound, the low pitiful murmur of Luis' sorrow.

"I know she died," said Salvador. After a prolonged pause, he continued in a low, sonorous voice. "She was a good woman. Kind, helpful. A saint, in many ways. I probably wouldn't have lasted as long as I have if it wasn't for her. Then, when old Jose died, I took to tending his goats and I saw less and less of Señora Gomez. Having the goats means I don't need the village as much now. Which is good for all of us, I think."

"She was murdered." Luis pressed the palms of his hands into his eyes, the tears at last come to an end. "Did you know that?"

"Yes."

"And children have disappeared. A little girl called Lourdes, a boy Francisco, both found dead. Enrique too, an old soldier who seemed to know something, perhaps more than he should, he has also been murdered." Luis dropped his hands onto his lap and took in a ragged breath. "And my mother and sister, they have gone missing. That's why I'm here, to find them."

"And kill the ogre."

Luis laughed, a sharp crack of sound, bereft of humour. "Only because I believed that it had taken my family."

"What do you believe now?"

"I don't know." Luis rubbed his chin. "I don't know anything anymore."

"Well, someone is responsible for all of this wickedness. Someone from your village." Salvador leaned forward. "It happened before, you know, years and years ago. Children were found murdered."

"They thought it was the ogre then. And now, a soldier comes into our village and tells us all that the ogre has returned."

"Yes, and they try to hunt it down. But they found no sign and my goats frighten them because those fools believe there are wolves roaming these mountain passes—idiots that they are! And then..." He exhaled loudly, "Then one of them is killed. In their desperation, tramping around amongst the trees making more noise than a troop of cavalry, they panic, run around like headless chickens and in the confusion one of them falls."

Luis waited a long time before he asked, "You saw what happened?"

Salvador's eyes were blank, without expression. "Yes. I saw everything, and I can tell you, it was no accident—because also saw who killed him."

Back at the cave, Luis gathered together his belongings, checked his pistols, buckled up his belt with the sword hanging from it.

"What will you do now?" asked Salvador.

"Go and speak to the mayor, tell him what I've discovered."

"You think he will believe you? I have my doubts."

"I don't know, but I have to try. I don't really have much choice."

"And your mother, your sister?"

Luis let his head hang down, weighed down by the black cloud of confusion and despair hanging over him, forever there to blight every passing second. "I have to find them, somehow, some way. My mother knows something, I'm sure of it. Hints, clues. When I pressed her she began to tell me the story and finally handed me a letter. From my father."

Salvador stiffened. "A letter? Your father was an educated man?"

"Self-taught, yes. He passed on some of his learning, so I too can read and write."

The man shook his huge head. "I am impressed. This letter, you have it?"

Luis nodded, reached inside his shoulder bag and held the single piece of paper between finger and thumb. "It talks of you, Salvador. I never really understood what father meant until... Until I met you, face to face. It details what happened, up until the time he..." Luis let his breath out slowly. "But no one would believe it. If I showed this to the mayor..." He shook his head and slowly folded the letter up again neatly. "I have a suspicion that the mayor would not wish this letter to become common knowledge."

"Then we have little choice—we have to find some way of telling the authorities in Malaga. That is the only thing we can do. I will come with you, into the village, confront them. Then, we shall go to Malaga and we will end all of this hypocrisy once and for all. They will send an investigator and he will leave no stone uncovered."

"You really think we can? Do you think they will believe us, a young boy and..."

"A cripple? Say it, Luis. Don't be ashamed. I *am* a cripple, deformed by nature, by a God that has played a huge joke on me. But I have survived, Luis and, damn it all, I'll not stand by and let them get away with this any longer."

Luis saw the man's determination etched into every line and crease in his broad face. It fired him, swelled out his chest, made him strong. "By God, Salvador, neither shall I."

"Then let us end it, Luis. Today!"

Chapter 22

Arrest

Together they returned to the village, making the long journey in silence, like a repentant band of holy brothers, head bowed, deep in thought. Still being early, few people were about but as the two turned into the square, some old men gathered around the fountain, took fright at Salvador's appearance and scattered screaming, a stampede of wild frenetic prey fleeing from predators. Salvador snarled, went over to the fountain and splashed water over his head. Luis flopped down next to him.

"You see how things have not changed? Their ignorance disgusts me."

Luis nodded. "What do we do now?"

"We wait," said Salvador, and sat down next to Luis. He motioned towards the scurrying men disappearing in a swirl of dust up the street. "Some of them are bound to go running off to the mayor. He'll be here in a few moments with a group of armed militia, mark my words."

They sat and waited, neither of them speaking. Sure enough, before the village clock had moved its hand to the next interval, the mayor came striding down the hill. Flanked by the old men and others armed with firearms, halberds and pikes. Luis heard them before he saw them, a gaggling band, talking as one in high, excited voices raised in alarm, laced with fear. They reached the square and fanned out, then stopped a few paces from where the two sat, weapons lowered at the ready, the mayor at their lead.

Before the Mayor spoke a word, Luis stood and pointed an accusing finger. "It's all lies," he began. "All this nonsense about ogres—lies! This," he gestured towards Salvador, "this is my friend. He took care of me, fed me. Told me many things, Señor Mayor. Things that I didn't know, things that we should all be ashamed of."

Muskets were primed menacingly, hammers drawn back. Luis experienced the first tremors of fear rumble deep inside. The mayor held up his hand, "Hold fast," he said to the men and stepped forward, his voice becoming quiet and serious, almost as if he were in mourning. "Luis, God help you. What have you done?"

Luis frowned, looked down at Salvador, then back to the mayor. "What do you mean, *what have I done*?"

"Luis, we were worried—where have you been?"

Something didn't feel right about any of this. Luis chewed at his bottom lip, "I've just told you." He wanted to continue with his bold words, his confident manner, but he couldn't. Something about the way the mayor looked at him, almost as if he were sad, hurt in some way.

"Luis," the mayor went to move closer. One of the men muttered a word of caution, but the mayor dismissed him with a wave of his hand, stepped right up to Luis, and stared deep into his eyes. "You've been gone all night, Luis. The men who found Enrique, they told me that they had seen you running off into the mountains. I feared for you, feared what you might find."

"Now you know." Luis's head began to fill up with mush. Perhaps it was the heat, the race down from the mountains. Or the mayor's manner. Concerned. "I found Salvador, he…"

The mayor placed a heavy hand on Luis's shoulder. "Why did you stay out until the morning light, Luis?"

"Eh? I, I must have fallen asleep." He turned to Salvador, frowning. Salvador stared down at his own feet. "He took care of me, I told you. Gave me food."

"You slept? All night? Where?"

"In a cave, up in the mountains. I found where he lived and when I got closer he…" Suddenly it hit him, like a mallet in his skull. A thought. A discovery. It almost felled him with its enormity and he sat down on the hard, unforgiving step of the fountain, mouth hanging open, staring into the distance, feeling so heavy.

"Whilst you slept, Luis," the mayor stepped back a little, reaching down to his waistband, bringing out a huge, ornately decorated pistol, "he came down to our village and murdered again."

The sound of the hammer engaging with a solid clunk forced Luis to snap up his head. He stared straight at the muzzle of the pistol. "Who did he kill?"

"Don't you know, Luis? Can't you guess?"

"Oh my God..." Yes, he could guess, but he didn't dare think it. He wanted to dismiss the thought from his mind, yet the words of the Mayor refused to go away. *Whilst you slept, he came down into our village and murdered again.* Dear God, could it be true? Luis put his face in his hands and wept.

"But don't worry, Luis," said the mayor as the others pressed in around them, "you've done a fine job bringing him to us. He'll hang this day, hang for all the murders he has committed. Especially for the murder of your poor, sickly mother."

As Luis sat in a daze, viewing everything from afar, detached and distant as if it were happening to someone else, the men began to lash leather bonds around Salvador, securing him tight. The big man offered up no resistance, resigned to his fate, all of the fight gone out of him. As they hauled him to his feet, he glanced over to Luis, a faint smile playing around his lips. Luis thought he saw the man shake his head slightly before the armed group marched him off towards the mayor's offices and the village jail that lay in the basement.

The mayor came over and sat down next to Luis. He fingered the mechanism of the pistol, a wheel-lock, intricately worked. A beautiful thing. "What did he tell you?"

Luis didn't answer him, his mind reeling with the revelation presented to him. Whilst he had slept, Salvador had slipped down to the village and... *murdered* his mother? No, that couldn't be right. Mother had gone missing before Luis even went up into the mountains, so how could Salvador have possibly known where to find her. To Luis, there could be only one answer to the conundrum—the mayor was lying. As he always did.

"*Luis!*"

Luis jumped, blinking away his thoughts and realised where he was. The mayor's face grew contorted with the same rage that coursed through him so easily. "Yes, Señor?"

"I asked you a question—what did he say to you?"

"Say to me about what?"

"About the deaths, Luis. About your mother, your father."

"He didn't say anything about them." Luis thought of the letter, what it contained, how Salvador had reacted when he read it, almost as if it were a confirmation of everything he had suspected. "He said nothing."

The mayor gripped Luis' knee hard, steel fingers pressing down into the flesh. Luis fought back the desire to yell, beg him to stop, but somehow he held on, biting through the pain. The mayor leaned forward, peered into Luis's face. "Are you sure, boy?"

Luis took his time, squeezing his eyes shut, blocking out the pressure on his knee. He had no fear of this man, just loathing. "I don't think he killed my mother, if that is what you mean."

Immediately, the mayor released his fingers and Luis fell back, gasping. "Then you're a fool!" The mayor straightened, hoisted up his pants and stuffed the pistol back in his belt. "Whilst you slept, he came here in the night and butchered her."

"No, you're wrong." The mayor's eyes narrowed, a dangerous black look crossing his features. "He couldn't have."

"You think not?"

"Mother had gone missing before I even found him. That was the reason why I went up into the mountains, to find her, believing she had been kidnapped. I now know that isn't true."

"You fool. Of course he kidnapped her, in the night and took her to his lair."

Luis titled his head, growing in confidence. He smiled. "But you just said he crept down in the night to—what was it you said? *Butchered* her. Which is it, Señor; did he murder her here, or drag her to his cave and then do it?"

Something flickered on and off in the man's eyes. A hesitation, a twinge of panic. Barely noticeable, but enough. Enough for Luis to have his suspicion confirmed. The man was lying. "You impertinent whelp, how dare you question me."

Luis set his jaw. He'd come this far, he was determined to push on. The mayor had mentioned death.

The death of his mother. How Salvador was involved. But he'd also said how he was involved in another death, so he pulled in a breath and asked, "What has my father got to do with this?"

"Your fa—*damn your eyes!*" The mayor's fists bunched, his face ablaze. "Tomorrow, that *thing* dies and this village can return to normal. You," he pointed his finger hard at Luis's face, "you get home and don't come out of your house until I send someone to fetch you." He turned on his heels and strode off towards his offices.

Luis watched him go, then slumped back, head against the fountain. He suddenly felt very tired and very much alone. They were going to hang Salvador, for a crime he hadn't committed, and there was nothing Luis could do about it.

Chapter 23

Another Betrayal

The mayor blasted through his front door, swept aside his manservant with a wave of the hand, and strode straight into his study and poured out a large goblet of *rioja* wine. He measured his breathing, trying to calm himself. That impudent whelp, to question him the way he had! He should have had him flogged, there and then.

He felt something tingling at the back of his neck. A slight burning, uncomfortable. Real. Slowly he turned and gave a little gasp.

"What did he say?"

"Good God," the mayor drained his glass. "How long have you been there?"

The man shrugged. "Long enough. What did he say?"

"He said that he had been with Salvador all night."

"So, he doesn't know the truth?"

The mayor turned away, chewing at his lip. "No, but he suspects. He has the letter."

The man brought his fist down hard on the table-top. "We must have it, damn you!"

The mayor waved his hand, "It means nothing on its own, but if he carries on unearthing things, then..." He let his voice trail away as he poured himself a second glass.

"I took the goblet from their house. The one *he* gave her."

"That was foolish—he'll wonder why. Luis is an intelligent boy."

"Too damned intelligent, perhaps, but no, he'll think it was a simple robbery. The only thing of value was that goblet, to have left it would have made him suspicious."

"I hope you're right."

"And I hope that you can persuade him of Salvador's guilt—otherwise, the boy must also die."

The mayor closed his eyes. "Has it come to this, demanding the death of another child?"

"You know what I will do, Lord Mayor. I will murder every child in this village if I have to—to gain what is mine."

"Yours? Dear God, you have a perverted outlook on the truth."

The man rose to his feet, his fists clenched. "I've waited half a life time, I'll not wait much longer. End this damned farce now, Señor Mayor," his fist pounded the table one again, "or by the love of God, I will!"

Luis didn't go home straight away. There was nothing there for him anyway. So he wandered, head down, towards the home of his old tutor, Señor Martinez, who opened the door to him on the first knock and immediately took Luis in his arms and held him tight.

The old man led Luis into his kitchen, where the remnants of a breakfast lay on a chipped wooden plate. Martinez shouted to his housekeeper, who came scurrying in wiping her hands on her apron. "Yes, Señor?"

"Make this boy some breakfast," he said, then put his arm around Luis and took him out into the large garden at the rear.

This was part of the tutor's house that Luis had never seen. A wide, sprawling piece of farmland, not a garden at all, spread out into the distance, the slight roll of the land descending down towards a stream that would, in winter, be a natural source of sustenance for the many plants and bushes that dotted the edges. Summertime, however, meant that everything struggled as the stream stood dry.

Martinez placed a hand on Luis's shoulder, "How are you feeling, Luis?"

He shrugged. "How am I supposed to feel?" He looked up at the kind face of his old tutor. His mother was dead. That was all there was to it. "She's gone."

Martinez didn't speak. Instead, he stooped down and picked a tiny, wild flower from the sparse, patchy grass. He held it under his nose. "Remarkable how, even in this harsh place, new life springs forth." He sighed. "Have you seen her?"

"No." Strange question. Why would he want to see her, she was dead. Murdered, *butchered* the mayor had said. "I want to remember her as she was, not how she is now."

Martinez nodded, as if understanding the depth of the horror Luis felt. "Yes."

"How did you know?"

The old tutor drew in a long breath, tossing the tiny flower away. "The whole village was full of it last night. The mayor sent men to patrol the streets, with torches, trying to find some clue. They came pounding on my door, asking questions about you."

"Me?"

"They wanted to know where you were. Constanza too. They still haven't found her."

"He didn't do it."

"Who? Salvador?" Martinez gave a little smile. "I know."

Luis did a double-take. "You know? How can you know?"

"Because I know *him,* Luis. I've known *about* him since the day he was born. He's my grandson. No doubt he told you."

Luis pulled a face, "He said you didn't know anything about him, that his mother hadn't told you—"

Martinez held up his hand. "She didn't, but I knew anyway. I always have."

"Then why... Why didn't you do anything?"

"I gave food to Señora Gomez so she could feed him. But if I'd have done anything more, the villagers would have found out and they would have gone up there, into the mountains and tracked him down." He shook his head. "I know he hasn't killed your mother, or any of the others."

"He didn't resist—they took him and he just..." Luis put his face in his hands. "Why didn't he say something?"

"He's tired, Luis. Tired of living his life the way he always has. Essentially, Luis, I believe he is tired of *life*. Fate has been cruel to him."

"But to just let them... he should have said something, Señor Martinez. They are going to hang him for things he has never done. It's an abomination!"

The old tutor nodded his head. "Yes, it is. But the harsh reality of this whole sorry tale is we can do little to prevent playing out the final act. The village will have its revenge, Luis, and nobody will be interested in justice or, indeed, the truth."

"I have to find Constanza," said Luis, gritting his teeth. "I think I know where to look."

"Luis," Martinez smiled sadly. "You should prepare yourself, for the worst. I do not profess to have all the answers, but of one thing I'm certain—whatever the reason for all these killings, they are not going to stop until..." He turned away and Luis saw the old man's eyes filling up with emotion. "There is something terrible going on here, Luis. And your poor mother and sister are the latest victims."

Luis shook his head, "No, Señor. Constanza is not dead. I know she isn't."

His eyes grew hard as he stared at his young student. "How can you know that, Luis? This madness which has gripped our village, it knows no bounds. No one is safe."

"Señor Martinez, you don't understand." Luis gave the old tutor a withering look, "I *know* who is responsible."

A footfall made them both turn. Luis was half-expecting to see the housekeeper standing there, plate stacked up with bread and cheese. Instead, it was the mayor, two armed men standing with him, a look of barely-controlled rage written across his features. "So, Luis. You know who is responsible, do you?"

Luis held his ground, as well as the mayor's gaze. "Yes. I know the truth, Señor and I will tell it unless you tell me where Constanza is?"

A thin smile broke out across the man's features. "How should I know?"

"Because you have taken her."

The mayor laughed. "Don't be ridiculous! For what possible reason?"

"To keep her with you. Now that Mama is dead, there is nothing left to stop you."

"What are you rambling on about?"

Martinez gripped the boy's arm. "Luis."

"I'm talking about *you*, Señor Mayor! You killed my mother and now you have taken Constanza."

The mayor narrowed his eyes, "You impudent fool! You have no idea what you're saying. That rabid creature in the village jail killed your mother."

"No, he couldn't have. You had people watch me and when I went up into the mountains, you, or your men, came into my home and..." He couldn't hold it any longer, the enormity of what had happened, the total horror of it all. He had kept it all inside, not allowing himself to succumb, but now it broke through his defences like a raging torrent. All the pent up emotion, the fear, the sadness, the hopelessness. He fell to his knees, head down, racked in body-shuddering sobs.

For a long time, no one moved, all of them watching Luis until at last his tears subsided and he looked up, eyes red rimmed, face smeared and drawn.

"I want this boy taken to the cells," said the mayor.

"What?" screamed Martinez. "You can't do that, what is the charge?"

"Murder, kidnapping, bearing false-witness. The list is long, master teacher."

"Are you mad? He is nothing but a boy."

"A very dangerous boy, just like his father was." the mayor signalled to his men. "Take him down." Martinez went to move and the mayor chuckled, hand falling to the butt of his pistol. "If you attempt to hinder my men, they will cut you down." To emphasise the point, one of armed guards pulled out his sword with deliberate slowness.

"Damn your hide," spat Martinez and turned to help Luis to his feet. "Don't worry, Luis. I will do what I can to put an end to this travesty."

Luis smiled, fell into Martinez's arms and hugged him tightly. Surreptitiously he reached out and crammed the letter into Martinez's pocket. The old tutor moved back slightly, a quizzical look on his face. Luis, with his back to the others, winked, then turned. "You won't get away with this," he said.

The mayor merely smiled, "I already have," he said quietly, then signalled to his men who each took hold of one of Luis's arms and marched him away to join Salvador.

Chapter 24

The Letter

For a long time Señor Martinez sat under the shade of a withered olive tree, hunched forward, hands on his knees, staring sightlessly into the ground. When, finally, his housekeeper came back he looked up at her. "Why?"

She titled her head, folded her arms. "That boy is wicked. You've never been able to see it."

"Wicked?"

"The way he struts around thinking he is so superior. His father was the same, his mother. Twisted, the lot of them."

"So you went to the Mayor and told him Luis was here."

"He killed his mother—you heard what the mayor said."

"You stupid fool, have you any idea what you're saying?"

"He's odd, Señor Martinez. He's not right. Every-one knows it—all the boys hate him."

"They hate him because they're jealous! Jealous because Luis has an opportunity to break free of this place, to better himself, make something of his life!"

"That's not for the likes of him—or us! This is our life," she jabbed her finger downwards, pointing at the ground. "This village, this is where we live, where we die. All of this nonsense about learning, it will do no good. Never has and never will."

"Yes, and that's the real reason why you went to the Mayor. You no more believe Luis killed his mother than I do—it's just your small-mindedness getting in the way, as usual. If there's something you don't understand or can't accept, you crush it with your ignorance!" He shook his head, despairing. "Just get out."

"I'll prepare your lunch and then I'll sweep out the—"

"No." Martinez had to battle hard to keep himself from leaping up and striking her. "No, I don't want you here. I want you to leave, get out."

"But Señor Martinez, I haven't—"

He squeezed his hands into tight fists and shook them, "*Get out, damn you!*"

She ran then, her face white with fear.

Martinez threw himself back and took in several deep breaths. Grateful for the overcast sky, allow-ing the temperature to not be as intense, he closed his eyes and regained some composure. Slowly, he reached inside his pocket and pulled out the letter.

For a long time he held it there, without looking at it, afraid of what he might discover. At last, he took the plunge, carefully unfolded it and began to read what it said.

'*My loves,*

If you are reading this, then I am no longer with you. It also means that these words have survived and that one day, God willing, the truth will be revealed.

Luis, it has always been my heartfelt hope that you would become educated, that you would break free from our situation and embark on a new life, full of discovery and wonder. If you can read this, my son, then your journey has already begun.

Let me begin by briefly outlining the story up to the present. It may help you to understand everything that has happened and, no doubt, all that will happen.

You had not long been born when, one fine morning, Pablo came riding into the village. You know Pablo well, I understand. Most do. A traveller, he ranges all across Spain and beyond, sometimes not coming this far south until many years have passed. This time he spoke of the War raging in the north, how the Catholic armies were being forced back, that France had joined the fray on the side of the Protestants. So incensed was I by this, that I decided to take my musket and join the Imperialist cause. Your mother, a good and kind woman, tried her best to persuade me, but I felt compelled to go, driven by a greater force. God. There is no need for any further explanation.

The journey north was hard and difficult and I will not detail it for it has little to do with what has happened. Pablo guided me for most of the journey and when I crossed into France, we parted ways. I moved east, crossing the borders of lands I never knew existed until at last, nearly a year after I had left our village, I came into Bavaria, and a town which I came to know as Donauworth. Here I met some men who were to change my life and the life of our village forever.

I fell in with a band of mercenaries, soldiers who sold their services to the highest bidder. The group I joined seemed solid enough, their captain a hard and resolute individual called Klaus Freiheim. This may or not have been his real name. Many such soldiers were criminals, fleeing from justice. However, Klaus made me feel welcome, inducted me into his company and was impressed with my use of the musket. He taught me some tricks with the sword and soon I was training with them on a daily basis.

News came that the armies of the Protestants under Bernhard of Sax-Weimer were marching towards us. We had defeated him, so Klaus told me, at a place called Nordlingen so confidence was high. But Nordlingen had been two years previously, and Bernhard was not the same man now. He crossed the Rhine and our forces struck but we were woefully beaten, our troops scattered, our artillery train and camp destroyed. We fled into the forests, many of us captured, stripped and hung on trees, pecked to death by crows. I, together with Klaus and six others, managed to escape and we spent weeks moving from one small place to another until, one fateful day, we came to a lonely monastery.

I wish to God that I had never set eyes on that place. It has been the bane of my life ever since.

They took us in, those fine monks, fed us, washed our clothes, gave us a place to rest and cared for our horses. I don't know the details, but some three or four nights later, I the most dreadful shouting woke me. One of the monks must have grown suspicious of us. Why, I do not know. But French soldiers came. A troop of them. Twelve men, heavily armed. Klaus and the others fought like demons. One of our group fell dead, but the French were despatched, only one managing to break out of the main gates. I ran after him, brought my musket to my shoulder, and brought him down. As I turned to move back into the monastery my eyes alighted on a scene from hell.

The men were incensed, Klaus amongst them. They were out of control, swearing and shouting, drunk with blood lust. They were set upon revenge, hunted out the monk that had betrayed us, cut open his body and pulled out his intestines in front of his living eyes. I stood transfixed in horror. Some other monks tried to stop them, but what could they do, men of God against bloodthirsty experts like Klaus? They butchered every last monk.

I stood and watched it all, unable to do anything. Fear and loathing had turned my limbs to stone. When at last the killing ended, the men began to loot the place. Soon a desire for gold replaced the desire to deal out death. And they found it, in abundance.

They piled the treasure up in the forecourt and I stood, wide-eyed, marvelling at the mass of gold at my feet. Coins and jewels mixed with ornate religious artefacts, all of them shimmering in the bright glow of the sun. Bedazzled, I couldn't help but laugh. We all laughed. Altar wine was broken open and we drank until we fell down, overcome with delirium. We were rich, rich beyond our wildest dreams.

Klaus had a plan, to split up, each of us taking a share of the booty. We would try our best to remain out of sight of the French, make our way south to Spain. I had told them stories of our village and they had asked me to draw maps, which I had done. Now, the plan was simple. We would all make our way slowly south then decide what best to do.

One or two of the others were not comfortable with this. They believed, quite rightly, that alone we would be easy-pickings for any wandering brigands. So we split into two groups. Klaus, myself and another called Ferdinand would form one group, and the remaining four formed the other. We packed the treasure onto pack mules that the monks had used to bring in produce to the monastery, and the following day we set off.

The journey was, for the most part, uneventful. However, as we crossed into Spain, Klaus grew sick. Dangerously sick. Ferdinand believed it was plague and he became like someone possessed. He wanted to kill Klaus, burn his body. I did my best, but nothing would deter him from his course. There was a terrible struggle. Ferdinand was a wild Italian, had fought in many battles and was a worthy opponent. But his body was weak-

ened by too many scars and his right arm was as good as useless. In the struggle, I drove a knife into his heart and killed him.

Klaus was very weak, but I knew it was not plague. I tended him, having burned Ferdinand's body— what an irony that was—but Klaus grew weaker with each passing day until eventually he told me to leave him, to make my way back home and wait there for the others. We had been good friends and, of all of them, I trusted Klaus the most. To leave him there, dying, in the middle of a strange and unfriendly copse, was the most dreadful decision I had ever made.

I returned to our village, three years after having left. You, Luis, would be almost four years of age and I remember picking you up and putting you on my shoulders, running around the plaza with you, everyone cheering. My wife, your mother, was so pleased to see me. When I had the opportunity, I told her about the gold and how we would be able to have a new life, as soon as the others came. Because now, of course, our share would be even greater. So, I hid the treasure up in the mountains, in a deep cave and tried to live my life as normally as I could. I waited and waited for the others to come, but they never did.

Then, one morning, I had a visit from the mayor. He wanted to know more about my story, where I had been, what I had done. There was something about his manner that struck me as odd. He seemed to want me to confirm suspicions he had. I wondered if he could possibly know about the gold. But how could he, I had told only your mother. And I knew she would not tell.

Then, one morning whilst I was out with old Jose, the goatherd, I saw the mayor standing outside his house talking to some men. As I came closer, I recognised one of them. He had not been one of our band, but I knew him from camp and when he set his eyes on me, his face went white. Then he pointed and shouted to the others to seize me. Jose pushed me away, tried to hold them back by herding the goats across the path and I made my escape, back to our house for my sword and musket. I knew now what had happened. The mayor had caught wind of the rumours that must have abounded. Many of the men that we had fought with had changed sides. Remember, they were mercenaries. They had no bonds of loyalty. Someone had discovered what had happened at the monastery. It was all clear to see. This soldier, this dog, a man called Manfred I think, must have caught wind of it all, come back here and enlisted the help of the mayor. The promise of gold drove them all on, changed them into demented beasts.

I ran up into the mountains but I did not want to lead them to the gold, so I took another track. Soon I came to an area that I had never visited before, high up amongst the mountains, a wild and desolate place. Here, I met Salvador. A more deformed and terrifying man I have yet to see. Many ungodly sights I had seen during my time away, but Salvador was worse than any. Despite all of this, he was kind and good, took me into his cave and gave me shelter. He told me his story and I was at once shocked and ashamed that my own people could treat a fellow human being in such a horrible and sinful way. Was it not our own Lord who had cured lepers and made cripples walk? So I promised myself that I would help Salvador, give him some of my vast wealth, restore some of his lost dignity.

But fate was against me, as it had always been since my return. Manfred and the others came upon me. There were three of them. Easy meat for me. Only Manfred managed to survive, scrambling away into a small wooded glade.

I returned to the village and the true horror of the situation came upon me then. In my house sat the mayor, a broad grin on his face. Next to him, my wife, your mother, held by an armed man, a knife to her throat. Playing on the floor, another armed man and you, Luis. The inference was obvious. I had to show them where the gold was, or you would both die.

When I told the mayor that there were others, far more skilful than I, who would be coming here to find what was theirs, he became nervous, frightened almost. The idea of soldiers, professional fighting men, coming into the village was something he had always feared. He had listened to Manfred's stories and he knew what these men were capable of. They could so easily repeat the horrors of the monastery here. So I hatched a plan. I would lead his two men to the cave and we would move the gold. Then we would wait for the soldiers to come and make our preparations to kill them as soon as they arrived. All I needed was enough gold to make our family life comfortable. The mayor agreed and I took the men up into the mountains.

I had become a changed man. War does that, Luis. It changes you. The value of human life, especially of those that you do not know, becomes as worthless as a grain of sand. I murdered them both, hid their bodies, then came back down to the village and told the mayor a dreadful story. The story of an ogre. I knew it was a wild tale, one that he may not swallow. But strangely, he did. It was as if he had always been aware of it and he became agitated, demanding that we go up into the mountains and seek the ogre out.

I am writing this now because tomorrow the mayor and I will go up into the mountains and confront the ogre. Salvador, in other words. I have my plan, and it is a dreadful one, but I have little choice. But I am afraid that my luck may run out. The mayor is a resourceful and callous individual and I do not trust him. I know he has his own plans, and they are to murder me and take the gold for his own. So, if I do not return, I have written this story down for your mother to keep and hopefully, one day, to pass onto you so that you may understand all that has passed. And when you do understand, Luis, I pray to God that you will know what to do.

Be watchful, Luis. Be wary of the mayor and his servants, and most especially be watchful for soldiers. Because when they come here, Luis, they will want only one thing. The gold.

Your loving father.'

Señor Martinez held the letter between his hands, staring at the ground. The words cut deep welts into his body, right to the bone. Now he had so many answers to the mysteries that had shrouded the village for years. The disappearance of Luis's father, how he had gone up into the mountains one day and had never been seen of since. The mayor must have murdered him, as he had many others. And the gold, that still remained hidden, far up in the mountains, in a deep cave. A cave that perhaps only Salvador knew the whereabouts of. That fact made him valuable, to the mayor and to the soldiers who had come. So hence the story of the ogre, one to keep people from wandering into the mountains and two, once they discovered the gold, the killing of the ogre would remove the last remaining obstacle. With Salvador dead, the gold could come into the Mayor's hands without hindrance. All that the mayor needed was the help of experts. Soldiers. And now, they had arrived. Of the curious individual known as Manfred, he had no clue to his true identity, but he had to still reckon in the overall picture in some way.

All that remained was Luis. Luis and his mother. The only others who had links to the gold because Luis's father would have told them. Or, so the mayor would believe. Martinez knew that this was not the case. The letter was the one piece of evidence remaining, once Salvador was dead. And now the gallows awaited him.

The final throw of the dice had been made.

Chapter 25

Jail

Riodelgado shimmered in the morning heat. Nestled amongst the mountains, in a large hollow rather than a valley, the few squat adobe houses stood silent. No one was at home. Everyone had gone to the *plaza* to see the hanging.

Standing on Salvador's shoulders, Luis could just make out the village square between the bars of the tiny window set high up in the wall. They were in the basement, below the level of the street, and he had to crane his neck to get a good view of the frantic activity of men preparing the gallows, hammering and sawing timber.

People's voices, raised in excitement, mingled with the creak and groan of carts as market owners prepared their stalls. A party atmosphere developing despite the early hour, anticipation thick in the warm air. He couldn't understand why they seemed so happy at the prospect of witnessing death. He tapped

Salvador on the top of his head and the big man let him down.

"They're building a gallows," he said. Salvador sat down on one of the simple wooden beds in the cramped, dimly lit cell. Luis slumped down on the opposite one and stared at his newfound friend. Salvador smiled. "They won't kill you. You're too young. But me..." He ran a gnarled hand through the thatch of his hair. "They'll have their fears and nightmares banished forever this day, for sure."

"They're murdering you because of the gold," said Luis in a quiet voice. He waited for some reaction, but Salvador merely gave a flicker of a smile and leaned back against the wall.

"Ah, the gold." Closing his eyes, Salvador laid his hands over his ample belly. "How much do you know?"

"Only what my father told me—in the letter he wrote."

Salvador shook his head slowly. "They'll burn it, Luis."

"No, they won't—it's in a safe place."

Salvador opened his eyes and frowned. "They'll find it. They won't rest until they have done so, believe me. Men like them always win in the end."

"Not this time. This time it is in a place they wouldn't dream of looking." He traced a line through the dirt on the floor with the toe of his boot. "What my father wrote all those years ago, after he had come back from the War, he meant those words for me. To help me understand what all of this is about, because some how he knew it would come to this. The deaths, the disappearances. But I'm still in the dark—I don't know what happened to *him*. He said he had a plan and it had something to do with the mayor... and you."

A moment of silence, during which Luis waited, studying the giant across the cell as he pondered Luis's words. Salvador blew out a loud breath. "The last time I saw your father, he came to the mountains with the mayor. I watched them from higher ground as your father led him to a remote area, well away from where the treasure lay stashed. I didn't understand why, but I assumed your father had some notion to kill him, as he had already killed others, with terrifying ease."

"The War changed him, as it changes so much, destroying not only lives, but spirits as well. I believe my father planned to kill the mayor, then blame you—or should I say, the ogre for the mayor's death."

"You can't be sure of that part, Luis."

"No. But the lure of gold made Father into someone dangerous and determined to get what he wanted. The mayor was an obstacle, which needed removing. And how better to cover everything up than by blaming it all on the ogre. People believed the stories because it was easier than believing the truth—they still do."

His voice sounded sad when he said, "Perhaps you're right after all. It would answer a lot of questions."

"So what happened?"

"I watched them, scrambling over the rocks. I'm not sure, even to this day, if your father knew where he was going. It was treacherous place, scree and shale making movement difficult. I could hear the mayor shouting. Perhaps he had become suspicious. Your father turned and I saw the glint of the blade. But the mayor is no country bumpkin. He was ready, and fired his pistol, shooting your father full in the chest, blowing him backwards across the hard ground." Salvador stared at the boy. "Are you sure you want me to go on?" Luis nodded, lips squeezed together, determined not to allow the grief to overcome him. Salvador continued, "The mayor buried him in a shallow pit, covering the body over with the shale. Then he did the most extraordinary thing."

"What?"

"He called out to me, almost as if he knew I was there. He told me he would find the gold and, when he did, he would return and hunt me down. Unless, of course, I showed him where it was."

"And did you?"

Salvador's eyes were suddenly wet, brimming up with tears. He pressed the heel of his palms into each eye. "I gave him some of it. I made a bargain. He would leave me alone to live my life and I would deliver gold to him, in small amounts, every few months."

Luis frowned. "But...I don't understand. If you made this bargain, why does he hate you so, want you dead? And why all the killings? The children, Señora Gomez? My mother?"

"The soldiers. Their arrival changed everything."

"*The soldiers?*"

"Aye. The same ones who murdered the monks and ransacked their monastery. The ones your father wrote about. They've returned and they want what is theirs."

Luis sat back. "They've been here before, haven't they?"

"The captain, the one called Klaus. He came, many years ago, not long after your father... But he was on his own."

"He took the gold?"

"No, Luis. The gold is still up there," Salvador motioned towards the tiny window. "None of them will ever find it, not without me."

"You won't tell them, will you?"

"As soon as I do, I'm a dead man." He laughed, a single, sharp crack. "I'm dead anyway, no matter what happens. Perhaps the mayor has found it already, who knows. He spends enough time up there, rooting around whilst the village sleeps."

"So that's why he killed people, to make them believe the ogre lived in the mountains, to fill them with fear, stop them from going up there."

"Aye. And with each killing, my guilt grew."

"*Your* guilt? You're not responsible, Salvador, not for any of it."

"No, possibly not, but the mayor, he was trying to force me to reveal the whereabouts of the gold, and every time I learned of another death, I knew I must tell him, in the end."

"Dear God." Luis stood up, punching his right fist into the palm of his left hand. "All this while, murdering innocent people, like Señora Gomez, the children..." He whirled around, feeling his face reddening. "We must stop all of this, Salvador—we have to tell the villagers your story, make them realise the truth, make them stop the mayor—arrest him!"

Salvador shook his head sadly. "Oh Luis... It's too late. The mayor knows everything. He has always known. He makes bargains with anyone he has to, to keep himself alive. He has everything sewn up. But now, now he is desperate. The War is over, Luis, but the mayor knows he is entering into the most dangerous part of his plan. These men, these soldiers, wish to make a life before it is snuffed out. That is why they are here. They will do anything to achieve their plans, and that includes denying the mayor his claims on the gold."

"Including killing him?"

"Luis, they will butcher every man, woman and child to find that gold."

"But..." Luis wrung his hands. "But my father said they had gold of their own. Could they have spent it?"

"Perhaps. But greed, Luis, greed is their constant bane, forcing them on, driving them to excess. You father possessed such treasure as you wouldn't believe. The gold candelabra..." he shook his head again. "I have never seen anything so beautiful. He took it with him, down to the village, no doubt to give it as an offering to the church, to God. Other things, too—such wonders, Luis. Gold and silver goblets, crucifixes inlaid with jewels and icons from the east. Beautiful things, breath-taking."

Luis felt his stomach turn over and he had to sit. "My God," he whispered. "Father Brialles."

"What about him?"

"Father Brialles, the priest. I saw him, at the church, packing away artefacts. They must have been what my father had given him, as a sort of penance."

"Yes, that would make sense. Perhaps your father was trying to buy his way into Heaven, seeking out forgiveness."

"But the soldier, the one you called Klaus, was there the next time I went. I'd gone to see the Father, to talk to him, ask him for advice, and Klaus was already there, but Father Brialles was not."

"Fled, taking the treasure with him."

"The treasure my father had given him."

"As I said, Luis—greed. It changes men, all men, no matter what their position."

"My father said war does that."

"And what is war other than someone's desire to take what another has."

"What are we going to do, Salvador? If they kill you, how will they ever find their gold?"

Salvador stared into the distance, his shoulders moved up and down, his expression serious, unflinching, as if he were wrestling with something terrible in his mind. When he spoke, his voice was small, frightened. "Oh Luis, they don't need me anymore, don't you see?" Those piercing eyes grew moist.

"They have something of much greater value—they have you."

Chapter 26

Gallows

The crowd stirred, voices raised in anticipation as armed guards led the two prisoners out into the sunlight, urging them forward with violent shoves in the back. People parted to let them through, licking slavering lips, mouths gaping wide in apish grins, eager for the spectacle to begin, the grim dance of the dead beneath the coarse rope of the noose. One or two cheered, others hurled insults. Luis couldn't tell who, nor did he care. They filled him with loathing, these fickle simpletons, clamouring for revenge, punishment, an end to the horrors visited upon them. He forced himself not to make eye contact with anyone as they jostled and pushed, gathering around the gallows, the whole village muttering, laughing, yelling, venting their hate, their joy. Someone pushed Luis hard in the back and he stumbled forward, cracking his knee on the hard ground. Cheers rang out and Salvador reached out both his hands, manacled together as they were, and pulled Luis to his feet. "Be strong," he said.

A guard stood at the foot of the steps that led up to the platform. He was grinning. Luis held the man's gaze, determined to do as Salvador had said. The guard grinned again, smelling Luis' fear, savouring the moment. A moment to enjoy.

The butt of a polearm between the shoulder blades forced him to mount the steps. He took his time, hands bound by rough cord, his mind whirled and his limbs become heavy, solidifying as the enormity of what was about to happen struck home.

"I'm with you, Luis," came Salvador's voice from below, and its solidity gave him courage, if only for a moment, and he stepped up onto the platform.

A great whoop of glee erupted when he pulled himself up straight. A huge man, his face covered by a black cowl, gestured to him to step closer, and Luis gazed at the pair of gently swinging ropes, waiting for their moment. His stomach lurched and he turned and looked out across the sea of faces, all of them upturned with expectant, wide-eyed expressions, many of them grinning. He recognised most. Some made a point of catching his attention. Carlos, chomping on a stalk of grass, raised both hands above his head and clapped his hands loudly, jeering, "Hey, girlie-boy, what's it like to be famous?" Many laughed at that. People he knew, people he'd always known. How could they have sunk so low, to come here to watch him dangling from the end of a rope? Was no one interested in the truth, were they so blind to believe the mayor's lies? Or was it simply their desire to be entertained?

Salvador stepped beside him, the guards close by, halberds poised ready. People whistled in derision and somewhere from the back, a voice shouted, "Kill the ogre!"

More laughter, as Carlos trilled, "The ogre and his master, come to give us a show!"

Cheering, applause, venomous curses and loud profanities, they felt secure now, this crowd of heartless, ignorant peasants. After all, the monster was snared, the end in sight. Luis wanted to be sick, the bile building up in his throat, burning him. He looked again at the two knotted ropes hung from a crossbeam and knew there was no going back, not now.

The executioner took Luis by the shoulder and pulled him towards the noose. It dangled a hand's width from Luis's face, his knees went weak and he knew he was going to faint.

"Hold fast, Luis," said Salvador quietly. "Don't let them see you are afraid."

"Oh God, Salvador." It was useless, Salvador may well have courage, but he didn't. This wasn't right, none of it. All he ever wanted to do was to find out the truth, and now, having come so close, for the curtain to come down, life snuffed out—damn it all, where was the justice!

The crowd cheered in a sudden eruption of sound and Luis turned to see the mayor stepping onto the platform. Arms raised in triumph, wide grin plastered across his glistening face. He allowed the moment to wash over him, drinking in the adulation before he stretched his arms out wide, and made a sort of flapping movement. The crowd gradually quietened.

"Citizens," he began, his voice a bull-roar in the tightly packed square. "Today we rid ourselves of our curse!" They cheered, hats thrown into the air, children yelling, old ladies bursting into tears. Again, the Mayor held out his hands, mimicking the flight of a bird. The villagers grew quiet again. "We have waited many years for this day and many of us have not lived to see it." There were murmurs from the back, someone shouted '*murdered*'. The mayor held up a hand. "This creature has lived in the mountains for years, preying on innocent souls, bringing terror and misery into our homes. And this boy," he turned briefly, his finger pointing towards Luis, "this *monstrous* child has fed him, kept him safe, done everything possible to aid the creature in his orgy of blood!" A tremendous cheer rose up, people were screaming, many applauded, some cries of, '*hang them*', others were yelling, '*burn them—they're too good for hanging!*'

A single voice boomed out over the din. It was Salvador. "God help you."

The mayor swung round, face a perfect mask of fury. He crossed the platform in two steps and struck Salvador across the face. "God help *me*? You dog, today you'll burn in hell!"

Salvador spat, a little trickle of blood dripping from his split lip. "Will I? Are you sure about that, Señor Mayor?"

The mayor's eyes narrowed. "Afraid are we?"

"Not as afraid as you will be, as you lie on your death-bed and cry out for forgiveness for the things you have done."

"That won't be for many years, ogre, and when the time does come, I will have made my peace with God. He knows the righteous."

Salvador nodded. "Aye, He does that." He looked towards Luis. "And the boy? You honestly intend to kill him as well, even though he has done nothing?"

"Nothing? Oh, I think he has done a great deal more than *nothing*. He murdered old Gomez, probably his mother too."

"Don't talk such nonsense—his own mother? If you believe that, then you truly are lost!"

The mayor leaned very close to Salvador, whispering into his ear so quietly that Luis had to strain to hear. "It doesn't matter what I believe, Salvador. It's the people who matter."

"And they believe you, is that it?"

"Oh yes," he smiled. "Every word."

The mayor stood so close to Salvador that their noses almost touched. Not as broad, but much taller, the mayor appeared to relish the fact that he could look down upon his charge. He grinned, and then it happened. Salvador brought his knee up with blinding speed, ramming it hard between the mayor's legs. The mayor screamed, like a stricken horse, a whinny of pain and shock. He folded in agony and Salvador rammed his great, solid shoulder into him, catching the mayor in the mouth, knocking him clean off his feet. Salvador turned just as the executioner lunged forward. Manacled though he was, Salvador still managed to maintain balance, pivoting slightly to the left to crack his foot into the executioner's shin, doubling him. In one movement, Salvador swung up his other foot, hitting the executioner under the jaw, sending him sprawling backwards.

The crowd, stunned into silence by the eruption of sudden violence, recoiled as one, a great shock wave rippling through them. They'd had no time to react, everything happening so unexpectedly, the first to recover was the guard next to the top of the stairs. He thrust hard with his halberd. Salvador danced to the right, surprisingly nimble for such a big man and the blade hit fresh air. In the same movement, moving so fast it was difficult to catch every flex of solid muscle, he snapped his foot back into the man's knee with an audible snap. The guard squealed, collapsing and rolling himself into a ball, clutching at the broken joint. Just then, the second guard came bounding up the steps, reaching to draw his sword. Salvador met him as he came over the last step, kicking him full in the face. The guard pitched backwards, hitting the ground below with a dull thud.

Salvador turned, grinning, and looked at Luis. "I'll come back for you," he said and turned again.

In that instant, Luis saw someone, moving like a ghost, silent and deadly. Luis shouted out, "*Salvador!*"

It was too late. Salvador didn't hear the warning, didn't see the soldier, the one called Klaus. Didn't see the pistol coming up, or hear the discharge. The ball hit him just below the hairline, right between the eyes. For a moment he teetered, swaying like a great tree in the wind and then, he toppled over, the platform shuddering with the impact as his huge body hit the decking, sending up a cloud of dirt and dust. A great plume of blood enveloped his large head, like a halo. A halo of death.

Luis fell to his knees, the strength draining from him, nothing remaining. From somewhere far away, he became aware of a figure standing over him and he looked up. The shape of man outlined against the bright blue sky. Klaus. He was reloading his pistol, very methodically, and all the time he had his lips pressed together, blowing out a tuneless whistle. A tune Luis didn't know, that he didn't care about because the blackness came, total and complete.

Chapter 27

Rescued from the Mill

A creaking sound, ill-fitted floorboards walked over, backwards and forwards, again and again, invaded his mind. He blinked open his eyes and almost screamed at the sight before him.

They had hanged Salvador.

He hung from the rope, the weight of his body stretching the noose tight. The hole in his head was of perfect dimension and his eyes were wide, staring into nothingness, all of the light gone out of them. He swung gently from side to side, a pendulum of death, the awful creaking of the rope sounding too loud, too horrible. It was this sound that had woken him.

Luis couldn't tear his eyes away, even when the rough hands pulled him up by the shoulders. Salvador's tongue held most of his attention, the way it lolled out of the corner of his mouth, purple, bloated.

They put the noose around Luis' neck, and he allowed them too, without resistance. There was no point anymore, defeat conquering him, death waiting, black and horrible and infinite.

The mayor stood a little way off, crouched over, patting his mouth with a neckerchief, trying to staunch the blood. Below, in the square, the crowd stood transfixed, silent, wondering what would happen next. Luis locked his eyes on Carlos, who merely shrugged, the laughter gone, his face a blank.

Stepping out from somewhere behind him, the executioner ran the back of his hand across his nose and sniffed loudly. Blood trickled from his nostrils. Salvador had almost succeeded, freedom so nearly achieved, if it hadn't been for Klaus. Luis closed his eyes. His mind still reeled, images coming in and out of focus.

"You have any last words?"

Luis stared at the executioner before turning his gaze to the mayor, who looked deathly pale, a bald-patch topping his skull, like a monk. "Why?"

The mayor frowned, dabbed at his mouth a few more times, and took an unsteady step. He appeared weak, swaying a little. Salvador's blow had chipped a tooth, sent the man's head spinning like a top. His breathing sounded laboured, his previous bravado gone. "You have a chance, a chance of mercy." He stepped closer, but not so close that Luis might have been tempted to repeat Salvador's attack. The mayor lowered his voice. "Your mother told me about the letter, Luis. Where is it?"

"I don't know anything about any letter."

"Don't lie to me, boy." He winced, clamped a hand to his abdomen, and sucked in a breath through his broken teeth. "I know you have it and I know you have read it. If you want to see Constanza alive again, tell me where it is."

"Constanza?" The mention of his sister's name brought a wail to his throat, like that of a wounded animal, struggling in the trap. He threw back his head and yelled at the top of his voice, "*Constanza!*"

Almost as if in a dream, the answer came, as loud and as clear as if she were standing next to him, "Louie! Oh, my Louie."

Everyone turned. The crowd, the mayor, executioner and Luis. All of them, staring in disbelief at the little girl who ran from the far end of the *plaza*, her tiny arms and legs pumping like pistons, head high and proud, laughing and crying at the same time.

The crowd, silent, awe-struck almost, parted to let her through. She ran to the gallows and took the steps with all the agility of a monkey and threw herself towards her brother, wrapping her arms around his waist and burying her face into his chest. "Oh Louie," she gasped, her voice muffled.

Luis' mouth opened and closed, unable to understand. He so wanted to hold her, but of course his tied hands prevented him, so he rested his chin on the top of her head and sobbed.

The executioner reached out to pull her away.

"Don't you touch that girl, damn you!"

Another figure strode across the platform.

The mayor gasped and the executioner stepped back as Pablo brought out a knife and cut through Luis's bonds. Brother and sister fell to their knees, holding each other, both of them crying uncontrollably.

Klaus pulled himself up into his saddle, sat astride his horse and looked out from his vantage point towards the *plaza*. "Damn his hide," he snarled, "I should have killed him years ago!"

He turned the horse around and spurred its flanks and galloped off towards his rendezvous.

Pablo held onto the two children, pressing them tightly to his sides. The mayor, breathing hard, turned to the crowd as they began to disperse, the show over. Many of them appeared disgruntled, muttering to one another. He looked back towards Pablo and the children. "I'll not be denied, Pablo."

"I've remained silent too long, Señor Mayor. They need to know the truth."

"No!" The mayor pulled out his sword and pointed it towards the traveller. "No. Not until this is over."

"It won't be over until you are rotting in hell, Señor Mayor."

The mayor's grip on the sword hilt tightened. "I'll run you through, damn you. Luis, where is the letter?"

Luis sniffed loudly and shook his head. "I'll never tell you. As long as I have it, we are safe. If you harm us, then the authorities will hear about what you've done."

"Done? I haven't done anything! All I want is the gold, Luis—a chance to make this village wealthy, to give the people what they need. I can turn this pathetic mix of broken old huts into a thriving town, Luis. That is all I want."

Luis frowned, not sure if what the mayor had spoken was truth or lies. He didn't know about anything anymore. He looked up at Pablo. "Give me your knife," he said quietly.

For a moment, a look of indecision crossed Pablo's face. He chewed the inside of his cheek then, making his mind up, passed over the blade. The mayor tensed, but Luis was not about to attack anyone. He turned the weapon around and presented it to the mayor, hilt forward. "Cut him down."

The mayor's eyes widened, but nevertheless he took the blade, stepped past Luis, and did as he was bid.

Salvador's body crumpled, hitting the decking with a deep, sickening thud.

"I want him buried," continued Luis, controlling his breathing, staying calm. "A decent burial, Señor Mayor. With a cross, marking his place for all to see, for all to remember."

"A *cross*—" The mayor bit his lip, exhaled loudly and went back to the edge of the platform and called over to some armed men who were standing there, looking bored. "I want you to take this body away." He turned to Luis, "Take it to the church. Lay it there, until we can arrange a funeral." Again, at the men, "*Now!*"

Luis allowed himself a smile and he relaxed his shoulders, pulling Constanza to him and holding her.

"Now, the letter."

Luis's smile broadened. "Not yet, Señor Mayor. The letter is my guarantee." He squeezed Constanza tight, "Our guarantee."

"How can I trust you?"

"That's rich, coming from you," spat Pablo. "You kidnapped this girl, murdered the mother... My God, is there no end to your depravity."

"I did none of those things, fool!"

"Even now, the tongue of a viper." Pablo shook his head, laying his hand on Luis's shoulder. "Keep the letter safe, Luis. It is your only chance."

"It is safe, Pablo. Very."

Pablo nodded. A dark look came over his face as he spoke directly at the mayor. "You will answer for what you've done. I swear."

"And I swear, it had nothing to do with me."

"You told me you had Constanza," said Luis.

"I lied. How else could I get you to hand over the letter?"

"Then..." Luis kissed the top of Constanza's head, got down on his haunches and, eyes level with her, said softly, "Where have you been, darling?"

"In a funny house."

"A funny...? What do you mean?"

"It was round and tall. A man said he made flour there, for bread."

Luis held her by the shoulders. "Man? What man, Constanza?"

"He said his name was Manfred."

Luis felt his stomach turn to ice. "Where was this funny house?"

She pointed, way off to the east, the direction that led inland towards Granada.

"How did you get away?" asked Pablo, stooping down, smiling.

Constanza seemed confused. "The other man opened the door and he put me on his horse. A nice big horse. Very nice ride. He took me to the main road then said he had to go."

Luis exchanged a quick look with Pablo.

"I found her on the highway," said Pablo, standing up. He winced, pushing his hand into the small of his back as he straightened himself. "She was on her own, so I spoke to her and she seemed to know who I was."

"She's a clever girl," said Luis and he kissed her on both cheeks. "You would know this *other* man, Constanza? The man on the horse."

She nodded. "I already saw him, Louie. He was here."

"Here?" Luis stood up, suddenly feeling afraid. "This man, Constanza. He was very big?"

"Yes."

"And did he smell, Constanza?"

"Smell? What do you mean, Louie?"

"Like old boots, Constanza. Leather."

"Like horses?" Luis nodded. "Yes, Louie, he smelled of horses and saddles and belts and all those things.

His clothes creaked, Louie. Like the door of our home." She looked around. "Where is Mama?"

Luis closed his eyes. Two things he had to do. Find out where Klaus was, because he now knew for sure that Klaus had rescued his sister. And two, he would have to tell Constanza the worst thing of all—that her mama was dead.

Chapter 28

To the Mill

The band the mayor collected together seemed a motley crew from where Luis stood. He glanced over them. Pablo stood some way off, holding Constanza. Beside him, three old men, two of whom held pitchforks, the other an ancient musket. Polishing a sword was Carlos. He was smiling and humming a tune to himself. Luis went up to him.

"Where is Alvaro?"

Carlos shrugged. "I don't know. He said he was going to find the ogre." He grinned, jutting his chin towards the gallows. "But we found him."

Luis kept his temper, although he had the sudden desire to smash Carlos in the face. "You really think Salvador was the ogre?"

"Of course." Carlos held his sword blade up and studied it, the blade glinting in the sun. With a flourish, he thrust it back into its scabbard. "Don't you?"

"You're a fool, Carlos."

The bully's eyes narrowed. "And what are you, little girl? I saw you up there, with that noose around your neck, snivelling and crying like the girl that you are. What are you going to do now, eh? Go back home with your little sister, cook her some beans? You're pathetic."

Not waiting for a response, Carlos swung around and strode off to join the mayor who sat by the fountain, head down, deep in thought. Luis glowered in silence, anger burning inside him. Even now, despite everything, Carlos hadn't changed. He would forever be the cruel, narrow-minded bully he had always been. Even the truth wouldn't change him.

Downcast, Luis went over to Pablo and Constanza. "Can you take her home, Pablo? Look after her for me?"

Pablo frowned, "Why, where are you going?"

Luis glanced away. The mayor now stood with his hand on Carlos's shoulder, gabbling on at him about something. "I'm going with them," said Luis. "I'm going to bring all of this to an end."

"It already is ended, Luis. What more is there to do?"

"This won't end until one of these maniacs has the gold."

"And then what? What do you think will happen once it *is* found?"

Luis reached forward and stroked his sister's hair. She cooed and grinned. "Hopefully, they will leave. Then we can get back to living our lives."

Alvaro was in two minds as to what to do. He had positioned himself behind some broken boulders, a good vantage point to view whatever went on below. He took a drink from his canteen. He had lain there for quite some time, watching the goings on at the old mill. Every now and then a man would appear, sometimes followed by another. They seemed to be waiting for something, or someone and, from the way they threw out their arms every so often in wild gesticulations, it was obvious they were growing impatient. Alvaro couldn't hear what they said, he was too far away, but occasionally a shout reached him. Anger.

He rolled over onto his back, undecided what to do. Should he go down, or return to the village? He had no idea who the men were, but one thing he was certain of—they were dangerous. He'd watch them cleaning their weapons, incessantly. Almost as if it were an obsession. Only men who fought cleaned weapons like that. Fighting men, soldiers. Mercenaries. Alvaro knew all about them. He'd spoken to the men of the village, the guards up at the Mayor's house, and their stories of battles and engagements filled him with excitement and wonder. His dream was to go away and fight. He was sixteen now, old enough. When the news trickled through that the War had ended he'd become morose and sullen. Once more, life had played its cruel tricks on him, or so it seemed. But then, the hunt for the ogre, the arrival of soldiers. Within the course of a few days, his dreams had started to become real.

The sharp sudden snap of a twig made him sit up.

A shadow fell over him and he rolled onto his knees, grabbing for the short sword at his belt. Before he took another move, the fist hit him in the side, just below his rib cage, and the wind rushed out of him and he creased up, coughing loudly, the pain like a red-hot poker in his side. His assailant was too fast, too big. Alvaro's thoughts span as if they were inside a whirly-gig. He went to stand, but his legs didn't have the strength and vainly, he raised a hand to ward off another blow. He didn't know where he was and, when the blow came, sharp and hard against the back of his head, he hit the ground with a slap and lay there, the pain consuming him, and he wondered for a second why these things always happened to him. Then his eyes became heavy and he slipped into unconsciousness.

Klaus reached down and hauled up the boy by the back of the collar. He was a big boy, but Klaus had little trouble throwing his limp body over the back of his horse. Taking the reins, he made his way slowly down the winding track towards the mill, lips pursed in a silent whistle.

Securing his saddlebags tightly, tugging at them to make sure they were sound, the mayor turned and addressed the small group of men.

"We'll take the direct route to the old mill," he said, his voice calm, flat. "I see no point in creeping around like thieves in the night. It has long been deserted and I expect no trouble."

"Where is Klaus?"

The mayor scowled, "Who?"

Luis stepped forward, pushing his way between two of the men. "Klaus, the soldier who came here first. The one who shot Salvador. Where is he?"

"How should I know?"

"He was the one who found Constanza and now he has gone. Strange, don't you think?"

"The only thing strange thing here," piped up Carlos, "is you!"

The others laughed. Luis ignored him, and the baying laughter. "Señor Mayor, it would be foolish to simply march up to the mill in the way you suggested, perhaps it would be best if—"

"The way *I suggested*?" The mayor's face reddened, "Why do you feel it necessary to always talk as if you are reading from a book, you mindless fop! If it wasn't for you, none of this would have happened. Despite that, if you need reminding, I am the one who makes the decisions, I am the one who made the plan, and I am the one who will lead us to the mill and end this farce once and for all."

"How?"

A stunned silence followed the question one nobody had considered in any seriousness. Gradually, the men muttered to one another and the mayor, who with eyes wide with rage, offered up no answer.

Taking his chance, Luis continued, "Every time you've gone out looking for the ogre, people have died. Either in the mountains, or here in the village. And now, you have only three old men and a boy to help you." He shook his head. "There is no one else stupid enough to do your bidding."

"We don't need anyone else," snapped Carlos, and he rushed forward and took Luis by the throat and shook him. "I'm not stupid, you prig. It's you that has done this, you and your meddling! I watch you every day, going up to that house you go to—the house of old Martinez. You strut around like a peacock, so superior, so self-righteous. What do you do up there, eh? Nothing useful, that's for sure."

Pablo, who had been watching the exchanges from some way off, strode forward, gripped Carlos's hand and tore it away from Luis's throat. Luis staggered back, clamping his hands around his neck as he gasped for air.

"You ignorant fool," spat Pablo, he whirled Carlos around and pushed him away. For a moment, it looked as if Carlos would pull out his sword, but then the mayor stepped forward, placing a restraining hand on the boy's arm.

"We're not ignorant," said the mayor very quietly. "We're simply afraid."

"Afraid of what?" Pablo looked every one of them straight in the eyes. "*What*? Anything you don't understand, anything you can't explain away with your pathetic, childish superstitions? Anything or anyone *different* you destroy. That's your answer, isn't it? Every single time?"

"Better than shutting ourselves away, whimpering in the dark like frightened children. Or running away, not able to face up to our responsibilities." The two men glared at one another before the mayor said, "I have to protect this village, by whatever means I can. All I have ever wanted was for us to prosper and for our people to feel safe. This boy," he waggled his finger towards Luis, "this boy and his family have caused more harm to everyone who lives here than anyone else."

Pablo sneered. "You mean his father, don't you? That's what all this is about, isn't it. When his father returned, he brought with him something you wanted, and that desire has poisoned your heart, Señor Mayor. That's the truth of it, as well you know. The rest is nothing more than a smokescreen to hide your true purpose."

"Shut up! You know nothing about any of it."

"I know more than you think, Señor Mayor. I know what Luis's father brought back with him from the war, and I know that you want it, have always wanted it. And because of your petty, ill-judged desires, evil, maligned forces have visited this village. Soldiers. Soldiers who have been corrupted by war and now want only to destroy and—"

"Quiet, damn you! The only evil thing that came into this village was that damned ogre— Salvador. And now he's gone. All that's left to do is find out what is happening down at the mill."

"You know what is down there."

"I'm warning you, Pablo, hold your damned tongue."

"Pablo." Luis touched Pablo's arm, trying to quieten him. But Pablo was incensed and he tugged his arm free, face scarlet with rage. "It's time everyone in this village knew the truth, Señor Mayor. The reason why people have died. And it has nothing to do with ogres."

Before Luis knew what was happening, the mayor screamed like a wild animal, leaping at Pablo. They fell to the ground in a mess of arms and legs, both snarling, struggling for advantage. Something flashed through the air and Pablo gasped. Luis threw out his hands, "No, no, stop it!"

It became quiet and the mayor stood up, his rattling breath the only sound. And when Luis looked, he saw the astonishment on Pablo's face. But only that. Felled like a tree, eyes already lifeless as he lay sprawled in the dirt, a great wound across his side, sliced through his jerkin, dead.

No one moved. Everyone stunned, grappling to understand what had happened. Luis, mouth moving but unable to find any words, went down on his knees and cradled Pablo's head in his hands. Constanza began screaming uncontrollably.

"You monster," mumbled Luis, still holding the traveller's head. He turned accusing eyes towards the mayor who stood, as if turned to stone, the knife still in his hand, blood dripping in a slow, thick trail from the long blade. "*You monster!*"

Luis's loud cry seemed to galvanize everyone, but it was Carlos who spoke out first, his voice as cold as the steel that had ended Pablo's life. "Come on, let's go to the mill and do what we need to do."

Carlos pushed past the mayor and strode off across the square, not waiting to see if any of the others followed. Back straight and resolute, he continued along the single, rutted track that led down to the bridge and the route to the mill.

Full of mutterings, the assembled men slowly followed in the wake of the boy, leaving the mayor to gawp at his knife, while Constanza cried and Luis gently cradled Pablo's head.

"We have to end this," said the mayor, in a low whisper, as if he were speaking to himself. "I've lived too long with this shadow hanging over me."

Luis gently laid Pablo's head to the ground, stood up and took Constanza into his arms and held her. He kissed the top of her head as she buried herself in his chest, whimpering. Luis felt empty inside. Everything around him was being destroyed, anyone who had ever meant anything to him killed. His voice had a hollow ring to it when he asked, "What is at the mill? Klaus, and the gold?"

Something stirred in the mayor's face, a sudden return to his usual self-assuredness. His eyes glimmered but then, almost as quickly, the light died away. His shoulders slumped, and he slowly put the knife back into his belt. "Our destiny waits there, Luis. Yours, mine... your father's."

"My father's? My father is dead, Señor Mayor. And you know how he died, don't you?"

The mayor nodded his head. "To my eternal shame..."

"And now Pablo's death to add to your list. Is the gold really worth all these lives?"

Without looking, the mayor turned in the direction of the others, who tramped along the path that led to the mountain passes.

"Is it worth *your* life, Señor Mayor?"

The mayor began to walk away, "Oh yes, Luis. It is well worth it."

Chapter 29

Preparations

Pedro brought up the pistol, then realised who it was and swore. "Where the hell have you been? And who is that?" He put the pistol back in his waistband.

Klaus grunted as he slid down from the saddle and pulled Alvaro from the back of the horse. He dumped the boy unceremoniously on the ground. "He's one of the village toughs. I found him spying on you." He turned, setting his jaw hard. "Why haven't you posted a guard?"

Pedro blinked. "A guard? Why the devil do we need a guard? They're peasants and there are not many of them left."

"There's the mayor. Don't underestimate him."

Pedro shook his head and stepped over to Alvaro. "What are you going to do with him?"

"Bait."

"Eh?"

"This ends today, Pedro. I've grown tired of waiting. I'm going to peg this lad out, right here in the open. When they see him they'll come straight down and then," he quickly drew a finger across his throat. "Finish."

"All of them?"

Klaus nodded. "We kill the mayor and his few followers, then we torch the village and turn our back on this God-forsaken place forever."

"And the gold, Klaus, don't forget the gold."

"The boy Luis knows where that is. He'll show us, have no fear."

Pedro grinned broadly, "So we won't need the priest any longer? Shall I kill him?"

"No yet. We'll kill him in front of Luis, that'll convince him that we're serious."

Klaus rubbed his chin. "How is the woman?"

"Still sick. The priest seems to know what he's doing."

"She's a little better then." Klaus couldn't keep the hope out of his voice.

"A little." Pedro bent down and turned Alvaro over. "I'll peg him out. How much time have we got?"

"Not long. I'll tell the others, get them in position. String this cur up in the centre of the yard so they can get a good view of him."

Pedro grinned again, clapped his hands together and rubbed them. "It's been worth the wait, Klaus. Rich at last, beyond our dreams!"

"Aye... beyond our dreams."

They stopped about four hundred steps from the old mill, crouching down amongst the rocks. Here they drank water and prepared their weapons. Carlos, who had two pistols, primed them both. Luis watched him whilst Constanza huddled up close, head down, her body trembling. "You're prepared to use those, Carlos?"

Carlos raised an eyebrow. "Why not? The mayor told us all about the soldiers—how they plan to come into our village, destroy everything. Soldiers," he spat, "I hate them."

Luis put his head back, his heart beginning to race. Soldiers may well be an object for their hatred, but they were still soldiers. Experts. What had the mayor managed to gather to fight them? Three men and two boys? He closed his eyes and tried to wish himself somewhere else.

"Mendez," whispered the mayor suddenly. "Mendez, I want you to scout ahead, see what they're doing, then come back and report to us."

Mendez nodded and slinked off without a word. Within a few steps he had disappeared amongst the rocks and undergrowth.

"What do you hope to gain?"

The mayor turned to Luis, a smile playing at the corners of his mouth. "You know full well, Luis, but for everyone else's benefit, we're going to kill the soldiers. They pose a threat to us all, Luis." He fingered the hilt of his sword. "That much, at least, is true."

"You can't hope to overcome them with so few men."

"Don't suppose that we are just a gang of blubbering peasants, Luis. All these men here, Mendez, Haime, Paco, they are all hunters, have been all their lives. I handpicked them. They can move without being heard and can shoot better than most."

"With only one musket between them? Are you certain you have thought this through?"

The mayor shook his head, and his smile grew broader. "Wait and see, Luis. Wait and see."

Alvaro opened his eyes and instantly turned his head away, squinting, as the sun, full in his face, burned through to his brain. Sweat broke out across his brow, accumulating in his eyebrows before running down his cheeks in tiny rivulets. Instinctively, he went to wipe his face, then realised he couldn't as the leather straps bit into his wrist. Fully conscious, the heat rising, he strained to look around him, try to regain some sense of where he was. As he did, the reality of what had happened brought with it overpowering panic, and he struggled uselessly against what bound him in abject terror of his situation.

He gave up, allowed his head to fall, and whimpered as if in mourning for the hopes he had, for the man he believed himself to be, for the pathetic sham he had become.

They had lashed him against two crossed pieces of wood, rammed into the ground. Stretched wide, the tendons in his arms and legs strained to breaking point, making escape impossible. In such fashion were the skins of slaughtered animals stretched out to dry. Now Alvaro hung as such a creature, not yet dead, but resigned to the hopelessness of it all.

He twisted his head and clenched his teeth as the pain screamed through his limbs. Breathing became difficult; panic welled up, threatening to take over him, his stomach turning to liquid. The bile rose to his throat, and he retched, about to be sick when a great rush of water hit his face with tremendous power. He jerked backwards, coughing and spitting, surprise mixing with fear. He shook his head. Perversely, the water revived him, its coolness settling his nerves. He blinked away the droplets from his eyes and gazed straight ahead.

The swarthy man in front of him grinned like a maniacal fiend, teeth gleaming in a face of blackened, cured leather, framed by ragged hair and beard. Alvaro allowed his eyes to drift over this tormentor. Dressed all in black, leather trousers tucked into high boots, black leather jerkin and crossed belts from which hung a sword and a short musket. A carbine, so Alvaro thought. A cavalryman. A soldier.

Deep-set eyes stared wildly as the man asked, "Hungry?"

Alvaro opened his mouth, finding it easier to breathe that way, and he took several short, shallow breaths, his mind scrambled. Heat, sweat, water. Pegged out, in the open, but for what purpose? "Eh?"

"Hungry. Are you hungry?"

Was the man offering food? His mind in a whirl, confused by this seeming kindness after being so humiliated, Alvaro managed a single nod. The man threw down the water pail he held and strode off towards the dilapidated mill that stood like a forefinger amidst the sun-baked yard in which Alvaro hung. Things came into focus. Horses tied up, drinking from a trough, a table set out with chairs, saddle bags and other equipment strewn this way and that. A makeshift camp, but no sign of anyone else.

He peered at the mill, its yellowing circular wall pot-marked, broken bits of plaster exposing the crude mud and straw structure beneath. He knew that as a boy it was a working mill, grinding out flour. As times grew hard it fell into disuse. Then Garcia came and made his own flour at his yard, using great stones turned by mules to grind the wheat. No one used or visited the mill anymore, and it stood derelict, the mayor condemning it as unsafe. From Alvaro's viewpoint, a captured beast ready for the slaughter, it looked anything but unsafe.

Klaus leaned against the doorframe, smoking his pipe. As the swarthy soldier eased past him, he said, "How long will he last, Johann?"

"Who knows? A day. If we feed and water him, maybe two. He's big, but he's young." Johann spat into the dirt. "I'll give him some cheese."

"No, I will. You take Franz and Pedro, get yourselves in position. Move the horses before you go."

Johann nodded. "You remember what you said, don't you Klaus? About the women?"

Klaus straightened himself, knocked out his pipe on the doorframe. "Once this is over, Johann, you can have whoever and whatever you please."

"I'd like the inn. Set myself up—retire."

"Retire…" Klaus let the word conjure up comforting images in his mind. He rarely allowed himself such luxuries but perhaps now, for the first time in too many years, he could allow himself a moment of whimsy. "My God, Johann, what a prize that would be."

"We deserve it."

"Aye." Klaus sighed, loud and long, "we do. For the moment, however, we have to go back to our old ways – for one last time."

Johann smiled and moved off. Klaus watched him go, then dipped inside the mill.

It took him a moment to adjust to the dark. In the corner he made out the slumped figure of the priest, huddled into a tight ball next to the bed. Klaus went over to him, taking a moment to look down at the woman who slept close by. Her breathing seemed easier, he thought, and in that half-light he allowed a flicker of a memory to stir, of a handsome woman, tall, slim, bronzed skin and raven-haired. His heart lurched as he saw what she had become. At their first meeting, he believed he had entered into the gates of paradise. Throughout all of his wanderings, all of his service for Catholic and Protestant generals, he had never laid eyes on a woman that stirred him as much as she had. A widow when he met her, she had willingly accepted his advances.

Now, here she lay, a wreck of her former self. Nothing much of her stunning beauty remained. A worn out shell, broken, close to decay. Vestiges of her loveliness remained, perhaps only discernible to him, and he smiled. He reached down and brushed away a lock of hair from her cheek and drew in a long, shuddering breath. He should never have left her.

"Regrets, mercenary?"

Klaus turned, his eyes narrowing to make out the features of the priest. Despite the murkiness, Klaus knew the man scowled, holding him in contempt, all fear gone now that he knew there was no hope.

"Don't lecture me, Brialles. If anyone is a mercenary here, it is you."

That stung, and Father Brialles shifted his position. "I did what I did to protect the sanctity of our church."

"You did what you did because you wanted the wealth for yourself. Don't fool yourself into thinking that you are any different to me."

Brialles raised his head. "I am *very* different to you—I don't kill for money."

"No, you run away instead." Klaus strode off, not prepared to listen to the man's pathetic moralising. He'd caught up with the priest on the road to Antequera, pack-mule weighed down with booty from the church. Brialles hadn't put up much of a fight. But then, he was a priest.

Klaus picked up a hunk of cheese and folded a piece of bread around it. He went outside, squinting at the daylight, and marched across the yard to Alvaro. The boy opened his eyes and Klaus crammed food into Alvaro's mouth. He munched it down with relish, ravenous. When the food had gone, Klaus brought out his canteen and pressed it against the boy's lips.

"Don't gulp," he said gently. "Take your time."

Alvaro drank, gasped and pulled away. His eyes shone with a renewed vigour. "Why are you doing this to me, stringing me up like a scarecrow?"

Klaus smiled, screwing down the top of his canteen before slinging it over his shoulder. "One, because you're bait for your friends and two, because you deserve it."

"Deserve it. What the hell do you mean?"

"I mean, you're a bully, a dog with no manners and not a care in this world for anyone else. I've watched you, boy. Watched how you inflict pain and misery. Now," Klaus brought his face close to the boy's, "now, you're receiving what's due."

Like a snake, Mendez slithered between the rocks and lay still until he recovered his breathing. The mayor rolled next to him and waited, rapping his fingers impatiently on his sword whilst Mendez drank fitfully from his canteen. He dragged his hand across his mouth. "There are four of them. One of them remains at the mill, the tall one, the captain." The mayor squeezed his eyes shut for a moment. Mendez continued, "The others are scattered around. Armed to the teeth."

"Damn it," spat the mayor, "they're expecting us. I should have killed that brigand Klaus the moment he shot Salvador!"

"There's more." Mendez sat up, blowing out his cheeks. "God, it's hot."

"Never mind that, damn you! What do you mean 'there's more'?"

"They have Alvaro."

Carlos, who had been dozing in the sun, wide-brimmed hat pulled down over his eyes, sat up at the mention of his friend's name, craning forward. "Alvaro?" His voice sounded frightened. "Is he dead?"

"Not yet." Mendez took another swig of his water. "They have him tied up, in the front yard. I think they mean to torture him, for some hellish reason. And..." He stared at the mayor, "Brialles' mule is there too."

"The priest?" The mayor's face turned ashen. He slumped back against a large boulder. "We have to think this through, Mendez. Felipe and Mario should be here soon, with more men, and weapons. We'll get ourselves into position and when night comes, we'll attack."

"I don't think Alvaro will last until night, Señor Mayor."

Carlos scrambled forward, gripping the mayor by the arm, "We have to attack now. It's our only chance."

"They'll cut us down like dogs, Carlos. We have to wait until dark."

"But Alvaro."

"Alvaro will have to wait." The mayor closed his eyes and pulled down his hat, obscuring his face. "As we will."

Chapter 30

The Attack Begins

By mid afternoon there was little or no shade, and they all grew increasingly restless as the scorching heat sucked the strength from their bodies. Luis sat with his hat pulled down over his eyes, kept his mind as blank as he could. For a long time he thought about Pablo, then Salvador. Finally, most painfully of all, images of his mother invaded his thoughts. He pushed them all aside. There was no point in torturing himself any longer. He'd learned so much over the past few days that there were times when he no longer recognised his old self. He'd witnessed death close up and the scars ran deep.

Carlos was the first to snap and he stood up, beating his thigh with his fist. "We can't wait any longer," he shouted, "We have to go and rescue Alvaro."

Luis peered at him from under the brim of his hat. Carlos appeared wild, his nerves shredded, close to breaking, and that meant he was dangerous, unpredictable.

"That's exactly what they want," said the mayor, who had remained in the same position for the best part of an hour. "The best thing to do is simply sit and wait."

"I'm damned if I'll wait any longer." Carlos pulled out a pistol and checked the priming pan. "I'm going down there."

"No you're not!" The mayor sat up, pushing his hat back on his head. His eyes were black-rimmed, his skin drawn taut around his cheeks. Stress taking its toll.

"Damned if I'm not."

Carlos went to move and it was Luis who now stood up and barred his way. "Carlos. We must wait. It's suicide to go down there."

"What do you know about it, you coward! When this is over, I'm going to finish you, Luis, once and for all." He took a step.

"Please Carlos." Luis put out his hand. Suddenly Carlos moved, knocking the hand away, then punched Luis in the solar plexus. Pain like a corkscrew spread through his lower body and Luis folded, the air spouting out of his mouth in a rush, and he fell to his knees, groaning.

"Louie!" Constanza ran up to him, flung her arms around his neck and held him.

Without a pause, Carlos eased back the hammer of his pistol and levelled the muzzle towards Luis's head. Through a mist of pain, Luis looked up.

"*Carlos!*" The mayor scrambled to his feet but then stopped in his tracks as Carlos turned the weapon on him. "Carlos, don't be a damned fool. It's a trap down there, don't you see?"

Carlos grinned, "I'm not a fool, Señor. I know exactly what I'm doing." Then, keeping the pistol pointed unerringly towards the mayor, Carlos edged his way past and began a slow descent towards the mill.

"Let him go," said Luis through clenched teeth. He rolled over and sat up. He closed his eyes, measuring his breathing whilst he put his arm around Constanza and drew her close. He'd managed to keep the sickness down, but he needed time to regain his strength. The blow had hurt him beyond imagining, and he felt light-headed, and a little ashamed. He never believed Carlos would react like that, despite what had happened in the past—the jeering, the name-calling, the constant torment. Carlos had never once laid a finger on him, until now. It was unexpected and hurt all the more for it.

The mayor rammed a canteen of water into Luis's face. "Drink that, you sap! Why the hell didn't you stop him?"

"It's not the boy's fault," said Paco from the between the rocks where he sat. "Carlos has always been a firebrand."

"He won't be much of anything by the time those soldiers have finished with him." Mendez sucked on a stalk of dry grass. "We'll have to go and help him."

"We'll be cut to pieces," said the mayor, watching Luis as he drank.

"Not if we crawl down, thinking of them as boar." Mendez hefted his musket, checking the powder. He stood up, kicking Haime who lay stretched out, fast asleep. The man grunted and turned over onto his side. Mendez kicked him again and Haime was suddenly awake, rubbing his eyes, looking around, confused.

"We must wait for Felipe," said the mayor. "He's coming, with more men. Muskets."

"Aye, but when?"

The mayor looked down at Luis and his sister. "Constanza. I want you to take a note to Felipe, the innkeeper. Can you do that?"

"She's only five," said Luis with some difficulty. A stab of pain lanced through him as he began to get up. "She'll get lost. I'll go."

"No, Louie," said Constanza, tugging at Luis's trousers. "I can do it. I know the way. I promise."

Luis looked at her for a long time, then turned to the mayor. "If any harm comes to her..."

The mayor dismissed him with a wave of the hand. "It's only a note, Luis. And besides, the ogre is dead, remember."

"Is he?"

The mayor frowned at Luis for a long time before turning away, scribbling something down on a scrap of wadding, usually used to pack down ball and powder in his pistol. He turned and pressed the wad into Constanza's hand. "Deliver this to Felipe. Tell him to come quickly." Constanza nodded, turned to Luis and hugged him tightly. Then she was running away, in the direction of the village, her tiny little body weaving in and out of the many outcrops of rocks that punctuated the path. The mayor smiled, "A brave girl."

Luis bit his lip. He felt as if steel claws had ripped open his chest, but the pain was nothing to the fear that now dominated his whole being. His sister, the only good thing in this most terrible of worlds... "Lord God, protect her I beg you," he muttered.

The mayor sneered, turned around and slowly drew out his sword. "Let's go and rescue those stupid boys."

Keeping low, they approached the mill from four different directions. The mayor, with Luis close behind, came down from the left. They had lost sight of the others almost as soon as they had begun their descent.

"My God, they're good," said the Mayor to himself.

Luis tapped him on the shoulder and motioned with his other hand to stoop down still further. Frowning, the mayor complied. Luis pressed a finger against his lips, whilst pointing with his other hand.

Way down below, the mill stood, a silent pinnacle, deserted except for the body of Alvaro stretched out on the crossed beams. As they watched, a figure, small and furtive, emerged from between the rocks on the far side. Carlos.

"What is he doing?" whispered the mayor.

Luis shook his head. "Wait."

They squatted transfixed as Carlos, quickly looking around, ran across the open yard towards Alvaro, boots kicking up clouds of dust. As soon as he got there he began to cut at the ropes with a knife. It proved hard work, his hand became a blur, sawing backwards and forwards, as he glanced repeatedly towards the mill door. Luis gripped the mayor's arm and motioned that they should continue down to the mill.

Paco was a good hunter. For years he had worked these hills with his father and grandfather, hunting down boar, which were a challenge, and rabbits, which were not. He loved the thrill of the chase, tramping through the bush, keeping himself as quiet as possible. Boars were a worthy adversary, courageous when cornered. He'd watched his father wrestle one once, knew their strength, their tenacity. He applauded it. It was what made the killing strike so worthwhile.

Now, crouched down beneath the branches of an old, withered olive tree, he licked his lips at the memory. The taste of wild boar. God, how he would have loved to be that boy again, out with his father, camping out under the night sky, away for days. Returning to his mother, to throw the carcass on the table. How they'd laughed. Such memories, such sweet, sweet memories.

His thoughts distracted him and he didn't hear the footfall until it was too late.

It was the last thing he ever heard.

From this close up, from where Luis sat, he could clearly see Carlos's strained expression as he worked away at the ropes with the blade of his knife. Alvaro was whimpering, begging Carlos to hurry. The mayor was already crossing the open yard. Luis held back, crouching down low he pressed up against a length of broken down fencing. He scanned the area. No one. As the mayor reached Alvaro and began to help Carlos in cutting at the ropes, Luis peered towards the open door of the mill.

"Where are they," he muttered to himself. Still crouched double, he made his decision and scurried across the yard to the door and went inside.

Chapter 31

The Attack Continues

It was black inside the mill, and cool. Luis dropped to his haunches, leaned against the door well and gave himself a moment, mouth open to hear more clearly, straining to pick up any clue that someone, anyone, lurked within the gloom.

Within a few minutes, his eyes grew accustomed to the lack of light and he could make out the bed. A face, turned towards him, a grey, ghostly visage. He took a sharp breath, recognising the squalid figure, draped in a black cowl. "Father Brialles!"

The priest emerged from the depths of the darkness, holding up his hand as if in warning, "Shush, Luis, they are here." He pointed upwards.

Luis stepped up to him and craned his neck. He could just make out the beginnings of a spiral staircase that ran up to the top floor, the area where once the gearing for the great sail-arms were positioned, driving the grinding stones below. No clues remained, only the bare earthen floor. Everything was stripped bare, except for the staircase. Keeping his eyes on it, Luis crept forward and stood next to Brialles. The priest put an arm around him and held him close. "Thank the Lord you are safe," he whispered.

Luis sensed they were not alone. He peered through the half-light to the bed against the far wall and the figure that lay upon it. He almost fainted with the shock.

It was the body of a woman and she was breathing very shallowly.

The woman was his mother.

Haime rolled over the outcrop of rocks and peered over the large boulder in front of him. He knew this place but many years had passed since he had been here. The old mill, which once worked every day grinding out flour, now stood silent and still, like an ancient monolith from a forgotten time. He sat and watched, but the angle of his position meant he did not have a clear view of the yard at the front. He knew the boy Alvaro was there, but he couldn't see him. In fact, he couldn't see anyone. It would be an easy thing to slip down there, press himself up against the wall and—

"*Buenas dias.*"

Haime span round at the sound of the salutation and froze in terror, taken completely by surprise by a figure appearing from out of the undergrowth, unheard. He gaped in disbelief as the stranger's blade drove into his chest. The pain was not what Haime expected. More like a fist, punching him hard. He looked down in abject horror as the dull metal of the sword slowly drew back out of his body, the flesh making a horrible sucking sound. The blood bubbled out, thick and very red. So much of it. He looked up to see a tall man standing before him, wiping the blade on a rag before putting it slowly back into its scabbard. He was grinning. Haime wanted to ask him who he was, where he had come from, how he had managed to sneak up on him unnoticed.

And then he died.

Luis stroked his mother's hair and quietly cried, relief mixing with despair. Another lie from the mayor, a lie which had crushed him, made him empty inside. Now, those feelings replaced by a new hope and overwhelming joy. He wanted to jump up and down and shout out to the world that his worst nightmares had not come true. His mother was alive, he brushed the hair from her brow and felt the heat of her skin. He gripped the thin cover which draped her body and bit down his tears. He had to remain quiet. He was here, in the old mill, and so were the soldiers, waiting to come and kill them all. But he could not keep it in. So he cried, for everything that had gone wrong and for the growing knowledge that soon time would run out. Only the hope that his mother might rally, that was the one thing that made everything worthwhile. If she could regain her strength...

"She seems better," he said in a low voice.

Brialles laid a heavy hand on his shoulder. "A little. I think the soldier has been tending her, giving her good food."

"The soldier... Klaus?"

"The leader? Yes, the one called Klaus."

"Why would he do that?"

"I don't know, Luis. Guilt perhaps."

Luis frowned. The priest's voice had changed, from being almost whimsical to acquiring a hard edge. Luis stared at him. Even in the gloom he could see that Brialles seemed uneasy. "Guilt about what?"

The priest went to move away. "Nothing. I've said too much."

"Father." Luis gripped the man's arm. "Guilt about what?"

A floorboard creaked upstairs and both of them froze. Brialles shot his finger to his lips and Luis turned wild eyes towards the spiral staircase, half-expecting to see the glint of steel or the fiery red discharge from a pistol.

Nothing happened, no one descended; not yet. He breathed a long sigh of relief and fell back against the side of the bed. The only sound was his mother's breathing. It didn't rattle any longer, it was slow and shallow. He was grateful for that, but the question still played on his mind and refused to go away. Why would Klaus be guilty about his mother? A man like that, without a care in the world except for his own survival? It didn't make sense.

Mendez had fine-tuned his senses over countless years of hunting. Known throughout the village as the possessor of an extraordinary ability to sniff out the whereabouts of prey when there were no apparent signs, his hunting prowess was beyond dispute. Possessed of an extraordinary ability to second guess any quarry, his intuitive instincts, honed through endless years, gave him the edge every time. Now, crouching down amongst the gorse, he knew someone was close, although he couldn't hear a thing. Furthermore, he knew it was no animal. The idea struck him, with cold, dreadful clarity, that he was the prey, the hunted.

His heartbeat raced and he listened, senses alert. He rolled over onto his back with a sound and slowly pulled back the hammer of his musket. Whoever it was, they were close, very close. So he remained completely still, and waited.

The man came out of the gorse at a rush, mouth open in a soundless scream, both hands filled with evil looking, curve bladed knives. Mendez shot him through the throat and the attacker faltered, blinked in total surprise, took a few tottering steps and fell down into the dirt, eyes wide open, a look of complete disbelief on his face.

The musket shot rang out across the valley like a thunderclap. From the surrounding gorse, pheasants exploded out from their nests, shrieking with fear, and in the yard Carlos and the mayor stopped and looked at one another, open-mouthed.

Luis scrambled over to the doorway and gazed across the yard, blinking through the harsh light, forcing himself to focus. He saw Carlos and the mayor return to their efforts, hacking away at the thick ropes that bound Alvaro to the crossed wooden stakes. They were now so close to slicing through them, the sound of the musket seeming to give them an extra spurt of energy until at last the ropes parted and Alvaro fell on his knees, gasping. The mayor bent down next to him and pressed a canteen of water to the boy's lips. He took a gulp, coughed, his body going into spasm.

Luis waved his arms desperately, trying to attract their attention. He knew for certain that one of the soldiers was upstairs, but he also guessed that whoever it was did not know Luis was there. He had to remain quiet or his life would be over. It was that simple. So he waved his arms from side to side, faster and faster. Surely the others would notice, catch the movement out of the corner of their eyes? One of them at least?

As if sensing the telepathic waves, Carlos looked. He gaped at Luis, but almost at once a dark cast spread over his features and he sneered, turning away in derision.

Luis, frustration rising, bunched his fists and pummelled the timber-framed door well. All he was trying to do was to help, give some warning of the danger upstairs. Well, if that was his attitude, to hell with him. Luis slammed his fist against his own thigh. *Damn him, damn them all!*

Suddenly a great cry came from the hills. Luis turned and saw Felipe, with Mario by his side, together with a small knot of armed men piling down the slope towards the yard. The mayor and Carlos supported Alvaro between them, keeping him upright, and they all watched in silence as the bunch of men came charging on, Felipe some way to the rear, holding onto someone. Someone small. A girl. Constanza.

Luis wanted to shout out, but he knew he shouldn't. Instead, he slid down the doorframe and sat in the half shadows, his fingers digging into the earthen floor. He watched in speechless horror as a nightmare began to unfold before his eyes.

A musket shot cracked through the air, from somewhere high above them. The lead ball hit Mario in the chest, spinning him around, his arms whirling out to his side in some mad pirouette. As he crumpled, the other men fanned out, crouched with swords, pistols and muskets at the ready. Another blast broke through the air, but this time the shot whistled harmlessly over everyone's heads and slapped into the now empty crossbeams where they had lashed Alvaro.

Two soldiers came running from behind the mill, one on each side, at full pelt, a horrible battle cry erupting from their lips. Both had swords and pistols. Before any of the men could react, the soldiers were amongst them. A few of the men managed to bring up muskets or a pistol, but it was a pathetic effort. They didn't stand a chance. The soldiers fought like demons, snarling and roaring as they despatched each adversary, with either a sword cut or a smash to the skull from the butt of a pistol.

Luis watched on his knees, hands propping himself up, a trail of saliva dripping to the ground from his open mouth. He couldn't believe the ferocity of the attack, the sheer animal rage of the soldiers, the ease with which they felled each of the assembled villagers. He saw too how Carlos and the mayor stood transfixed, locked in terror, unable to move, fear their master. It was beyond anyone's experience.

Then, as suddenly as it had begun, it was over and a preternatural stillness settled. The soldiers stood in the centre of that charnel house, breathing hard, sweat raining down their faces, arms hanging limp, their upper bodies drenched in the blood of the killed. Around them, bodies hacked and split, internal organs spewed, life, memories, thoughts, dreams and hopes spent. The day of judgement visited in a blind, insane turmoil of violence.

Slowly, their heads came up and settled upon Carlos and the mayor.

They let Alvaro go from numbed fingers and he slumped to his knees. Everyone waited and the soldiers grinned through mouths like gaping demons, demented by the lust of killing. They slowly began to close.

A figure walked past Luis, ignoring him completely. It was another soldier, the one positioned upstairs, busily reloading a short musket as he stepped out into the intense heat of the afternoon. Luis watched the man's broad back as he advanced upon the hapless Carlos and mayor.

"My God," murmured the mayor, his mouth slack and quivering. "God in heaven help us."

Luis knew he had to do something. The carnage had been too great, it had to stop. But what to do and how to do it. He was merely a boy, what possible good could he be against such professional killers. Not daring to think what would happen next, he got to his feet and fumbled for the pistol in his belt.

A figure came into his line of sight, appearing from around the back of the mill. Luis gasped. It was Mendes. Determined, strong, focused on what needed doing. He positioned himself next to the door where Luis stood, brought up his musket to his shoulder, inhaled and discharged the weapon. The broad-backed soldier, still moving towards Carlos and the mayor, took the blast between the shoulder blades and flew forward, face first, and slammed into the hard packed earth.

For a moment, everyone was too stunned to move, all eyes turned to the dead man on the ground. Carlos reacted first, screaming, he flung himself at the nearest soldier like a wild cat, grappling him around the throat. They both went down in a confused tangle of arms and legs.

The mayor drew his sword and closed with the second soldier as Mendes ran forward, musket held aloft like a club. Inexplicably, the tide had turned.

As sword blade rang against sword blade, Mendes brought the stock of his musket down hard onto the soldier's head. It split like a melon, a great spurt of blood and brain erupting from the smashed skull and the man crumpled as the mayor, making sure, thrust his blade into the man's exposed throat.

Carlos screamed a cry somewhere between frustration and panic. Too late, Mendes turned. The remaining soldier had regained his ground and cuffed Carlos away as if he were an insect. He span in a tight circle, sword held in reverse manner, and rammed it deep into Mendes' gut, the blade sinking into the flesh without resistance, as if it were an over-ripe peach. Withdrawing the sword, his other arm came round in a wide arc, the pistol butt striking the mayor across the temple, pitching him backwards, over Alvaro, dumping him to the ground.

Without a moment's hesitation, Luis broke into a run, head down, arms pumping, eyes focused on the soldier. He crossed the yard in a matter of seconds. The soldier must have realised and turned just as Luis collided with him full in the midriff, hitting him with enough force to send him crashing backwards, his breath rushing out of his body in a loud gasp.

Rolling forward, Luis came up again, only this time, he had in his hands both his pistols. He took a deep breath and screamed, "Stop!"

For a moment, Luis thought that the soldier would attack. He was on one knee, gulping in air, blood trickling from his mouth, eyes like beads, black as night. His sword lay on the ground beside him and he very slowly reached out a hand to take it.

"Please," begged Luis, his hands shaking with the weight of the pistols.

The soldier climbed to his feet, breathing hard. He stretched his back and looked around. Luis saw a flicker of indecision crossing his face, but only briefly. The man tensed, flexed his arms and went into a low stance, sword ready.

Luis closed his eyes. The soldier would never stop. He was a mad dog, possessed by a force beyond imagining. A bloodlust, cruel and heartless, ran through him, consuming him. Luis saw it all in the blink of an eye. He knew he couldn't shoot and he knew, in that moment, that the soldier would kill him.

From nowhere, in a blur, a hand reached out and snatched the pistol from his grip.

Luis's eyes sprang open. Felipe, coming up behind him, had taken the pistol. He stretched out his arm and pointed the weapon unerringly towards the soldier. "I'll kill you," he said, voice even, controlled, utterly believable.

The soldier sneered and slowly shook his head. "Cock your piece, peasant!"

The horribly realisation struck both Luis and Felipe at the same time. They froze in that moment, but it was all the time the soldier needed. Felipe gave a cry, began to pull back the hammer, and the soldier crossed the space between them in one stride, sword in hand, the blade running Felipe through to the hilt, the point exiting through the innkeeper's back.

Luis groaned and fell to his knees, heard but didn't see Felipe landing next to him in a lifeless heap. It was over now, all hope gone.

He looked up. The soldier towered over him, teeth set in a maniacal grin. The man had lost every shred of humanity, mercy and compassion.

He drew back the blade with exaggerated slowness, enjoying the moment. Luis held his breath, knowing this was the end and he readied himself for the burning pain of the blade, the blackness of oblivion, the terrible uncertainty of what waited for him beyond the veil of death. He opened his mouth to give up a short prayer just as Carlos landed on the soldier's back. He wrapped his legs around the man's waist, hands pulling back his head by the hair. The soldier gave a great roar and thrashed around, trying to rid himself of the pathetic parasite clinging to him, his hands trying to gain some hold on Carlos, to pull him away.

"Louie!"

Luis turned, saw Constanza running down the slope, her little legs eating up the ground between them. She was crying and Luis knew he had to protect her. Protect his family, fight for the world that he had known, that these vile villains had broken into and attempted to pillage. For too long he had remained motionless, unprepared to raise a single finger. Well, not any longer. He had come so close to the death, had experienced a glimmer of what true horror was. Life and his family were too precious for him to simply roll over and let it all end like this.

He whirled around. The soldier wrestled frantically with Carlos, turning this way and that, hands gripping the boy's wrists, squeezing them. He stumbled, fell. Luis strode forward.

"Enough!" he shouted, rammed the muzzle of his pistol into the man's open mouth, and squeezed the trigger.

They all stood like statues, none of them believing what had happened. Carlos stumbled backwards, like one drunk, arms out wide, desperate to regain his balance. His eyes were wide, mouth agog. No words came from him.

Luis stood, the pistol in his hand. He had done it, he had discharged his piece. He hadn't even begun to think of the consequences of taking another human being's life, how he would cope, how he would explain it, how he would ever clear his conscience. The soldier was a monster, a killer, a man who deserved to die. God alone knew how many lives he had blighted with his casual violence, but to kill such a man. Was there ever any justification for that?

The soldier fell back and sat there, stunned. Gradually, he began to recover and he started to laugh.

The pistol had not been primed.

Luis cursed himself for never preparing the weapon. It was his father's piece, the one he had found at home in the bottom of the cabinet. He had always meant to load it but somehow, in all the confusion, he had forgotten. He looked down at the weapon, saw his hand begin to tremble. Then his whole body joined in and it was if some great invisible hand had seized him by the shoulders and was shaking him madly.

"My God." The soldier stood up, dusting off his pants. "You damned, ignorant peasants. You can't do a damned thing right, can you? What a waste of time and energy you are, the whole damned lot of—"

His head exploded an instant before the blast was heard, the force of the shot enough to spin him around in a tight circle. He thudded to the ground and remained still.

All eyes turned and looked at Alvaro, the pistol still smoking in his hands. Then he looked up and he smiled.

Chapter 32

Aftermath

"They're all dead."

Luis sat on the ground, Constanza in his lap weeping softly. He stroked her hair and looked up at the mayor. He appeared dazed and the bruise on the side of his head was the size of a piece of shoe leather, and about the same colour.

Carlos staggered over to Alvaro and helped him sit up. The pistol slipped from his fingers. He, along with everyone else, appeared drained, thoughts elsewhere, no one able to come to terms with the nightmare events, nor believe it was over.

After a prolonged pause, the mayor went around each of the bodies, prodding them with the toes of his boot, paying particular attention to the soldiers, turning them over, studying their waxen faces.

"He's not here," he said, his voice sounding strange, as if his tongue was too big for his mouth.

Luis realised that the swelling on the man's face was making talking difficult. "Who isn't?"

"Klaus." The mayor looked again at each dead soldier, balking at the ones whose heads had exploded so horribly.

Something moved at the edge of Luis' vision and he looked past the mayor, towards the hillside from which they had all descended, and saw something. He narrowed his eyes. No doubt about it, there was a figure there, amongst the gorse, heading back towards the village. Luis pointed quickly, "There!"

The mayor span round and followed the direction of Luis's finger. "Damn his hide!" He straightened up to his full height, touched his cheek carefully and hissed, "We'll not catch him now, not in the state we're in."

A shuffling sound made them all turn. Through the open door of the mill came Father Brialles, the long tail of his black habit trailing in the dust of the yard. He shuffled forward, head down, openly crying as he gazed upon the scene of death all around. "Merciful God in heaven," he said, voice croaking with emotion.

"You will say some words Father," said Carlos, who still sat on the ground with Alvaro leaning against him.

"Words?" The priest shook his head, clasping his hands together in front of him. "What possible good will words do now?"

"It might help their souls, father." Slowly Carlos's face crumpled and he broke down, held onto Alvaro's arm, pressed his face into his friend's shoulder and wept.

"Dear God," muttered the mayor, and reached to take the pistol from Luis's numbed fingers. The mayor looked into the boy's eyes. "Luis…"

Luis looked away, letting his head rest on top of Constanza's. There was a deep sadness in the mayor's eyes, something which Luis had never seen before. Could it be that he had misjudged the man, that there actually was a hint of humanity hidden somewhere deep within him, at last beginning to surface? Luis pondered on this, but couldn't be sure. Too much had happened and he needed to retreat into himself, think things through.

A curious atmosphere settled over the yard. No one moved, no one spoke. Even those who had been weeping gradually stopped. The silence which followed was intense. Nothing stirred, or made any sound at all. Even the light wind did not rustle the leaves of the few trees that stood here and there. It was almost as if everything held its breath, waiting for something to happen.

And then it did.

He came unheard, moving across the yard like a whisper in a breeze, floating not walking. Years of fighting had honed his skills, skills which had served him well, kept him alive. He moved behind Brialles and before anybody knew what was happening, the soldier sank his blade through the priest's back, the point slicing upwards, cutting through vital organs until it reached the heart. Brialles died without a sound, until his limp corpse hit the ground, and then everyone turned, and moaned as the horror resurfaced.

Klaus stood and glared at them, directing most of his red-rimmed gaze towards the mayor. As if stunned by the venomous look, the mayor slinked backwards, face ashen, a trembling hand covering his mouth, a curious groaning coming from deep within his throat. His sword slipped from unfeeling fingers and clattered at his feet.

"It's time," said Klaus, his voice as sharp as glass, with no emotion, just hard and simple.

Luis frowned. *Time for what*? How had Klaus managed to get behind them without being seen? The man moved like a ghost. Perhaps that was what he was, had been all the time. Luis went to stand up.

"Stay there." Klaus held up his hand, the look on his face doing the rest. Those eyes would truck no argument. Luis fell back down, transfixed. "You need to hear this, Luis."

"No," mumbled the mayor, falling to his knees, his hands coming together in front of his chest, as if in prayer. "Please, Klaus. *Please.*"

"I came here, Luis," began Klaus, taking a step forward, the blade of his sword hovering in front of the mayor's face, "with your father, when you were a tiny boy."

"My father? But..." Luis, confused beyond words, felt a massive cavern opening up inside him. A sudden sickness rising into his throat. He felt afraid, anxious.

"We had a plan, your father and I. We would wait for the others," Klaus nodded briefly towards the fallen soldiers. "When they came, we would kill them and share the gold between us. Your father, he had an idea that we should give some of the gold to the church and the rest we would split. I would go my way and he would go his. Become mayor, perhaps, of a new prosperous village…" He smiled. "But you had other plans, didn't you, Señor Mayor? When I went away again, to meet up with these brigands," he kicked at one of the dead soldiers with his boot, "things began to fall apart. Isn't that right, Señor Mayor? You see, Luis, the mayor wanted the gold for himself. Who wouldn't, after all it was a fortune. So he followed your father into the hills, saw him meeting Salvador, and devised his plan. The story of the ogre."

"But you…" Luis wiped his dry mouth, "It was you who told the village of the ogre!"

"To my shame, Luis, I broke my bond with your father. I made a new pact with Señor Mayor. He murdered your father, buried him up in the mountains somewhere. I told him if he didn't bring the gold to me, then I would subject the village to my wrath. He did not give me the gold."

"You dog," spat the mayor at last, regaining some of his old courage. "I didn't know where the damned gold was! I still don't." He turned his desperate face to Luis. "It's not true, Luis, I swear. I didn't kill your father."

"Salvador saw you."

"No," the mayor shook his head. "No... he *thought* it was me. You see, I had planned to meet your father and I was in the mountains. But so was..." He shook his head.

Klaus pointed with his sword once again, the blade inches from the other's face. "You're a liar, Señor Mayor. You killed his father. You should have discovered the whereabouts of the gold first, that was your one big mistake."

"No, he wouldn't tell me. So we arranged to meet. I threatened him, told him I would kill his family, his wife. That much is true. So I went to meet him, but he didn't show."

Luis noted a slight twitching at the corner of Klaus's mouth. A tiny chink in the man's self-confidence. Could it really be the case that the mayor's words were true, that someone else had murdered his father? Or was it simpler than that, that the mayor was willing to say anything to spare his own, miserable life?

"I swear, if you're lying..." Luis felt his face growing hot. He bunched his fists.

"And I swear to you I am not," said the mayor. "Why should I lie? I planned to kill him, that is the truth. He was going to take me to the gold and I was going to kill him. There! That's it. But someone else had already done the deed."

The silence yawned over them. Luis, cradling Constanza's head, tried to come to terms with the enormity of the mayor's words, and slowly the dawn opened up bright in his head. If the mayor had not murdered his father, then it could only be one other person. He turned to Klaus, "You killed him, is that it?"

"No," said Klaus. "Your father and I were friends, Luis. He was perhaps the only real friend I have ever had." He frowned deeply. "No... If what the mayor says is true then there is someone else in this village..."

"It cannot be Salvador," said Luis quickly, before anyone else jumped to that conclusion. "Salvador saved me. He wouldn't have done anything to my father, I'm sure of it."

"Your father was a formidable adversary," said Klaus. "Not many could overcome him. Even Salvador might have struggled. Unless, he was taken by surprise..."

"Or knew the person." Luis pressed his lips together hard. "That's it. My father met someone up there in the mountains, someone he didn't suspect—wouldn't suspect. Because he knew him."

"Or her."

Both Luis and Klaus turned to Carlos, who now stood up, hands on his hips. "I've been listening to all of this, taking it all in. It's obvious isn't it? Obvious who it was who killed your old man, Luis. The same person who killed them all, the children, Señora Gomez, old Enrique, Francisco...anyone who might have guessed at the truth."

"Who are you talking about, Carlos?" Luis felt his whole body become taut as he waited impatiently for Carlos to speak.

"The one person whom nobody would ever suspect." He grinned, arrogant, confident in his revelations. "Your own mother, Luis."

Chapter 33

A Mother's Tale

"You rancid cur!"

Before anyone could move, even blink, Luis shot to his feet and landed such a blow across Carlos's jaw, that the bully was more surprised than hurt. As he teetered backwards a step or two, Luis hit him again. And again. Over and over, driving Carlos backwards, the ferocity of the blows too much for a reaction. All the years of anger, the pain, the humiliation Luis had suffered. It all came out in that single burst of violence. He held nothing back, pounding the other boy's face and stomach, until Carlos, screaming for mercy, crumpled to the ground, face pummelled into a bright red, bloated ball of blood and bruises. He rolled himself up into a ball, crying incessantly, defeated and battered.

No one moved. Luis stood there, his fists raw from the punches he had landed, gulping in a great lungful of air, sweat pouring down his face, legs apart, tense and ready to continue the attack.

Alvaro crawled over to his friend and held him as if he were a baby. Held him against his chest and gently rocked backwards and forwards. It was a pitiful sight and Luis turned his back, glowering towards Klaus. "It's not true."

"No," said Klaus without a pause. "It isn't."

Luis fumed, "Then who killed my father, damn you. Was it Brialles? Is that why you killed him?"

Klaus blinked. "Brialles? No, I killed him because he was a liar and a thief. He only helped your mother out of some perverse belief he could escape with the gold."

"Then who was it who murdered my father?"

"I don't know."

Luis considered this for a moment. It was difficult, but somehow he knew that Klaus spoke the truth. He went over to Constanza and reached out his hand. "We're going home."

"Wait," said Klaus, stepping closer, the sword now lowered, the threat diminished. "There's something you need to know."

"Klaus," said the mayor, a voice of warning, "not now."

Luis went onto his knees and held Constanza close. He pressed his face into hers, closed his eyes and said, very softly, almost resigned to anything now, "Yes, Klaus. Tell me, now."

"It's not right," interjected the mayor. "There's no need to stir up any more of the past, not like this."

Klaus exhaled slowly, turned away for a moment, then bent down to stroke Constanza's hair. "There are many things I am ashamed of, Luis. Things I've done; terrible things. But one thing will always fill me with courage and a sense of well-being. One thing for which I will never feel shame, only love."

"Tell me what it is." Luis was only a breath away from the soldier, clearly able to see the many scars that criss-crossed his face, the evidence of battles fought, the pain he had experienced. Without thinking, he reached out and touched his arm. "Please."

Klaus snapped his head around, as if the touch was the cruellest pain he had ever known. He squeezed his eyes shut, then sprang them open again as he gasped. Luis frowned, then reeled back in horror as a trickle of blood drooled from the man's mouth. Scrambling to his feet, dragging his sister with him, Luis looked with disbelieving eyes and saw, in all its terrible, uncompromising truth, that the mayor had plunged his sword deep into Klaus's body. His mouth hung open, a strange gurgle emitting from Klaus's throat, his eyes rolled up into his head and he fell forward. Stunned, Luis watched the mayor place his foot on the Klaus' back and withdrew the blade with a flourish.

Speechless, Luis felt as if, in a single moment, all he ever wanted had been stripped away. He began to shake, and holding onto Constanza he pressed her face into his body, averting her eyes, but not his own. He looked down at the still body of Klaus and the enormity of what had occurred hit him as hard as any blow he had landed on Carlos. Now he would never know the secrets that Klaus had been about to reveal. Another chapter closed, unread. He bit down on his lip, frustration mixing with anger. Once more denied the truth. He measured the mayor with a cold stare.

With Constanza whimpering, Luis took her slowly back to the mill, leaving the others to grapple with their own thoughts. Luis had had enough of them, of everything they stood for. He knew now, with total clarity, what he had to do.

In the coolness of the darkened room, Luis went over to the side of the bed and knelt down. With Constanza beside him, he stroked his mother's arm. She murmured, her fingers uncurled and her eyes flickered open. Even in the gloom, Luis could see her smile. "Luis." Her voice was tiny, like a fragile bird's.

"And Constanza, Mama. We're both here."

Their mother laughed, more like a small bark, and she took a strand of Constanza's hair and played with it for a moment. "My darlings," she said. "My two darlings."

"Mama," Luis moved forward, "Mama, I need to ask you something. Are you strong enough to talk?"

"I am feeling much better, Luis. Much better."

Luis could tell it was a lie. Her voice trembled, her breathing shallow. But he knew he had to press on. He ran his tongue over his lips, not at all sure if his questions would receive the answers he wanted. "Who took you from our house and brought you here? Was it the mayor?"

"The mayor?" She shook her head, just the once. The action seemed to cause her some pain, but it soon passed. "It was Klaus."

The soldier's name hit him like a slap. Klaus? Why would Klaus bring his mother here?

"Where is Father Brialles? He made me a potion; it seemed to help me. Restored my strength."

"He's…" Luis couldn't bring himself to tell his mother the truth. He patted her hand, "He has gone back to the village, Mama. With the others."

"Oh." She closed her eyes. For a long time she said nothing and Luis thought she had slipped back into sleep. He continued to stroke her hand. "I'm so tired," she said suddenly, her voice very low indeed. "So very tired…"

He waited, preparing himself for the one question that burned through him, the question that needed asking. "Mama, how do you know Klaus?"

The name hung like a heavy weight in the quiet of the room. Luis dared not speak again. She caught her breath for a moment, releasing it slowly, rattling it through her mouth. Luis waited, knowing she had heard the question, but wondering why she struggled with the answer. He squeezed her hand and she swivelled her head towards him and smiled.

"He was a friend of your father's, many years ago, when you were very small. You don't remember?"

"No, Mama. Nothing."

"Well, as I said, you were very small. He came to visit us, many times. He was a kind man, a good man. A soldier, yes, but unlike any other. We would talk

for hours; his stories thrilled me. When your father...
when your father disappeared, Klaus comforted me.
He was so kind, so good. So giving. He said he would
return and he would help us. Gold. That was what he
promised. I didn't believe him, of course. And as the
years past, I forgot him. We struggled on, just you
and me... Others tried to help, but there was little
anyone could do. Señor Garcia, he was very kind. He
would visit us often, bring us bread and milk." Her
breathing became laboured, the act of talking an increasing effort.

"Mama, rest now."

"No, I'll be fine. Just give me a moment or two."

Luis waited, watching her face, the way she mod-
erated her breathing, her lips slightly parted, eyes
closed. Constanza muttered something and Luis put
his arm around her and held her close.

A movement behind him made Luis turn. Silhou-
etted in the doorway stood the mayor, the sword in
his hand still. Although Luis could not see the man's
expression, he could guess at what it held.

"We are going back to the village, Luis. I will send a
cart to carry your mother in the morning. After that,
we will burn the dead. We want no plague here."

Luis watched him go, then turned back to his
mother. She was staring straight at him. "They are
all dead, all the soldiers?"

"Yes. Lots of others too. And Father Brialles." Luis
closed his eyes, instantly regretting that he had forgotten to carry through his promise of not telling his

mother of the priest's death. When he opened his eyes he could see the sheen of tears on her cheeks.

"So much waste," she said, her voice laboured, trembling with emotion. "All these years, waiting for things to change, to improve... All for nothing." All of a sudden, she gripped Luis's arm with surprising strength. "Listen to me, Luis. Towards the rear of this compound, beyond the tree line, there is a dried-up old well. You will need a rope. And a strong nerve."

"A rope? Mama, I don't—"

"*Listen!*" Her grip tightened. "You must climb down and bring back the treasure that is there."

"Treasure? You mean, the soldiers put their gold down there, in the well?"

"No, not the soldiers. Brialles. Klaus overtook him, brought him back here. The treasure he took from the church was the part of the gold your father gave. So, by all accounts, it is yours, Luis. By right."

Luis pulled himself away from her. "Mama, I cannot do such a thing, it's... it's not right! That gold belongs in the church. To take it would be—"

"Would be nothing, Luis. It is yours. That damnable priest, do you think he cared that it belonged to the church?"

"He may not, but I do. I will take it from the well and then I shall return it, to where it belongs."

"Then you're a fool."

"Maybe. But an honest one, at least."

She exhaled loudly through her nose. "My God, so like your father—a stubborn mule! Very well... Upstairs, in the loft, you will find Klaus's share. It is not as much as it might have been, but you can take that. There is enough to set you and Constanza up for the rest of your lives."

"How do you know all this, Mama? How do you know about Klaus leaving his gold up there? Why would he tell you things like that?"

"Because he loved me once."

Luis felt his heart almost stop. Even Constanza, who had sat silently throughout the exchange, now sat up, sensing that something momentous was about to happen.

"Mama... what are you saying?"

She held her breath, her fingers digging into Luis' flesh. "I'm saying that Klaus is Constanza's father."

Chapter 34

The Village Awakes

They spent the night at the mill. In the morning, Luis rose early and went outside. The air was already warm and so thick you could cut it with a knife. Something else hung in the air; the bitter, sharp stench of death.

When the smell, like nothing he had ever experienced before, hit him he almost vomited right there and then. It invaded his nostrils and he gagged, turned back into the room and groped around for some water. Constanza and his mother still slept. He was glad of that.

He found a water gourd amongst some abandoned belongings in the far corner, near the foot of the spiral staircase. Splashing himself, he found a bandana and wrapped it around his mouth and nose and went outside again. The heat was intense. Out in the open, exposed with no shade, the yard received full sunlight throughout the day, a cauldron, baked dry, all goodness sapped out of the earth, as it had from him. Cast to the elements, remaining shreds of innocence and naivety lost forever. He pressed the bandana against his nose, held his breath and looked around. Flies settled in black, seething mounds on the corpses, the noise and the smell proving too much, and he went back inside. Never had he seen such horror.

He stood for a moment, blinking through the dimness, aware of the unsettling rumbling in his guts. More than the images of death, there had been something else.

It began as a stirring deep inside him as he ran the images through his mind again. The bodies, various pieces hacked off, heads split open, bloody entrails strewn across the dusty ground, bodies thrown in impossible angles. The grim visage of death. Terrifying, base—a butchers' yard, lives destroyed in an instant, without pause for thought, concern or conscience. The bodies of the dead.

The most terrifying thing of all—Klaus was not amongst them.

The mayor hardly slept through the night. He sat, slumped at his great dining table, dressed in the clothes he had worn when he had gone to the mill, his sword thrown across the floor. The nightmare kept repeating itself.

When the pounding started at his door, he thought it was only the awful memories that kept swirling around in his head. He had dozed a little, the knocking bringing him back to reality. He sat blinking for a moment unaware of where he was. Slowly, the mist parted and he got to his feet, taking his time, sucking in deep breaths, leaning on the table until he felt able to move.

He had dismissed his servants the previous evening when he had returned, telling them to go to their families. He would notify them when he required their services again. He doubted if he ever would. Too much had happened; his world had changed now. So, with no one to answer the knocking, he walked out of the dining room, across the great hall, to the door and opened it.

He gaped at the man standing in front of him. And the cold fingers of fear gripped his throat when he saw the knife in the man's hand.

The house felt like a stranger's. Gone was the welcome cosiness, the comforting sense of familiarity. Unknown, unwelcome hands had violated his family's possessions and ransacked his home. He stood, surveying the scene, and felt crushed. He had no desire to clear anything away, only a burning wish that all of it would simply disappear and his old life return.

He did his best to tidy his mother's bed. The rest, he couldn't face and he went back outside and made his way down to the village *plaza*.

A curious melancholy came over him and he found himself yearning to see once more the group of boys by the fountain, hear their painful words, suffer their cruel jibes. He couldn't help but give a little laugh at the irony of such thoughts. How quickly everything had changed.

He intended to visit his old tutor, Señor Martinez. No one was about, the streets were deserted, deathly quiet. At the tutor's house, it was the same story. No one home. Luis rapped on the door, but the only reply was the sound echoing through the empty rooms and corridors within. Exasperated, he stomped back to the plaza and, after a momentary hesitation, he went over the bridge towards the mayor's residence. Luis needed to check that the cart was ready to return to the mill and bring his mother back home.

Luis stopped as he stepped through the gate to the house. Peering down the path, he could clearly see that the main door of the building was open. A sudden chill ran through him, despite the heat of the day. Something wasn't right. Taking a deep breath, he forced his legs to move, feeling he was entering into the very pit of fear.

The mayor retreated a few steps, hands held up in defence, eyes on the knife brandished in front of him. He licked his lips, "I know why you're here. But we're too late, it's all gone."

"Gone? Don't lie to me, damn you!"

"It's true, I swear it. Look around if you don't believe me—do you seriously think I'd be sat here, like this, if I had the gold?"

"What happened?"

"Everything." The mayor ran a hand over his face. It was awash with sweat. "Everything that could go wrong, did. It was disastrous."

"Convenient more like."

The mayor held his breath. "Not for those who died."

"That's nothing new—many have died. Many more will, unless you bring me the gold."

"You can't keep threatening me—I've done everything you've asked of me, and more."

"Except deliver the gold."

"I've told you… the gold is *lost*! I have no idea where it is."

"But she does, doesn't she."

"No, I don't believe so."

"Then we will have to ask Klaus, won't we."

"Klaus is dead. Along with the others. Felipe, Mario, Mendes, Brialles, all of the soldiers—they are all dead."

A pause whilst he considered this. "And the boy? What of him?"

"He lives. He is with his mother, back at the mill. I said I would take a cart to bring her back."

"Then, you must do it. And when he returns, I will have the gold, or I will slit all of their throats. Enough is enough, Señor Mayor. My patience has run out." He slowly slid the knife back into its scabbard. "Get the woman and then we will end this, for good."

He turned to go and gaped at what he saw.

Luis stood, petrified, rooted to the spot, unable to believe his eyes. He had heard every word, listening just outside the main door. But now, as the man turned, Luis stepped forward to confront him. His heart missed a beat when he saw the look on the man's face, a look of sheer hatred.

"My God, Luis..."

Luis shook his head, his mind a jumble of distorted, unconnected thoughts. "Señor Garcia, what are you...?"

Very slowly, the baker drew out his knife.

Chapter 35

The Baker, The Soldier and Their Secrets

Klaus staggered up to his waiting horse, held onto the reins and waited. The animal whinnied, alarmed, stomping at the ground. Klaus breathed hard, his head down, hand pressed against his side where the wet rag oozed blood. He had tried to staunch the flow and had, at first, succeeded, but with every step the wound would open anew. Klaus knew he had lost too much blood. He needed to rest, to regain his strength. Eat and drink something. Anything.

Moving through sheer instinct, he managed to climb into the saddle and steer the horse through the brittle, scorched scrub. He clung onto the beast's neck, forcing himself to remain conscious. He had no water and his tongue felt huge and painful in his mouth.

At last, he came into the *plaza*. He slid from the horse and slumped down onto the fountain steps and plunged his face into the cool, sharp water. He sat, letting the water drip from his nose and mouth, until his eyes cleared and something like awareness returned to his limbs and mind.

Time was his enemy now. It was too hot, and his blood loss meant he was weak, too weak to protect Luis. But he had no choice. He had promised his mother as much many years ago and it was a promise he was determined to keep. Even if it meant dying in the process.

The approach of horses caused him to sit up. He winced, fingers as weak as a child's as he grasped for his pistol. He failed as another wave of pain ran through him, reaching into the very core of his being where it remained, brewing. God damn that mayor! For it all to end like this.

He became dimly aware of cavalrymen fanning out around him, some with drawn pistols, others with hands on the hilts of their swords. One of them dismounted and moved closer.

"Klaus?"

A voice he knew, from years ago. He raked a hand across his eyes and looked up to see him. He grinned, "Señor Martinez."

"Where is Luis?" The old tutor squatted next to Klaus, his voice heavy with concern.

Klaus shook his head, and scanned the mounted men. There were a troop of twelve cavalrymen, all armed. By the look of them, drenched in sweat and dust, they had been riding for a long time. Horses whinnied, desperate to get closer to the fountain and water.

Martinez gripped Klaus' forearm. "Klaus... are you hurt?"

Klaus shrugged, pulled away the sopping wet rag, and smiled. "A flesh wound."

Martinez took one look and turned on the others, "Quickly, this man needs attention!"

Soldiers jumped out of their saddles and ran over, just as Klaus toppled forward, his face turning green. Martinez grabbed him, supported him until the others took over. They lifted him back against the fountain steps and stretched him out on his back.

"Let me die, Señor," said Klaus, his voice barely above a whisper.

"Nonsense! We need you alive. Now listen to me, Klaus. Where is Luis?"

As Martinez waited, the others tended to Klaus, cutting away his leather jerkin to expose puckered flesh, the wound vicious, blood congealed around the edges but still seeping through the centre.

Klaus smiled again, "Why bother yourselves with an old rogue like me? Eh, Martinez?"

"Luis," the old tutor leaned closer. "Where is Luis, Klaus?"

"I don't know. I left him down at the mill, with his mother and the girl."

It was Martinez's turn to smile. "Your girl. Your daughter. Did you tell him?"

"Well... things, they..." He winced, "But I'm sure when he knows, he will take it well."

Martinez reached inside his jacket and brought out the letter Luis's father had written. "This will seal the fate of the mayor. I have Don Manuel Laquilla with me, senior deputy to the Lord Advocate in Malaga. The mayor is to be taken into custody, to face charges of murder. We need your testimony."

"Ah... now I understand why you're anxious I live." He grimaced as the soldiers applied a coarse bandage to his wound. "Damn his eyes, this is the mayor's doing. He took me unawares."

"All the more reason to bring him to justice."

"Well, that is something long overdue. Although, from the words he spoke, I'm not so sure if my suspicions," he nodded towards the letter, "or your evidence are centred on the right culprit."

Martinez cocked an eyebrow. "Who else could it be?"

A tall, thin man, wearing a luxuriant black wig, came over to them. The most beautiful embroidered gloves encased his hands and his clothing, also black, was inlaid with gold thread. "This is not the news I wanted to hear, Señor Martinez."

"No, I'm sure that the mayor is culpable. When we question him, we shall have the truth."

The scream brought them all to a halt. For a moment no one spoke, then Martinez—the first to react—pulled out his sword and yelled in a voice that echoed his fear, "*Luis!*"

"I don't understand."

Luis could have run, if he had wanted to. But this development was beyond his reasoning. He had to discover the truth. So he stood and waited whilst Garcia slowly advanced on him.

"You never have," he snarled. "My God, for someone so clever you've been unbelievably stupid."

"I can't... This cannot be true. You? What have you got to do with all of this?"

"He followed your father, Luis." The mayor seemed about to faint, but held onto the wall, propping himself up, taking out a kerchief to mop his brow. "I wanted to tell you everything, but I couldn't. If you'd have known..."

"If I'd have known... What?"

"I followed your father, Luis," said Garcia. "Up into the mountains. He didn't know I was there. I've been hunting in these mountains for years. I saw the good Señor Mayor talking, then leaving, and I waited. Watched. My patience was rewarded. I followed your father high up, to a tiny cave where I saw him pulling out the bags stuffed with booty. I slit his throat, buried him in the cave, then returned with the gold."

Luis heard the rush of blood into his ears, felt the churning of his guts, the weakness in his knees. He wanted to be sick, to cry out, to run around the village demanding that everyone listen. But he did none of those things. Instead, he let his head hang low, lips quivering, and he opened his mouth and began to cry.

"Not content with what he had, he wanted it all." The mayor pushed himself off the wall. "So he blackmailed me. If I didn't get in touch with Klaus, have him return with everything, then he would begin to murder the children of the village."

"Murder…" Luis shook his head, wiping his nose with the back of his hand. He'd stopped crying, the burning embers of disbelief, anger and sadness simmering in the very core of his being, but now he had control. And a desire for the truth.

"Yes," continued the mayor. "But he grew to enjoy it, Luis. He'd missed his vocation had our good master baker. He relished the thrill of it all, became like a man possessed, needing more and more, like a drunk craving drink."

"You'd make a good preacher, Señor Mayor!" Garcia gave the mayor a scathing look, then rounded on Luis. "I was with them, way back, when we plundered the abbey. When we split up, I made my way here, arriving before any of them—even your damned father. My real name is Manfred Kepel, and I served under Field Marshall Wallenstein in our struggle against the Protestants. I met with Klaus, your father and the others, and after our army was broken, we wandered aimlessly, until we stumbled upon that damnable place, with those accursed monks, and that gold! Gold which has weaselled into all of our hearts. After I came here, heard the stories, met your father and Klaus once more, I knew I had to have it all. And I knew that I would have to wait, possibely even years for the secrets to be disclosed. So I became part of this village, cast off my old identity, became Garcia the baker. A quiet man, a good man. I lived amongst you, became one of you, and all the while I've waited. Well, I'll not wait any longer. Your damned mother knows where the rest of the treasure is—she always has, and I would have got it out of her if it hadn't been for that damned Gomez woman."

"You, you murdered Señora Gomez?" Luis, the sweat springing from his forehead, could no longer contain his fury. All of his fear evaporated in that single moment and he screamed at the top of his voice, launching himself at Garcia, wrapping his fingers around the man's throat with such ferocity and suddenness that the baker was taken completely by surprise. They fell to the floor, Garcia's blade clattering across the hard, marble tiles.

"Which way do we go?" demanded Laquilla, throwing himself up into his saddle once again.

"We must split up," said Martinez, helped into the saddle by one of the soldiers attending Klaus. "Some of you to the inn, some of you search the mayor's office. Don Laquilla, you and I, to the mayor's house."

Laquilla nodded, gave out the orders, finally pointing to the soldier next to Klaus. "Stay with him. You," he pointed to the second soldier, "you come with us." Then he spurred his horse as Martinez took his own mount up the steep hill and headed towards the bridge.

Luis had no control now, unable to focus or think, so consumed by hatred and the need for revenge. Everything focused in on his fingers, knowing he must maintain the pressure, squeeze the life out of this creature beneath him. It was all that mattered. Even when the first blow hit him in the stomach, he bit through it, kept his grip secure. The second blow, however, hit him hard in the groin. He yelped, a rush of nausea racing through him, and for a moment everything went black. Strong hands pushed him aside and when he blinked open his eyes, his fingers were no longer around Garcia's throat. The pain swept over him, his stomach turned to mush, throat filling up with bile. He vomited, wretched and rolled around, both hands clamped to his groin, the pain like fire, overwhelming. Squeezing his eyes tight shut, tears sprang forth, but not of anguish or pain, but of despair. Despair at being defeated.

Something hit him in the side, lifting him off the ground, to slam him against the wall. The breath knocked out of him, he slid down and through a mist of red, searing pain, he watched Garcia advance. The man, clutching at his throat, coughing hoarsely, reached down for the knife which lay on the floor. But the mayor went for it first and the two men became locked in a violent struggle, wrapping arms and legs around one another. The Mayor managed to get a palm under Garcia's chin, forcing the head back. But Garcia, stronger and fitter despite his bruised throat, brought up his knee, striking the mayor hard between the legs. Squealing, the mayor fell backwards and Garcia kicked him in the ribs with the toe of his boot. Screeching like a terrified caged bird, the mayor doubled up, pain over-coming him.

In that moment, Luis saw it all, played out before him in a jagged series of flickering images. He saw Garcia pick up the knife, slice through the mayor's throat, then turn to finish Luis, plunging the blade into his heart. A life finished, no justice done. And mother and Constanza, left to the vile, unfettered excesses of this man. The man who had brought so much misery to this village, reaping a harvest of murder and mayhem. All for the sake of gold.

He saw it all, and he knew he could not allow it to happen. He went forward, on his knees, and picked up the blade, the knife the men had fought for and forgotten in their struggle. He got to his feet as Garcia struck the mayor hard across the jaw, finishing him. Then the baker straightened, threw his head back and laughed. Victory, so sweet. With a look of exultation written across his features, he turned and Luis plunged the knife deep into the man's chest.

Garcia gasped, eyes registering disbelief. He teetered backwards, fingers desperately trying to gain purchase on the hilt of the knife as it lay buried in his flesh. But his fingers were useless, the strength draining from them. He gurgled horribly, blood frothing from his mouth, and his eyes began to become dull, registering northing and he fell backwards, crumpling over the unconscious body of the mayor.

Luis stared, hands hanging heavy by his side. He had killed. He had wanted to before, with that soldier, but now he really had. The enormity of it, the dreadful realisation of what he had done came at him in a rush, too fast for him to understand, or consider. The horror of the moment, the corpse, the knife. The blood. All feeling drained from his limbs, his legs turning to liquid, just as the door flew open and Señor Martinez took hold of him before everything went into freefall and Luis fainted.

Chapter 36

Of Mayors and Things

Luis limped into the cells in the basement of the mayor's building. They had tended to Klaus and a cart had been sent to the old mill. Mother and Constanza would soon be home. As for the mayor, he was in bed at his home. When he well enough to travel, he would go to Malaga to await trial. As Luis trod his way carefully down the narrow, well-worn steps, he wondered what would become of everyone else. A village without a leader was like a ship without its rudder. It would drift, become lost, finally break up. The future for Riodelgado was not good.

He peered through the bars of the cell towards Klaus, who lay on a rickety bench, one knee propped up, arm behind his heads, staring at the ceiling.

Luis gestured to the keeper, who frowned.

"Open it," said Luis.

The man went to say something, thought better of it after seeing the look in Luis' eyes, and came over, put the great heavy key in the lock and turned it.

Luis stepped inside the tiny, cold cell and waited for the jailer to engage the lock once more. Klaus opened one eye and smiled. "Ah, Luis. My little friend."

Luis coughed. He didn't know how to begin. He had so much he needed to say, but finding the words when he felt so confused, so emotional, was going to be difficult. He coughed again. "They have looked after you well?"

"Well enough. I won't die, if that's what you mean."

"It's not—and you know it."

"Do I? Don't you hate me Luis?"

He searched Klaus's face for any hint of humour, but there was none. Luis sighed, looked around and settled upon a small, rickety stool in the corner. He pulled it out and sat down. "I don't hate you, Klaus. I just wish you had been honest with me, right from the start."

"If I had, the mayor, or more likely Manfred would have killed you. And your family."

"*Our* family, don't you mean."

Klaus smiled. "Yes. I suppose I do."

"What will they do to you, Klaus? Once they take you back to Malaga?"

"That much is in God's hands, Luis. But I doubt if they will hold me. Martinez will vouch for me. He knows most of the truth... but not all."

"What do you mean?"

"The gold, Luis."

Closing his eyes, Luis let his head drop. "I don't want anything to do with it, Klaus. Leave it where it is, at the bottom of that well."

"The well?" He sniggered and sat up, making a face, obviously still in some pain. "Ah yes, that's what I told your mother. I knew she'd tell you."

"What are you saying, that it's not there?"

"It's not there, Luis. I'll tell you where it is and once all of this has settled, you can take it. Start again. You'll need it to rebuild this village, make it a place fit for decent people to live. Pay for a good doctor, to make your mother better."

"So that when you return, you can what, begin again with her?"

"Something like that." He groaned slightly as he swung his legs over the bench and sat with his elbows on his knees, staring at the floor. "Would you object to that, Luis? Your mother and I... and Constanza?"

Luis thought. "But you're a soldier, Klaus. You'd never be able to live the life of a *normal* family man."

"Perhaps not." He winked, "But I'm willing to give it a damned good try!" Then, still smiling, he leaned forward and told Luis where the treasure was hidden.

Outside again, standing there in the bright, burning sun, Luis looked around the *plaza*. People were on the street, life slowly returning, normality once again in evidence. Walking along, in deep conversation, were Alvaro and Carlos. Carlos still bore the bruises of the battering he'd received. When he saw

Luis, he stopped and offered a raised hand. A truce, perhaps? Or something more.

"I want to thank you, Luis," said Alvaro, coming towards him. He held out his hand and Luis took it. They stared into each other's eyes. "I misjudged you, Luis. I'm sorry."

Luis gave a ghost of a smile, "I should thank you, Alvaro. For saving my life."

Alvaro nodded his head slowly. "I think we've both gone to places where we should never have gone, Luis. Don't you?"

Luis watched them go. Two old enemies, old hatreds now buried. He breathed a long sigh of relief. He started as a figure moved up behind him, then smiled when he recognised his old tutor, Señor Martinez.

"So, Luis. Here we are."

"Here we are, indeed, Señor Martinez. I've talked to Klaus. What is going to happen?"

"We'll try the mayor, of course. His part in all of this..." He pressed his fingers into the corners of his eyes. "Dear God, the man was corrupted by Satan! To have known the truth, all these years, and to have never spoken a single word..." He shook his head, his face drawn.

"He could not, Señor. Garcia had a hold on him, forged by the threat of murder. The murder of my family. The mayor prevented that, and for that there should be some recognition, even some mercy."

"Perhaps. Perhaps."

"And Klaus? What of him?"

"I think we can reach... an understanding."

Luis nodded, knowing it was the best he could hope for at that moment, and went to move past his old tutor. Martinez placed a gnarled hand on his shoulder and stopped him. "We'll need a new mayor, Luis. You're old enough... and God knows, you've proved your mettle."

"*Me*? But I'm not yet sixteen, Señor Martinez!"

"But you soon shall be. I'll be recommending you." He grinned broadly. "It has a good ring to it, don't you think?"

"What?"

"Your new title, of course. *Don* Luis."

Five Years Later

Luis did become mayor and the old, sleepy village of Rio Delgado thrived. No one questioned where the new prosperity came from, no one cared. Everyone benefited. A new church was inaugurated, houses and roads repaired, a village militia raised, and the old mill came into working once again. As the war between Spain and France raged, the Iberian peninsula fell into chaos. At one point it looked as if Spain might fragment and split into the kingdoms of old. France became the dominant power in Europe and would remain so for nearly two hundred years. By careful preparations, Rio Delgado remained unscathed for the most part and the people thanked their mayor for his wise and careful leadership.

After a brief spell in Malaga, Klaus returned and made good his promise to help Luis's mother and sister. Mama recovered, growing stronger by the day, and Constanza began her education, just as Luis had done, learning to read and write, preparing herself for a better life. Together, Klaus, Mama and Constanza lived in a splendid house on the hill, overlooking the village, and every night Luis would visit and they would talk and laugh. Of all things, it was that laughter that was most welcome.

And so this story turned to legend. The story of a remarkable boy, looked down upon by his peers, mistrusted by his elders, who rose above the calamities visited upon him and became a good and great man. A man who overcame adversity, injustice, tyranny and greed and found peace and made Riodelgado into a place to settle, grow and live a fulfilling life.

One evening, as the Sun dipped below the jagged mountain tops, Don Luis veered from the path of his nightly stroll through the countryside. His mind was clear; the day had been long and hard, he was tired, eyes gritty and his legs heavy. When he looked around him, he realised he was close to the part of the mountains where he had first come across Salvador. His heartbeat quickened slightly as memories returned, rushing into his head, vivid images of violence, death, fear. He sat down on a nearby fallen tree trunk, took out his water bottle and drank fitfully.

As he gasped, patting his mouth with the back of his hand, something moved just beyond his vision, way off in the olive grove. He peered forward, eyes screwed up. At first, there was nothing, but as he stared he became aware of the sudden change in the air, as if charged with threat.

And then it came.

A shape, big, lumbering, moving through the trees with a nonchalant ease. Too big to be a boar, and bears did not come down this far south, he knew. The shape slipped between the undergrowth, much larger than the sleek, lazy shape of a wolf. So something else. Something unknown.

He stood up, a tightness in his throat. As he brought up his water bottle again, to slake his thirst, he saw it for what it was.

A man. But unlike any man he had ever seen in his life. Where Salvador was heavy across the shoulders and weak in the legs, this creature was sheer bulk from top to toe. A massive head, almost no neck at all, braced against shoulders so wide it wouldn't be able to pass through a double door without difficulty. It was stooped somewhat, its long, muscular arms dangling down, hands almost scraping the ground. It sniffed the air, paused, seemed to find something unlooked for, and grunted with what sounded like surprise.

Then it turned, and its great, bulbous eyes fell upon Don Luis.

Luis had no sword or musket, merely a short dagger, of no help at all. But nothing would have aided him at that moment. Rooted to the spot, the fear seized his limbs in a tight, unrelenting grip. Mesmerised, he locked eyes with the creature. Luis's mouth fell open, but no matter how he tried, he could emit no sound. His whole body trembled, as if shaken by some unseen hand, and then the thing took a step towards him.

"Don Luis."

The sound of its terrible, booming voice galvanised him into action. The strength surged back into his legs and suddenly he was running, crashing through the undergrowth, mindless of the tree branches which whipped across his face and sliced through his flesh. Adrenalin charged, he sprinted down towards the village and the relative safety of his home. He dared not look back, his only thought to get away, to leave the mountainside, to get to the village, through the streets to his home. He didn't stop until, lungs bursting, he reached his gates, flung them shut, and pushed across the great bolt, something he had sworn never to do. He wished everyone to know that he was there, for anyone at any time.

Not this day, however. This day he had to keep the beast at bay.

He ran into his home, taking the stairs three at a time, crashing into his room and taking down the musket which hung on the wall. With shaking fingers, he checked the priming pan, reached out for the bag of shot, then stopped.

The only sound was his breathing, fast, heavy. He had had no time to think, to rationalise what he had seen. And what had he seen, exactly? A large, brutish man, or something more. Something so terrifying, beyond imagining that it simply could not be so.

Don Luis went over to his window and looked up towards the mountains. Could it be true, after all these years? The legend, the myth? Was Salvador merely an accidental bystander in a story that was real?

He let the musket slip from his fingers and it fell to the floor with a clatter. His eyes had given him a glimpse of the reality, of the true horror of what had always lurked amongst those jagged mountain tops.

The ogre. Not a figment of anyone's imagination or a story conjured up by Klaus and the others. An actual living thing.

The stories of Don Luis had barely begun.

THE END

Dear reader,

We hope you enjoyed reading *Ogre's Lament*. Please take a moment to leave a review, even if it's a short one. Your opinion is important to us.

Discover more books by Stuart G. Yates at https://www.nextchapter.pub/authors/stuart-g-yates

Want to know when one of our books is free or discounted? Join the newsletter at http://eepurl.com/bqqB3H

Best regards,
Stuart G. Yates and the Next Chapter Team